THE
WIND
KNOWS
MY
NAME

THE WIND KNOWS MY NAME

ISABEL ALLENDE

TRANSLATED FROM
THE SPANISH BY
FRANCES RIDDLE

BLOOMSBURY PUBLISHING
LONDON · OXFORD · NEW YORK · NEW DELHI · SYDNEY

BLOOMSBURY PUBLISHING
Bloomsbury Publishing Plc
50 Bedford Square, London, WC1B 3DP, UK
29 Earlsfort Terrace, Dublin 2, Ireland

BLOOMSBURY, BLOOMSBURY PUBLISHING and the Diana logo
are trademarks of Bloomsbury Publishing Plc

First published in 2023 in the US as *The Wind Knows My Name*
by Ballantine Books, an imprint of Random House, a division of
Penguin Random House LLC, New York
First published in Great Britain 2023
This edition published 2023

A catalogue record for this book is available from the British Library

ISBN: HB: 978-1-5266-6031-2; TPB: 978-1-5266-6034-3;
WATERSTONES SIGNED EDITION: 978-1-5266-6855-4;
EBOOK: 978-1-5266-6036-7; EPDF: 978-1-5266-6035-0

2 4 6 8 10 9 7 5 3 1

Typeset by Integra Software Services Pvt. Ltd.
Printed and bound in Great Britain by CPI Group (UK) Ltd, Croydon CR0 4YY

To find out more about our authors and books visit www.bloomsbury.com
and sign up for our newsletters

To Lori Barra, Sarah Hillesheim,
and so many others working for a
more compassionate world

Here is my secret. It's quite simple: One sees clearly only with the heart. Anything essential is invisible to the eyes.

— *The Little Prince*, ANTOINE DE SAINT-EXUPÉRY

There's a star where the people and the animals all live happily, and it's even better than heaven, because you don't have to die to go there.

—ANITA DÍAZ

THE ADLERS

A sense of misfortune hung in the air. From the early morning hours, a menacing breeze had swept through the streets, whistling between the buildings, forcing its way in through the cracks under doors and windows.

"Just winter settling in," Rudolph Adler murmured to himself in an attempt to lighten his mood. But he couldn't blame the weather for the tightness in his chest, which he'd felt for several months now.

The stench of fear, like rust and rotting garbage, clung to his nostrils; neither his pipe tobacco nor his citrus-scented aftershave lotion could mask it. That afternoon, the stink of dread stirred up by the wind was suffocating, making him feel dizzy and nauseous. He decided to turn away the patients left in his waiting room and close up early. Surprised, his assistant asked if he was ill. She'd worked with the doctor for eleven years and had never known him to shirk his duties; he was a punctual, methodical man.

"Nothing serious, only a cold, Frau Goldberg. I'll go home and rest," he answered.

They tidied the office and disinfected the instruments, then said goodbye at the door as they did every evening, neither suspecting that they'd never see each other again. Frau Goldberg headed to the streetcar stop and Rudolph Adler walked the few blocks to the pharmacy at his usual brisk pace, hat in one hand and doctor's bag in the other, his shoulders hunched. The sidewalk was damp and the sky cloudy; it had been drizzly and he predicted they'd soon see one of those autumn rainstorms that always caught him unawares, without an umbrella. He'd walked those streets a thousand times and knew them by memory, but he never stopped admiring his city, one of the prettiest places in the world with its Baroque and Art Nouveau buildings coexisting harmoniously, the majestic trees that had begun dropping their leaves, the equestrian statue in the neighborhood square, the bakery's window display with its spread of delicate pastries, and the antiques shop crammed with curiosities. But that afternoon he barely raised his eyes from the pavement. He had the weight of the world on his shoulders.

THE TROUBLING RUMORS HAD begun that morning with news of an assault in Paris: a German diplomat shot five times and killed by a young man, a Polish Jew. Spokespersons for the Third Reich called for revenge.

Since that March, when Germany had annexed Austria and the Nazi Wehrmacht paraded its military pomp and circumstance through the heart of Vienna to a cheering, jubilant crowd, Rudolph Adler had been plagued with fear. His worries had begun a few years prior and only worsened as Nazi power was consolidated through increased financing and a growing stockpile of weapons. Hitler used terror as a political tactic, taking advantage of discontent over economic woes after the humiliating defeat in the Great War and the Great Depression in 1929. In 1934, Austrian chancellor Engelbert Dollfuss was assassinated in a failed government coup, and since then eight hundred others had been killed in various attacks. The Nazis intimidated their detractors, provoked disturbance, and pushed Austria to the brink of civil war. At the start of 1938, internal violence was so untenable that Germany, from the other side of the border, exerted pressure to annex the troubled country as one of its provinces. Despite the concessions that the Austrian government had made to German demands, Hitler ordered an invasion. The Nazi party had laid the groundwork for the invading force to be met with open arms by the majority of the population. The Austrian government surrendered and two days later Hitler himself entered Vienna, triumphant. The Nazis quickly seized total control. Opposition was declared illegal. German laws and SS and Gestapo oppression, as well as antisemitic policies, went into immediate effect.

Rudolph's wife, Rachel, who had always been rational and practical, without the slightest tendency toward catastrophic thinking, was now almost paralyzed with anxiety and only functioned with the help of medication. They both tried to keep their son, Samuel, in the dark about what was happening, to protect his innocence, but the boy, who was about to turn six, had the maturity of an adult; he observed, listened, and understood without asking questions. Rudolph had initially prescribed his wife the tranquilizers he used to treat anxious patients, but when they seemed to have no effect, he turned to other, more powerful drops, which he obtained in opaque unmarked bottles. He could've used the sedatives as much as his wife, but he would not risk jeopardizing his professional acumen.

The drops were provided to him in secret by Peter Steiner, a pharmacist and friend of many years. Adler was the only doctor Steiner trusted with his own family's health, and no government decree forbidding interaction between Aryans and Jews could change the respect they had for each other. In recent months, however, Steiner had been forced to avoid Adler in public, since he couldn't afford any trouble with the neighborhood Nazi committee. In the past, they'd played thousands of games of poker and chess, exchanged books and newspapers, and taken regular hiking and fishing trips together to escape their wives, as they said jokingly, and in Steiner's case to flee from his horde of children. Now Adler no longer participated in the poker games in the back room of Steiner's pharmacy. The pharmacist met Adler at the back door of his shop and provided the medication for Rachel without registering it on the books.

Before the annexation, Peter Steiner had never questioned Adler's roots and considered the doctor to be just as Austrian as he was. He knew the family was Jewish, as were 190,000 other Austrian citizens, but that meant nothing to him. He was agnostic; the Christianity he'd been raised with seemed to him as irrational as all other religions, and he knew that Rudolph Adler felt the same way, though he upheld some Jewish customs out of respect for his wife. Rachel felt it was important that their son be raised in the Jewish community and traditions. On Friday evenings, the Steiners were often invited to Shabbat at the Adler home. Rachel and Leah, her sister-in-law, spared no detail: the best table linens, new candles, the fish recipe that had been passed down from a grandmother, fresh loaves of bread, and abundant wine. Rachel was close to Leah, who had been widowed young and had no children. Leah was devoted to her brother Rudolph's small family, and although Rachel begged the woman to move in with them, she insisted on living alone, visiting often. Leah was sociable and participated in various programs at the synagogue to help the neediest members of the community. Rudolph was the only brother she had left, since the youngest had emigrated to a kibbutz in Palestine, and Samuel was her only nephew. Rudolph presided over the Shabbat prayer, as was expected of him as head of household. With his hands on Samuel's head, he asked God to bless and protect him, to grant him grace and peace. On more than one occasion Rachel caught a wink exchanged between her husband and Peter Steiner after the prayer, but she let it slide, knowing it wasn't meant in mockery but merely a gesture of complicity between two nonbelievers.

The Adlers belonged to the secular and educated middle class that characterized Viennese society in general and Jewish society in particular. Rudolph had explained to Peter that for centuries his people had been discriminated against, persecuted, and expelled from many lands, which was why they valued education over material wealth. They could be robbed of their belongings, as had occurred repeatedly throughout history, but no one could take away their intellectual assets. The title of doctor was more highly prized than a fortune in the bank. Rudolph came from a family of craftsmen, proud to count a physician among them. The profession afforded him prestige and authority, though in his case it indeed did not translate to material wealth. Rudolph Adler was not a sought-after surgeon or a professor at the storied University of Vienna, but a family physician, hardworking and generous, who treated more than half of his patients for free.

THE FRIENDSHIP BETWEEN ADLER and Steiner centered around mutual affinities and deeply held values. Both men had the same voracious curiosity for science, were lovers of classical music, inveterate readers, and clandestine sympathizers of the Communist Party, which had been outlawed in 1933. They also shared a visceral repulsion to Nazism. Ever since Adolf Hitler had moved from chancellor to proclaiming himself absolute dictator, they would meet in the back room of the pharmacy to lament the state of the world and the century they'd been born into. They consoled themselves over glasses of brandy so strong it could've corroded metal, which the pharmacist distilled in the basement, an underground cavern neatly organized with everything needed to prepare and bottle many of the medications sold in the pharmacy above. Sometimes Adler would bring Samuel to the basement to "work" with Steiner. The boy could entertain himself for hours mixing and bottling leftover powders and liquids of all different colors, which the pharmacist gave him to play with. None of the pharmacist's own children was granted such a privilege.

Steiner was deeply pained over each new law aimed at destroying his friend's dignity. He'd purchased the doctor's apartment and office, in name only, to keep them from being confiscated. The office was very well located on the ground floor of a stately building, and Adler lived above with his family. The doctor's life savings were invested in those properties; transferring them into someone else's name, even if it was his friend Peter, was an extreme measure that he took without consulting his wife. Rachel would've never agreed to it.

Rudolph Adler had long tried to convince himself that the antisemitic fervor would soon die down. This vulgarity had no place in Vienna, the most refined city in Europe, birthplace of the world's greatest musicians, philosophers, and scientists, many of them Jewish. Hitler's incendiary rhetoric, which had become increasingly extremist in recent years, was yet another expression of the racism that his ancestors had suffered, but it had not kept them from living together and prospering. Still, as a precaution, he'd removed his name from the sign outside his office, only a minor inconvenience since he'd been treating patients there for many years and was well known in the neighborhood. He'd lost his Aryan patients, who'd had to stop seeing him, but he was certain they'd return once the political climate shifted. Adler was confident in his professional abilities and his well-earned reputation. Nevertheless, as the days passed and things grew ever more tense, he began to weigh the notion of emigrating to wait out the tempest unleashed by the Nazis.

.　　　　.　　　　.

RACHEL ADLER DROPPED A pill into her mouth and swallowed it without water as she waited for her change at the bakery. She was dressed fashionably in beige and burgundy tones, with a jacket that cinched at the waist, hat perched on one side of her head, silk stockings, and high heels. She was not yet thirty and very pretty, but her grave expression made her look mature beyond her years. She tried to hide her trembling hands in her sleeves and respond lightly to the baker's comments about the attack in Paris.

"What was that boy thinking, killing a diplomat? Stupid Pole!" the man exclaimed.

She'd just come from the final class with her best student, a fifteen-year-old boy to whom she'd taught piano since age seven, one of the few who took music seriously. "Sorry, Frau Adler . . . you must understand," the boy's mother had said when she let Rachel go. The woman paid Rachel three times what was owed for the class and leaned in for a hug before seeming to think better of it. Yes, Rachel understood. She was thankful that the woman had employed her for several months more than she should have. She swallowed her tears and walked away with her head high; she was fond of the boy and didn't judge him for proudly donning the black shorts and brown shirt bearing the slogan "blood and honor" of the Hitler Youth. All the young men belonged to the movement; it was practically obligatory.

"Look at the danger that Polish boy has put us all in! Have you heard what they're saying on the radio, Frau Adler?" the baker continued pontificating.

"Let's hope they're only empty threats," she said.

"You should get home quickly. Groups of boys are causing a ruckus on the streets. You shouldn't be out alone. It'll be dark soon."

"Good evening. See you tomorrow," Rachel muttered, placing the bread in her bag and depositing the change in her coin purse.

Once outside she filled her lungs with cold air and tried to shake off the sense of foreboding that had plagued her since dawn, well before turning on the radio or hearing the alarming rumors circulating through the neighborhood. She looked up at the black clouds that threatened rain and tried to recall the errands she had left. She still needed to buy wine and candles for Friday, when her sister-in-law would be coming over for Shabbat, as she did every week, along with the Steiners and their children. But she worried that despite the medication she'd just taken, her nerves might betray her—she needed her drops—so she decided to leave the shopping for another day. Two blocks farther she arrived at their building, one of the first built in the pure Art Nouveau style at the end of the nineteenth century. When Rudolph Adler first purchased the office on the street level for his practice and the apartment for his family above, the organic lines, curved windows and balconies, and delicate stained-glass flowers had been considered bad taste to polite Viennese society, accustomed to Baroque elegance. But Art Nouveau soon caught on and the building quickly became something of a landmark.

Rachel was tempted to stop into the office to confer with her husband but immediately discarded the notion. Rudolph had enough worries of his own without her loading him down with her troubles as well. Also, it was time to pick Samuel up from his aunt's house. Leah was a teacher and had begun giving classes to a group of Jewish children who could no longer attend school. Samuel was a few years younger than the others but was easily able to keep up. So many children had been badly mistreated in school that the mothers of the community had arranged to have the younger ones instructed privately at home, while the older students received an education at the synagogue. It was a temporary emergency measure, they were certain. Rachel continued on her way without noticing that her husband's office was closed up at that unusual hour. Rudolph generally treated patients until six o'clock in the evening, except for Fridays, when he went up for dinner before sunset.

.　　.　　.

LEAH'S APARTMENT, MODEST BUT well located, consisted of two rooms filled with secondhand furniture, framed photographs of her prematurely deceased husband, and souvenirs from the trips they'd taken together. On the days she received students, the air always smelled of fresh-baked cookies. Rachel Adler walked in to find three other mothers who had come to pick up their children and stayed for tea. They were listening to Samuel play "A Song of Joy." The child was adorable, small and thin with scraped-up knees, untamable hair, and a wise expression of concentration, swaying to the music of the violin, unaware of the effect he had on the audience. A chorus of exclamations and applause exploded with the final notes. It took Samuel a few seconds to stir from his trance and return to the circle of mothers and children. He thanked them with a slight bow and as his aunt rushed to give him a kiss, his mother hid a smile of satisfaction. It was a fairly easy piece, which the boy had learned in under a week, but Beethoven always sounded impressive. Rachel knew that her son was a prodigy, but she hated boasting of any kind so she never mentioned it, waiting instead for others to do so. She helped Samuel put on his coat and place his instrument safely in its case, bid her sister-in-law a quick goodbye, and left for home, estimating that she'd have just enough time to pop the roast in the oven and have it ready by dinnertime. For the past few months she hadn't had any domestic help, since her Hungarian housekeeper, who had been with them for several years, had been deported. She hadn't had the heart to search for a replacement.

The mother and son passed the doctor's office without stopping and stepped into the building's wide foyer. Water lilies on the glass lampshades lit the space in blue and green tones. They walked up the wide staircase, waving to the concierge, who watched from her cubicle at all hours. The woman made no response—she rarely did.

The Adlers' apartment was spacious and comfortable with heavy mahogany furniture designed to last a lifetime but that clashed with the delicate, simple lines of the building's architecture. Rachel's grandfather had been an antiques dealer and his descendants had inherited an array of art, rugs, and adornments, all of exceptional quality, all out of fashion. Rachel, raised with luxury, managed to live in elegance despite the fact that her husband's salary, supplemented by her music lessons, did not compare to her grandparents' wealth. Hers was a discreet refinement, since ostentation repulsed her as much as arrogance. The risks associated with provoking envy in others had been instilled in her from a young age.

In the corner of the living room, near the window overlooking the street, sat her grand piano, a Blüthner that had been in her family for three generations. She used it to give most of her lessons and it was also her main source of entertainment in her hours alone. She'd played it with great skill from a young age, but in adolescence, when she'd realized she lacked the talent necessary to become a concert pianist, she turned to teaching, for which she had a natural ability. Her son, on the other hand, possessed a rare musical genius. Samuel had sat at the piano from age three and could play any song by ear after hearing it only once, but he preferred his violin, because he could take it with him wherever he went. Rachel could not have more children and she had invested all her motherly love in Samuel. She adored her son and couldn't help indulging him because he never gave her any trouble; he was kind, obedient, and studious.

Half an hour later, Rachel heard a commotion on the street and peered out the window. It was getting dark. She saw half a dozen young men shouting Nazi slogans and insulting the Jews, calling them disgusting bloodsuckers, parasites, and murderers—epithets she'd heard many times and even read in the press and in German propaganda. One of the boys was carrying a torch and others were armed with sticks, sledgehammers, and pieces of metal pipe. She ushered Samuel away from the window, closed the curtains, and headed for the stairs to call her husband, but the boy clung to her skirt. Samuel was accustomed to being alone but was now so frightened that his mother could not leave him. The noise outside soon quieted and she assumed that the crowd had passed. She took the roast out of the oven and began to set the table. She didn't want to turn on the radio. The news was always terrible.

PETER STEINER CHATTED WITH his friend in the back room of the pharmacy, where the game of chess they'd started the previous afternoon sat beside a bottle of brandy, half full. The well-respected Steiner Pharmacy had been in the family since Peter's grandfather established it in 1830, and each subsequent generation had worked to maintain it in perfect working order. It still had the original carved mahogany shelves and counter, the bronze accessories brought over from France, and a dozen antique crystal jars, which more than one collector had offered to purchase and which, according to Steiner, were worth a fortune. The window displays were framed with painted flower garlands, the floors were Portuguese tile worn down from more than a century of use, and a tinkling of silver bells on the door announced each customer's arrival. The Steiner Pharmacy was so picturesque that it was visited by tourists, and had even appeared in magazines and a book of photography, as a symbol of the city.

Peter had been surprised to see Rudolph Adler so early on a workday.

"Is something wrong?" he asked.

"I don't know. I can't breathe. I think I might be having a heart attack."

"You're too young for that. It's just nerves. Have a drink; it's the best remedy I know," Steiner replied, serving his friend a double shot.

"We can't live in this country anymore, Peter. The Nazis have us fenced in, they're drawing tighter and stricter circles around us. We can't even enter certain restaurants and stores. They bully our kids in school, they're firing us from jobs in public office, confiscating our businesses and properties, prohibiting us from exercising our professions or loving a person of another race."

"The situation is utterly untenable. It will have to get better soon," said Peter, without much conviction.

"I'm afraid you're mistaken. Things will only get worse. It takes selective blindness to think that we Jews will ever be able to live here with anything resembling normalcy. Violence is inevitable. There are new restrictions every day."

"I'm so sorry, my friend! Is there anything I can do?"

"You've done a lot already, but you won't be able to save us. To the Nazis we are a malignant tumor that has to be excised from the nation. My family has lived in Austria for six generations! The humiliations only pile up. What else can they take from us? Only our lives. We have nothing else left."

"No one can take away your medical degree. And your assets are safe. It was a good idea to put your office and apartment in my name."

"Thank you, Peter, you've been like a brother to me. But I'm very worried. Baser instincts seem to have taken root. Hitler is going to be in power for a long time and he wants to conquer all of Europe. I think he's leading us straight into war. Can you imagine what that would be like?"

"Another war!" exclaimed Steiner. "That would be collective suicide. No, we learned our lesson from the last one. Remember the horror . . . the defeat . . ."

"We Jews are the new scapegoat. Half the people I know are trying to get out. I have to persuade Rachel that we should go too."

"Go? Where?" asked Steiner, alarmed.

"England or the United States would be the best options, but it's almost impossible to get visas. I know of several people who have gone to South America . . ."

"How can you think of leaving! What would I do without you?"

"I suppose it will only be for a time. And I still haven't made up my mind, nor will it be easy to convince Rachel. She can't imagine leaving this life we've built over years of hard work, abandoning her father and her brother. My sister won't like the idea either, but I can't leave her here."

"It seems like a very drastic decision, Rudy."

"I have to think of Samuel. I don't want my son to grow up as a pariah."

"I hope you don't have to leave, but if you do, I will take care of your things, Rudy. When you return, it will all be safe, waiting for you."

They were on their second glass of brandy when they heard the commotion outside. They looked out the door and saw a crowd had filled the street: men, boys, and even some women shouting obscenities and Nazi party slogans as they brandished sledgehammers, clubs, and other heavy objects. "To the synagogue! To the Jewish Quarter!" shouted the ones in front. Rocks flew through the air and they heard the unmistakable sound of breaking glass, met with a clamor of celebration. The mob moved in unison like a single animal blazing with murderous glee.

"Help me close up the pharmacy!" Steiner exclaimed, but Adler was already in the street, running toward his house.

TERROR INVADED THE NIGHT. It took Rachel Adler all of ten minutes to comprehend the gravity of the situation. She had closed the curtains so that the noise outside was muted and at first she thought that the gang of boys had returned. To distract Samuel, she asked him to play some music, but the boy seemed paralyzed, as if he were witnessing a tragedy that she was still unwilling to acknowledge. Suddenly something exploded against the window and glass rained across the floor. Her first thought was of the cost to replace the beveled glass. Immediately a second rock crashed through another window and the curtain fell from the rod, hanging loose from one corner. Through the splintered glass she glimpsed a fragment of orange-tinted sky and inhaled a whiff of smoke and fire. A wild racket howled through the apartment and then she understood that they were dealing with something much more dangerous than a group of drunk boys. She heard furious shouting and shrieks of panic amid the continuous din of shattering glass. "Rudolph!" she exclaimed, terrified. She took Samuel by the arm and dragged him to the door, the boy reaching for his violin case on the way out.

Only the wide marble staircase with its bronze handrail separated the apartment from the doctor's office below, but Rachel didn't make it there. Theobald Volker, her neighbor from the apartment above, a retired military officer with whom she'd exchanged barely more than a few words, was standing in the hallway, blocking her path. He gripped her shoulders. Flattened against the wide chest of the old man, who was muttering something incomprehensible, Rachel struggled and called for her husband. It took her over a minute to understand that Volker was trying to keep her from going downstairs because the building's carved wood and stained-glass door had been beaten down. A violent group had gathered in the foyer.

"Come with me, Frau Adler!" he ordered with the voice of a man who knew how to lead.

"My husband!"

"You can't go down there! Think of your son!" he answered as he urged her up the stairs to his apartment, a place she'd never set foot.

Volker's home was identical to the Adlers' but had nothing of its brightness and elegance. It was somber and cold, with sparse furnishings and no decoration other than a few photographs on a shelf. The man led her to the kitchen, as Samuel, hugging his violin, followed behind, mute. Volker opened the narrow door to the pantry and instructed them to hide inside without making a sound until he came for them. Then he closed the cabinet and Rachel and Samuel stood huddled together in the small, dark space. They heard Volker drag a piece of heavy furniture across the floor.

"What's happening, Mama?"

"I don't know, my dear. We have to be very still and keep quiet . . ." she whispered.

"Papa's not going to be able to find us when he gets home," said Samuel without lowering his voice.

"It's only for a little while. There are some bad men in the building, but they'll leave soon."

"They're Nazis, aren't they, Mama?"

"Yes."

"Are all Nazis bad, Mama?"

"I don't know, son. There might be good ones and bad ones."

"But there are more bad ones than good ones, I think," the boy said.

THEOBALD VOLKER WAS ALREADY a career military man when he'd been called on to defend the Austro-Hungarian Empire in 1914. He had come from a family of farmers with no military tradition, but he made a name for himself, moving up the ranks. He was six foot two with the physical strength and disciplined nature of someone born for battle, but he wrote poetry in secret and dreamed of a peaceful retirement in the country planting crops and raising animals alongside his childhood sweetheart. In the four years the war lasted he lost everything that gave meaning to his life: his only son, who died on a battlefield at age nineteen; his beloved wife, who, stricken with grief, committed suicide; and his faith in his country, which in the end was nothing more than an idea and a flag.

When the war ended, he was fifty-two years old, had reached the rank of colonel, and was heartbroken. He couldn't remember what he'd been fighting for. He was forced to accept defeat, tormented by the ghosts of twenty million dead. There was no place for him in that ruined Europe, where the broken remains of soldiers, women, children, mules, and horses all rotted together in mass graves. For a few years, he supported himself through a series of undignified jobs, enduring his misfortune, until old age and ailments forced him to retire. Since then he'd occupied himself by reading, listening to the radio, and composing lines of verse. He left his apartment only once daily to purchase a newspaper and enough food to make his meals. His war medals were still pinned to his old uniform, which he put on once a year for the anniversary of the armistice agreement that had dissolved the empire he'd defended during four horrific years. Each year on that date he shook out and ironed his uniform, shined his medals, and cleaned his guns, then opened a bottle of aquavit and got drunk, cursing his loneliness. He was one of the few Viennese citizens who had not taken to the streets to cheer for the German troops on the day they annexed Austria. He did not identify with those goose-stepping soldiers. He'd learned from experience to distrust patriotic fervor.

The adults in the building avoided the colonel, who didn't even respond to a passing wave, and the children feared him, with the exception of Samuel Adler. Rachel and Rudolph were often busy with their respective jobs and the housekeeper who used to come left at three o'clock each afternoon. When he wasn't with his aunt Leah, the boy would have to spend a few hours alone, doing his schoolwork and practicing music. He soon realized that whenever he played the piano or violin, his neighbor discreetly brought a chair down to the first floor and sat in the hall to listen. Without a word, Samuel began to leave the door open. He made an extra effort to play perfectly for that audience of one listening in respectful silence. They'd never spoken, but when they passed in the building or on the street they exchanged a slight nod of the head, so imperceptible that Rachel had never noticed the tenuous friendship between her son and Volker.

After stowing his neighbors safely away inside the pantry and moving the kitchen table to hide the door, the colonel quickly dressed in his gray uniform with its gold epaulets and array of war medals. Then he holstered his Luger, old-fashioned but in perfect working order, and posted himself at the door to his apartment, waiting.

IT TOOK PETER STEINER several minutes to close the wooden shutters over the pharmacy's display window and lower the metal shade over the shop entrance. He put on his coat and rushed out the back door, eager to find Rudolph, but the narrow alley behind the shop was already crowded with shouting rioters. He flattened himself into a doorway to hide from a rowdy group of troublemakers and waited until they disappeared around a corner before peeking out. He was a robust man, with ruddy skin, stiff blond hair like a brush, eyes so light they looked like cloudy water, and the arms of a weightlifter; he could win any trial of strength. Excepting his wife, no one intimidated him, but he decided it was best to take a longer route to avoid that unruly horde of hooligans, praying that Rudolph had done the same. But within minutes the pharmacist understood that there was no way to avoid the chaos that had taken the city by storm. He didn't think twice. He joined the throng. He ripped a Nazi party banner from the hands of a boy who didn't dare to object, and, waving that detestable flag, he let himself be pulled along by the tide of humanity.

In just a few blocks, Peter Steiner was able to get a more precise measure of the havoc that had been unleashed upon the quiet neighborhood where a large part of the Jewish community had traditionally lived and worked. Not a single storefront window remained intact; bonfires blazed as looters set fire to items pulled from houses and offices, everything from books to furniture; the synagogue had flames shooting from all four sides as the firefighters looked on passively, ready to intervene only if the blaze jumped to other buildings. He saw a rabbi being dragged by his feet, his bloodied head bouncing against the cobblestones; he saw men being beaten, women with their clothes torn off and hair ripped out, children smacked, the elderly trampled and urinated upon. From some balconies, bystanders cheered the aggressors on. From one window an arm extended waving a bottle of champagne, but the majority of the houses and apartment buildings were darkened with the curtains drawn.

The pharmacist quickly realized, to his horror, that the crowd's raw, savage energy was contagious and even exhilarating. He had to reject the impulse to transform into a monster, to destroy, burn, and shout till he had no air left in his lungs. Panting, covered in sweat, his mouth dry and his skin tingling with the rush of adrenaline, he crouched down behind a tree and tried to catch his breath and compose himself. "Rudy . . . Rudy . . ." he murmured. He continued repeating the name aloud until he'd returned to his senses. He had to find his friend before Rudy fell victim to the mob. He stood and continued on, safeguarded by the Nazi banner and his pure Aryan blood.

Just as Steiner had feared, Adler's office had been vandalized, painted with graffiti spelling out slurs and party symbols. The door had been beaten down, and all the windows broken. Furniture, cabinets, lamps, medical instruments, jars, the entire contents of the doctor's office lay strewn across the street. There was no sign of his friend.

COLONEL THEOBALD VOLKER MET the first rioters firmly planted in the doorway to his apartment with his arms crossed over his chest.

Fewer than fifteen minutes had passed since they'd broken down the front door and scattered like rats through the building. Volker supposed that either the concierge or one of the other tenants had reported the Jewish neighbors, maybe even pointed out their apartments, because later, as he walked the floors, he noticed that some doors had been broken down while others were left intact. The Adlers' door hadn't been destroyed because it had been left open.

Half a dozen men and boys drunk on violence, wearing party armbands, appeared on the stairway landing shouting. One of them, who seemed to be the leader, faced off with the colonel in the hallway. He carried an iron pipe raised high, ready to strike, but he was momentarily paralyzed by the sight of this gigantic old man in his outdated uniform, looking down on him with an air of authority.

"Jew?" he barked.

"No," Volker replied calmly.

Voices shouted up from below, frustrated over finding the Adler apartment empty. Two slightly older men appeared on the stairs and addressed Volker.

"How many Jews live here?"

"I couldn't tell you."

"Step aside, we're going to check your apartment!"

"On whose authority?" the colonel replied, moving his hand to his holstered Luger.

The men talked briefly among themselves and decided that it wasn't worth their time to bother with this old man. He was clearly just as Aryan as they were, and he was armed. They went down to the Adlers' apartment and joined the others in ravaging the place, smashing the china and the furniture, tossing antiques out the broken window. Several men began to drag the piano toward the balcony with the intention of throwing it to the street below, but it was heavier than they expected, so they settled for simply smashing it apart instead.

The destruction lasted only a few minutes but the effect was as if a grenade had exploded inside the apartment. Before leaving, they emptied the contents of the trash cans onto the beds, ripped up the furniture's upholstery with their knives, stole all of Rachel's treasured silver, poured gasoline on the rug and set it ablaze. The troop then marched back down to the street and rejoined the bloodthirsty mob.

The colonel waited long enough to be sure that the vandals had left and then went down to the Adlers' ruined apartment. Fire smoldered on the rug, and with his characteristic precision and calm, he lifted one corner and folded it over, suffocating the flames. He then took blankets from a bedroom and pressed them against the rug to ensure that the fire had been fully extinguished. Picking up a chair that had been knocked to the floor, he sat down heavily, struggling for breath. "I'm not what I used to be," he murmured, lamenting the merciless passage of time.

He sat waiting for the drumbeat in his chest to slow as he assessed the scope of the damage. It was much worse than he'd imagined hours prior, when he first heard the call to protest the Jews who were supposedly conspiring against the government. The German minister of propaganda, speaking on Hitler's behalf, had announced that the Party itself would not be organizing demonstrations in response to the assassination of the German diplomat in Paris, but that protests were permitted. The rage of the German and Austrian people was fully justified, he said. It was an open invitation to rioting, destruction, and massacre. The colonel suspected that the mob, which at first glance appeared to be out for senseless violence, included men who were not acting purely on impulse but who had been trained, men who had been given clear targets and total impunity. They must've had instructions to avoid damaging Aryan property, which would explain why they only looted the apartments belonging to the Adlers, the Epsteins, and the Rosenbergs. Volker wasn't fooled by their civilian clothes. He knew they were young Nazi militiamen, the groups that had employed violence as a political strategy in recent years and terror as a form of governance ever since the annexation.

He was still gathering his strength when he heard footsteps in the hall and an instant later was faced with a madman brandishing a Nazi standard, wielding it like a spear. "Adler! Adler!" the man shouted at the top of his lungs. The colonel stood clumsily and unsheathed his Luger.

"Who are you? What are you doing here?" the madman demanded. "This apartment belongs to Rudolph Adler!"

Volker did not respond and he didn't flinch when the man waved the flagpole inches from his face.

"Where is he? Where is Adler?" the man shouted.

"Who wants to know?" Volker asked, swatting the stick away like a fly.

That's when Peter Steiner noticed the man's advanced age and his uniform from the Great War. He realized that he was not dealing with a Nazi officer.

Volker watched as the agitated man dropped the banner and brought both hands to his head in a gesture of desperation.

"I'm looking for my friend Rudolph. Have you seen him?" Steiner asked, his voice hoarse from shouting.

"He wasn't here when they looted his apartment. I don't think he was in his office either," Volker replied.

"And Rachel? Samuel? Do you know where his family is?"

"They are safe. If you find Dr. Adler, let me know. I live in apartment twenty on the second floor. I'm retired Colonel Theobald Volker."

"Peter Steiner. If Adler comes home, tell him I'm looking for him, to wait here. I'll be back. Remember my name, Peter Steiner."

THE VIOLINIST

VIENNA, NOVEMBER–DECEMBER 1938

Rudolph Adler would never return to his home and would never again see Rachel or Samuel. The night of November 9, 1938, the Night of Broken Glass, it never got dark. Fires lit the sky until dawn.

Peter Steiner obtained a swastika armband and, brandishing the Nazi banner torn and filthy with dust and ash, he scoured the neighborhood in all directions, taking a mental inventory of the destruction. Finally, around three o'clock in the morning, he was informed that an ambulance had rounded up the more seriously wounded. So he went to the hospital, where he passed himself off as the director of a paramilitary brigade and was allowed to enter. Victims lined the hallways as doctors and nurses rushed to help as many people as possible. They had not received orders to deny treatment to Jewish patients. Amid the confusion, a nurse explained to Steiner that there was no official register of everyone who had recently arrived, and she suggested that he check the emergency room and the hallways crowded with beds.

Steiner combed one room after another, exhausted. He was about to leave, prepared to give up, when he heard his friend's weak voice calling out to him. He'd walked right past without recognizing Rudolph Adler, who was lying on his back, his head wrapped in a bloody bandage and his face so swollen that his features were indistinguishable under the swelling, cuts, and bruises. Several of his teeth were broken and he could barely speak. Steiner had to place his ear next to the wounded man's mouth to understand what he was murmuring.

"Rachel . . ."

"Shhh, Rudy, save your energy. Your family is all right. Just rest, you're in the hospital, you're safe here," Steiner replied, tearing up from fatigue and relief.

In the hours that followed he remained with his friend, nodding off on the floor beside the bed, as the injured man whimpered and raved. A few times in the night a nurse stopped to check that the patient was still breathing, but no one inquired about the identity of the victim or the man sitting beside him. The swastika armband was enough to keep anyone from asking questions. When the sun came out and he felt the streets would be safe, Peter Steiner stood on shaky legs, aching all over and thirsty as a camel.

"I'll let Rachel know I found you. Then I'll come back and stay with you until you're released," he told his friend. He received no response.

Frau Steiner was waiting anxiously for her husband at home. She hadn't slept all night either, sitting up beside the radio, which claimed that the disturbances had been provoked by the Jews. Between sips of coffee laced with brandy, Peter told her the truth as he'd seen it. After washing up and changing into a clean shirt, he returned to the Adlers' building. There he saw a group of men wearing the dreaded brown shirts presiding over a few women on hands and knees scrubbing paint and bloodstains from the pavement, as curious onlookers taunted them. He recognized Frau Rosenberg, who had been a regular customer at the pharmacy. For an instant he felt an impulse to intervene, but the urgent need to speak to Rachel won out and he rushed past, trying not to call attention to himself.

The windows on the front of the building had all been destroyed and crude black swastikas had been painted on the walls, but the broken glass was already being swept up and a man was measuring to replace the windows. Upstairs, he saw that the door of the first-floor apartment across from the Adlers' was dented and hanging by a single hinge; he peered in and saw that it had been looted too. At apartment twenty on the second floor, Theobald Volker greeted him freshly shaven and with wet hair, wearing his decorated uniform.

"I have to speak with Frau Adler," Steiner said.

"I'm afraid that won't be possible," the colonel replied, unwilling to share her whereabouts with anyone, much less a man who had a Nazi flag the night before.

"Do you know where she is?" Steiner insisted.

"I couldn't tell you."

"Listen, sir . . . I mean, Colonel, you can trust me. I've known Rudolph Adler for twenty years; I'm a close friend of the family. Samuel is like a son to me. I need to speak to Rachel. Her husband is in the hospital, badly injured."

"I'll give her the message, but I don't know what she can do in these circumstances," the military man replied.

"Tell her to prepare to leave immediately. As soon as we can get Rudolph out of the hospital, they should leave the country. Thousands of Jews were fleeing before; Rudolph had plans to do so as well. After what happened last night, it is clear none of them are safe here. They have to leave. Samuel's future depends on it. Do you understand?"

"I understand."

"You have to convince her, Colonel. Rachel is quite attached to her father and to her home, but we've reached a point of life or death. I'm not exaggerating, I assure you."

"I have no doubt about that, Herr Steiner."

"Tell her that they won't lose the apartment or the office. She doesn't know it, but they're in my name so they won't be confiscated."

STEINER RETURNED TO THE hospital. In the light of day, the extent of the city's destruction was on full display. The streets were strewn with garbage, broken glass, and rubble; coals still glowed in the bonfires; there were holes in many shop fronts and homes where the buildings had been battered with sledgehammers. Agents of the Security Service were searching house by house and filling their vehicles with documents that had been confiscated from offices and synagogues before setting the buildings on fire. There was an order to deport all Jewish men and long lines of prisoners advanced toward the trucks that would drive them to the concentration camps, while their families bid them sobbing farewells from the sidewalks. Most Viennese residents chose to remain shut inside their homes, but there were some who spit at and insulted the lines of detainees, either out of racist hate or in order to ingratiate themselves with the Nazis.

When he got to the hospital, Steiner found that the situation there had changed. The chaos of the night before had been replaced with a military discipline; security had been set up and no one was allowed to enter or exit. The authorities were taking inventory of the patients and deporting all Jewish men who were well enough to stand. He wasn't able to find out whether Rudolph Adler was among them but assumed that his severe wounds had prevented him from being moved.

In the days that followed a certain degree of normalcy returned. Among many inhabitants of Vienna, the orgy of fire and blood had left behind a profound sense of shame. The Jewish community was forced to pay a fortune in "damages to the German nation" and, just as Rudolph Adler had feared, their properties and other assets were being confiscated by authorities or appropriated by Aryans. Jewish businesses and offices were closed and the children were forbidden to attend schools. When word got out that the men sent to the concentration camps could be freed if they emigrated immediately thereafter, lines formed day and night outside the offices and consulates that could issue passports and visas. Thousands and thousands of families, having lost everything, fled with nothing more than the contents of a suitcase.

Rachel Adler had been warned not to go to the hospital to ask after her husband, because she might be arrested if she did. She instead delegated the task to Peter Steiner and his wife, who took turns going twice daily to fill out requests to see the patient, to no avail. She didn't even attempt to remedy the shipwrecked ruin of her apartment; she simply gathered a few necessities and moved herself and her son in with Volker. The Steiners had offered to accommodate them, but they had six children and a grandmother all living in a small house, and Rachel wanted to be nearby when her husband returned. She had managed to convince Leah to go to a home outside the city, set up by the synagogue, until the family could leave together. There she would be more or less out of harm's way for a while, but in reality no Jew was safe.

As Rachel spent the days going from office to office, line to line, trying to get the documents needed to emigrate, Volker took care of Samuel. The old colonel, who had spent so many years isolated in his grief and disillusionment, found in the precocious five-year-old the grandson he might've had if his son had survived the war. He took the role so seriously that he wouldn't leave the boy alone for a moment, even though it meant modifying his fixed routines. In his eagerness to compensate for the trauma of recent days and the uncertainty surrounding Samuel's father, the colonel took the child to the park, museums, concerts, and even to the cinema to see *Carnival in Flanders,* a romantic comedy that neither of the two understood. Samuel for his part was careful to repay the man's kindnesses with violin concerts, which the colonel listened to in rapt silence. Volker knew that his precious days with the boy were numbered.

A few days after the pogrom, when there was no longer any doubt that the iron shackles that fettered the Jews would quickly strangle them, Rachel returned with news that she had a meeting with the Chilean consul the next day.

"Chile? That's the other end of the world, Frau Adler!" Volker exclaimed.

"Well, Colonel, it's the only meeting I was able to get. I was informed that this particular functionary sells visas, but he doesn't accept money, only gold and jewels. Luckily I still have the diamond ring and pearl necklace I inherited from my mother. I hope that will be sufficient . . ."

"It sounds like this man has very few scruples, madam. He may try to swindle you."

"That's why I'd like to ask you to accompany me. Would you mind? He wouldn't dare to pull out any dirty tricks with you there in uniform. We'll get the visas and as soon as Rudolph is back, we can leave."

They had a plan, but that very night Peter Steiner arrived with the news that Rudolph Adler had been deported to a concentration camp in Dachau.

"They sent him several days ago, but we only found out today. He's in no condition to survive that horrid place," said the pharmacist.

"We have to get him out of there right away!" Rachel exclaimed, terrified.

"If you can prove that you're going to emigrate immediately, we may be able to, Rachel. The Nazis don't want any Jews here at all."

"I hope to get us visas to go to Chile."

"To where?" asked Steiner, surprised.

"Chile, in South America."

"It might take time," Volker added.

"Maybe you should go now, with Samuel, and Rudolph can follow later . . ." Steiner suggested.

"No! I'm not going anywhere without my husband."

AS THE DAYS PASSED and her chance to save her husband was further delayed, Rachel became increasingly desperate. Circumstances for Jews in Austria were worsening by the hour and she didn't even want to imagine what conditions must be like for Rudolph. She had gone to the meeting with the Chilean consul in such a state of nerves that Volker had to answer the questions for her.

The consulate was located in a row of identical dark offices, in one of the few ugly buildings in the city center. There were several people standing in the waiting room, which only had a few chairs and a desk, behind which sat the secretary, a gruff little man with an air of false importance. They would have stood there for hours before being seen if Volker hadn't discreetly slipped the man a few bills, which enabled them to skip the wait.

From the start, the consul seemed guarded and suspicious. When Rachel finally got up the nerve to suggest paying for visas for herself, her husband, her son, and her sister-in-law, the man responded dryly that he would make note of her request but that he had to follow the normal bureaucratic process, which took between one and two months, and he would let her know in due time. She understood then that it had been a mistake to bring Volker. The imposing military man intimidated the Chilean consul, who tried to be careful in his illicit dealings.

"We'll visit the other consulates," Volker said as they left, but Rachel had noticed the way the consul examined her, clearly impressed, and decided she would try again.

A few days later, without telling anyone, she returned to the Chilean consulate alone. She was wearing a knit dress that was cut on the bias and hugged her figure, high heels, a fox stole, and the pearl necklace and diamond ring with which she planned to bribe him.

The diplomat was a pretentious man, with a carefully groomed mustache and slicked-back hair, who used platform shoes to compensate for his short stature. He received her in his office with its tall ceilings and dark, worn leather furniture. The walls were adorned with a portrait of his country's president and paintings of battles. The curtains were drawn, even though it was midday, and the only light came from a lamp on the heavy desk. He took her hand in a greeting that he lingered over for endless seconds. He spoke only basic German and Rachel thought she'd misunderstood when he said that jewels were, in reality, offered as more of a tip for the consul's troubles. Nevertheless, he said, he was sure a woman as pretty as she was could find a way to get whatever she wanted. He was a romantic, he added, leading her by the waist to an overstuffed chocolate-colored sofa. Rachel Adler was prepared to pay whatever price the man demanded.

The humiliating experience lasted fewer than ten minutes and Rachel vowed to forget it immediately. It was another unfortunate episode in the tragic reality she'd been enduring for months now. Afterward, the consul smoothed his clothes, ran a comb through his hair, tucked the ring and the pearls into a desk drawer, and asked her to meet him at a hotel the following week, when he would turn the visas over to her. Rachel was in no position to negotiate. Saving her family was all that mattered.

.   .   .

IN EARLY DECEMBER 1938, Rachel Adler had attended three meetings with the Chilean consul and was still waiting for him to give her the visas she and her family would need to enter his country. She feared that the man would not hold up his end of the bargain until he'd had enough of her. She didn't even want to consider the possibility that he might not give her the documentation he'd promised even after raping her and taking her jewels. She could only barely function thanks to the drops and pills that Peter Steiner provided; she walked around with a knot in her stomach, sucking in sips of air like a drowning person, unable to hide the shaking of her hands. She had not told anyone about what went on in the hotel room where she met the Chilean, but Colonel Volker was beginning to suspect something.

"Have you had any news of your husband, Frau Adler?" he asked.

"Peter got word that he is very weak, he hasn't recovered from the beatings, but that he's still surviving for now. He assures me that Rudolph receives my letters, even though he can't respond to them."

"You'll excuse me, madam, but I think this whole Chile issue is taking too long. I don't trust that man. He may be simply swindling you. I think you should try to get Samuel to safety."

"I'm doing everything I possibly can, Colonel."

"I don't doubt that, but it can't be delayed much longer. As you know, Great Britain has offered to receive ten thousand children under the age of seventeen. Many English families have signed up to host the children. Samuel could spend some time there, just until you and your husband obtain visas to go to Chile, or somewhere else, and you can be reunited."

"Send Samuel away on his own? How could you think of such a thing?"

The old colonel would be devastated to lose the sweet boy, for whom he had a deeply rooted affection, but he felt better able to as-

THE WIND KNOWS MY NAME • 31

sess the danger they faced, and he knew that any window of opportunity to escape would be very brief; they had to act before the Nazis forbade anyone else from leaving. He was certain that Hitler's nationalist rhetoric would lead to another war and when that happened it would be much harder, if not impossible, to save Samuel.

"The first group of two hundred children has just left Berlin," Volker said. "It's a short trip and they have chaperones with them. People are waiting to welcome them as soon as they arrive in England. An amazing Dutch woman, a Frau Geertruida Wijsmuller-Meijer, has gotten permission from the Nazis to take six hundred children out of Austria. I understand that they give priority to orphans, children from poorer families, and those who have fathers in concentration camps. Samuel falls into that category. I beg you, Frau Adler, to consider your son's well-being."

"You're asking me to ship my son off to another country, alone!"

"It's only a temporary measure. It's the best way to protect Samuel. You should make up your mind soon—the train is leaving in just a few days."

Peter Steiner agreed with Volker. Between the censorship and propaganda, it was hard to know the truth about what was happening across Austria. But there was more information on the similar situation in Germany, which Peter learned about from certain customers at the pharmacy and from his poker buddies.

Rachel, desperate, consulted with her father and brother, in the hopes that they would be able to come up with some alternative, but they both insisted that she should try to secure the boy a spot on the Dutch woman's train with the other children. England was close, they said, she could visit him. They were trying to get to Portugal and from there to any other country that would accept them; the exodus of Jews from Germany and Austria was escalating rapidly and it was ever harder to obtain visas.

"The family is falling apart," said Rachel, sobbing.

"Right now the most urgent thing is to get Samuel to safety," her father decreed.

"We have to stick together; with so much uncertainty all around us, if we separate, we may never see each other again," she argued.

"Once you secure your passage to Chile with Rudolph, we can leave Portugal and meet you there, as soon as you're settled."

"I can't leave Samuel!"

"It's for his own good. It's a sacrifice you have to make, Rachel. Other families from the congregation are also considering the Kindertransport," her father said.

Even though Rachel tried to hide her terror and anguish from Samuel, he was aware of what was going on. He waited until his mother was out and asked the colonel why they were planning to send him far away. Volker sat him down at the kitchen table and unfolded a map to show him where England was located in relation to Vienna and explained how he would get there. He assured the boy that the separation from his parents was necessary, but it would only be for a little while, and that he could think of it as a grand adventure.

"I have to wait for my father. When is he coming back? Where is he?"

"I don't know, Samuel. You're a young man now. You have to help your mother, who has a lot of worries since your father isn't here. Show her that you're happy to go on this trip with the other kids."

"But I'm not happy, Colonel. I'm scared . . ."

"All of us are scared sometimes, Samuel. Even brave men get scared, but they face their fears and do their duties."

"Have you ever been scared?"

"Many times, Samuel."

"I want to stay here with my mother and with you until my father returns."

"I'd prefer for you to stay here with me too, but you can't. One day you'll understand."

Once Rachel Adler, with her heart in pieces, finally accepted what had to be done, things began to move quickly. A representative from the Jewish community visited Volker's apartment the next day to evaluate their situation. The fact that Samuel's father was in a concentration camp, and the wives of prisoners were in danger of being deported too, meant that the boy could be added to the list of passengers. They explained that the Kindertransport was being organized with great care by several Jewish committees, rescuing children from Poland, Hungary, and Czechoslovakia as well. Other countries had offered to receive the young refugees, but none had opened as many homes to them as Great Britain. Samuel would travel by train to Holland, near Rotterdam, and from there he would go by ferry across the channel to the English port of Harwich.

ON DECEMBER 10, VERY early, Rachel and the colonel took Samuel to the train station. Rachel shuffled along like a sleepwalker, sedated by an excessive dose of Steiner's drugs. The day before, she had suffered a panic attack so severe that Volker had called Steiner. The pharmacist, alarmed, ordered Rachel in the most urgent terms to collect herself, to keep from passing her fears to her son. The little boy was making a commendable effort to remain calm and she had to help him; she had no right to break down this way in front of him, the pharmacist insisted. Then he injected her with a powerful tranquilizer that put her to sleep for nine hours. In the meantime the colonel packed a little suitcase for Samuel with clothes he'd purchased, one size too big so that he could wear them for as long as possible. He put a ten-reichsmark bill in the pocket of the new little coat and he pinned one of his war medals to the lapel.

"It's a medal of bravery, Samuel. I received it many years ago in the war."

"For me?"

"I'm only loaning it to you, to remind you to be brave. Whenever you are frightened, close your eyes and rub the medal and you'll feel a huge strength grow in your chest. I want you to keep it until we see each other again, then you'll have to give it back to me. Take good care of it," the colonel told him, his voice breaking.

That day a large group crowded the station. There were children of all ages, even some who could barely walk being led by the hand. Many of the youngest cried and clutched their mothers, but in general the mood was calm and the organization impeccable. Dozens of volunteers—almost all women—registered the children, as guards in Nazi uniforms monitored the periphery, without intervening.

Rachel and Volker led Samuel to a table where a young Englishwoman checked that the boy was on the list and hung an identification badge around his neck. Then she patted his cheek and told him sweetly that he couldn't take the violin, because each passenger was allotted only one piece of luggage; there was no space for any more.

"Samuel never goes anywhere without his violin, miss," Volker explained.

"I understand. Almost all the children want to bring something extra, but we aren't allowed to make any exceptions."

"They let that one through," Volker said, pointing to a small child clutching a teddy bear.

The young woman tried to reason with the colonel, explaining that she was only following orders. There was a long line of children waiting and a circle had formed around them. Some people were annoyed at the holdup and others commented that it wouldn't hurt anyone to let the little boy take his violin, while the Englishwoman insisted that she had to follow the rules.

Suddenly, Samuel, who hadn't said a word since they'd left home, set his dented violin case on the ground, removed the instrument, placed it on his shoulder, and began to play. In under a minute a hush had fallen around the young musical prodigy as the air filled with sounds of a Schubert serenade. Time stood still and for a few brief, magnificent moments the sad crowd, weighed down by uncertainty, felt comforted. Samuel was small for his age and the coat, which was too big, lent him an endearing, fragile quality. Seeing him play with his eyes closed, swaying slightly to the rhythm of the music, was a magical spectacle.

When the song finished, Samuel received the applause with his habitual calm and carefully returned the violin to its case. In that instant the crowd parted to make way for a large woman dressed all in black, her name circulating in a murmur all around her: It was the Dutch woman who had organized the Kindertransport. Impressed by the music, the woman bent over Samuel, shook his hand, and wished him a good journey.

"I'll show you to your seat," she said. "You can bring your violin."

Kneeling on the pavement, Rachel hugged her son tightly, incapable of holding back her tears, muttering instructions and promises she wouldn't be able to keep: "I'll see you soon, my love. Don't forget to drink your milk, and brush your teeth before bed. Don't eat too many sweets, and be respectful to the people who take you in, remember to say thank you. I'll see you soon, as soon as your papa gets home we'll come to get you. We're going to bring Aunt Leah and maybe your grandfather too. England is a very pretty country, you're going to have a lot of fun. I love you so, so much . . ."

The most vivid image of his past, which would remain intact in Samuel Adler's memory until old age, was that last desperate embrace and his mother, bathed in tears, held up by old Colonel Volker's firm arm, waving her handkerchief at the station as the train moved away. That was the day his childhood ended.

SAMUEL

LONDON, 1938–1958

The journey from Austria to England took three days, which to little Samuel felt eternal. For the first part of the trip the children sang cheerily and played with the volunteers, but as the hours passed they were gradually overcome by fatigue and homesickness. The littlest ones cried out for their parents. By the second day they were slumped against one another on the hard wooden benches and floors, dozing fitfully. Samuel, however, remained stiffly upright, immobile, gripping his violin, silently following the repetitive *trac-trac-trac* of the iron wheels against the rails. The train stopped frequently for soldiers to inspect it, threateningly, but they were no match for Frau Wijsmuller-Meijer's icy authority. Finally they reached the frozen, somber Dutch port, where they filed off the train through the afternoon rain and climbed aboard the ferry, heads nodding with exhaustion. The petrol-colored water was choppy and many of the children, who had never seen the ocean, cried in fear. Samuel became seasick and vomited violently over the railing, his face splattered with salty spray.

When they arrived in England they were greeted by the families who had agreed to take in the tiny refugees, each one identified by the sign hanging around their neck. Samuel was met by two women, a mother and daughter, who had requested an older girl to help with domestic chores and spent a good while arguing with the organizers, as he stood against the wall holding his little suitcase, his violin, and his coat stained with vomit. He stayed with the women only a short time. They both worked in a military uniform factory and even though they were twenty-something years apart in age, they seemed like twins due to their identical affected way of speaking, their tight curls, manly shoes, and bad breath. They lived in a tall, narrow house crowded with porcelain figurines, cuckoo clocks, fake flowers, crocheted doilies, and other objects of dubious taste and practicality, all meticulously arranged in an inalterable order. Samuel wasn't allowed to touch anything. They were very strict and always in foul moods, with an endless list of house rules, even going as far as to count the sugar cubes and dictate who could sit in certain spaces at certain times. They didn't understand a word of German and the boy did not speak English, which contributed to their exasperation. Additionally, Samuel spent hours in silence, crouched in the corner, and he wet the bed at night. When his hair began to fall out in clumps, they shaved his head.

It was soon evident that this was not the right home for Samuel Adler and so he was handed over to another family and then another and another, repeatedly rejected because of his sickly, depressed disposition. After a year of this, he was placed in an orphanage on the outskirts of London, a beautiful region of meadows and forest. Against that bucolic backdrop, the horrendous stone building, built as a hospital during the First World War, stuck out like an eyesore.

The orphanage was meant for children much older than Samuel and was run with the discipline of a military barrack. The boys had wooden bunks with thin mattresses and lived on rice and beans, as pretty much everyone did in that time of war. They studied in classrooms that were freezing in winter and suffocating in summer and spent a lot of time playing sports, because the institution's objective was to form young men who were strong of both body and mind. Disputes were resolved in the boxing ring, those who misbehaved received the rod, cowardice was the worst defect imaginable. At first Samuel was exempt from certain activities and punishments because he was asthmatic and much younger than the other boys, but those privileges soon expired.

Through all this, the boy kept his violin. He wasn't allowed to play it, but he composed melodies in secret and imagined how they would sound in the silence of his room at night. He cherished the war medal that Colonel Volker had pinned to his coat before taking him to the station, keeping it safely tucked inside his violin case. He had confirmed on more than one occasion that it was in fact magical, just as the colonel had claimed: His fears abated whenever he rubbed it. He guarded the medal jealously, aware that it was only on loan and that he'd have to return it one day.

Across England, optimism was the rule of the day. Victory was all but assured, they said, although the war effort had an abysmal cost in blood and resources. The German bombings, which killed more than forty thousand civilians and reduced entire neighborhoods to ash, had failed to achieve their ultimate goal of terrorizing the British population into surrendering. Minutes after the enemy planes retreated and the sirens announced the end of a bombing, people emerged from their hiding places, smoothing out their clothes, feigning a calm that no one felt, and began the work of putting out fires and searching for survivors among the rubble. Everything was rationed, food was scarce, there was no fuel for any mode of transport or heating in wintertime, the hospitals overflowed with wounded victims, and the streets were crowded with amputees and starving children. Still, people tried to live with dignity, determined not to make a fuss, to maintain a stiff upper lip and bear the danger and discomforts with a sense of humor, as if it were all happening in another dimension. *Keep Calm and Carry On* was the slogan printed everywhere.

IN 1942 SAMUEL GOT pneumonia. In his wrought-iron hospital bed, among a dozen other patients lined up along the ward, he struggled to breathe, oscillating between blazing fever and cold sweats that left him shivering. At one point he thought he was dying and decided to tell his parents. He had written to them several times but he received only two brief letters from his mother during his first year in exile. In moments of lucidity, he wrote, with great difficulty, to his parents on a piece of notebook paper a nurse had given him. No one could help him write it because the letter was in German. *Dear Mama and Papa: I am sick. I want to tell you in case you go to get me at school and you don't see me there. The hospital is very big and everyone knows where it is. Sometimes I feel like I'm floating and I can see myself lying on the bed. They don't know if I'm going to die, but just in case, I want to leave you my violin so you have something to remember me. I also want to ask you to give the medal back to the colonel who lives on the second floor. It is inside my violin case. Please excuse the errors, I almost forgot how to write in German. Your son, Samuel.* He addressed the letter to *Herr Rudolph Adler und Frau Rachel Adler, Vienna, Austria,* and asked a nurse to post it for him. Knowing that it would never reach its destination, the good woman handed it over to Luke Evans, because he and his wife were the only people who visited the boy.

Luke and Lidia Evans were a Quaker couple who had spent years volunteering to help children in war zones, first during the Spanish Civil War and then working with Jewish organizations around Europe. Samuel thought they looked very old, but they were only in their early forties. Due to the intense love they had for each other, they'd gradually begun to look more and more alike and could almost pass for twins, both short and slim, with straw-colored hair and round glasses. Lidia suffered from Parkinson's, which in time would lead to semi-immobility, but when Samuel met her it was not yet noticeable. Her illness had forced the couple to abandon their work on the front lines and return to England, where they tried to help young refugees such as Samuel. The Evanses didn't have children of their own and quickly became attached to this intelligent, painfully sensitive boy. And so, when he was released from the hospital several weeks later, they took him home with them. Samuel never again returned to the orphanage; he'd finally found the home he so desperately needed.

The Evanses became his family. They sent him to a Quaker boarding school, but he spent weekends and vacations with them. Conscious of his origins and eager to give him a background in religion, they enrolled him in classes at the local synagogue, but the effort lasted only a few months. Samuel felt he no longer belonged to that community, and religion in general did not interest him, despite the rabbi's best efforts. He was not attracted to Christianity either, but the school was liberal in that respect and did not force him to convert. His reserved nature fit perfectly with the Quaker values of simplicity, peace, truth, tolerance, and the power of silence.

The Evanses and the school provided Samuel with much-needed stability; soon his asthma attacks and nightmares became less frequent and his alopecia, which had tormented him for years, cleared up on its own. The bald spots on his head filled in and he grew the mop of curly hair that, for the rest of his life, would be his most distinguishing physical characteristic. He was a good student and decent rugby player, which helped him to integrate with the other boys, but he did not make friends. Athletics were required and he liked that rugby enabled him to let out his frustrations through shoving, tack-ling, and rolling in the dirt, but it was the only time in his life that he would play sports. As a teenager he joined the school orchestra, where his talent shone, but he'd gone too long without practicing and although his love for music remained intact, he was no longer the prodigy he'd once been.

SAMUEL WAS TWELVE YEARS old when the war ended in May of 1945. He would forever remember the bells ringing in celebration, the parties that spilled out of the houses and schools into the streets, ev-eryone joyful, hugging, shouting, laughing. When the festivities fi-nally subsided, Europe began to take stock of the bloody victory, with cities destroyed, land laid to waste, massacres, countless victims, and hordes of refugees searching for a place to sit and rest. The con-centration camps, where the Nazis exterminated eleven million peo-ple, more than half of them Jews, were now abandoned. Samuel hoped he might find his parents, who would surely be searching for him. He imagined they'd arrive at his school and ask after him, and when they saw him they wouldn't recognize him; but he would rec-ognize them, because he had their photograph stuck to the inside of his violin case beside Colonel Volker's medal. His childhood violin had been replaced, but those other relics of his past still went every-where with him. He imagined his parents unchanged by the six and a half years they'd been apart. In the photograph, his father had glasses, a mustache, and a serious expression that contrasted with his moth-er's open smile, beautiful dark eyes, and wavy hair. He wore a formal suit with a vest, somewhat outdated, and a bow tie; she wore a white blouse, a dark jacket with a brooch on the lapel, and a fashionable hat.

Several more years would pass before he received any news of his family. In 1942, the Nazi leadership had agreed on a "final solution," as they called it, to exterminate the Jews, but the details of the Holocaust would not come out until much later. The Evanses contacted one of the organizations dedicated to helping the millions of people displaced by the war, but their efforts to locate the Adlers were in vain. They tried to keep Samuel from seeing the reports about the concentration camps, but one Saturday the boy went to the cinema and a newsreel played scenes of the horror: piles of cadavers and bones, skeletal survivors. Terrified, he refused to believe that his parents could be among the victims.

UPON COMPLETING SCHOOL, BOYS his age were required to go into mandatory military service, but Samuel was exempt due to his asthma and a back injury he'd received playing rugby. Instead, he attended, on a full scholarship, the Royal Academy of Music, which had been the most prestigious conservatory in England since its founding in 1822.

Through a cruel twist of fate, the bright, sunny day Samuel excitedly began his in-depth study of music turned out to be one of the blackest days of his life.

He walked back to the Evanses' house, so euphoric that he felt drunk. He arrived around seven o'clock in the evening and as soon as he crossed the threshold he felt a dark premonition, as if he'd been punched in the gut. Lidia stood blocking his path.

"Wait, Sam . . ." she said, gripping him by the vest, but the boy didn't let her finish. In the living room sat a large young woman, so blond she looked albino.

"Samuel . . . ? I'm Heidi Steiner. Do you remember me?" she asked in German. "No, how could you, you were so little when we saw each other last. I'm Peter Steiner's daughter."

Samuel hadn't spoken German in years, but he could still understand it. Neither name meant anything to him. He waited for the woman to continue, the knot in his stomach tightening. Because she spoke to him in German, he deduced that the visit was about his parents.

"I was able to find you because I knew you'd been brought here to England on the Kindertransport and the organizers kept a register of each child. Your file listed all the houses you stayed in and the orphanage where you lived before the Evanses took you in. The Quaker school was listed too."

She added that she hadn't been able to seek him out before because it took years for the inhabitants of the defeated countries to put their lives back together. Germany was in ruins, humiliated, and impoverished. Austria had shared a similar fate.

"In the early days we had to rummage for food in the garbage," she said. "The hunger was so severe that there were no cats or dogs left alive, we even ate the mice."

Peter Steiner, Heidi's father, understood that his freedom was at risk under the Nazi regime; he had some well-connected friends who warned him that the Gestapo had him in their sights, suspecting him of being a Communist sympathizer. He hid money away to protect his family in case something were to happen, never imagining that the Nazi defeat would transform the bills into useless slips of paper overnight. Along with his savings, he kept the deeds to Rudolph Adler's clinic and apartment, as well as a note explaining that it had been a symbolic transaction, and that Adler was in fact the legitimate owner.

"I'm sorry, Samuel, but your home was destroyed in a raid," Heidi said.

Samuel suspected that the woman was trying to buy time with this long preamble. Why would he care about some property in Vienna? She couldn't have come all this way to give him news of an apartment building.

Heidi went on to tell him about two of her brothers, recruited as teenagers, who never returned from the battlefield. One of her sisters died of typhus and the other disappeared when the Russians occupied Austria. Of the six Steiner children, only she and the youngest brother remained, along with their mother, who now lived in an asylum.

"My father was arrested in 1943, accused of being a Communist. They confiscated the pharmacy and our home. He died in Auschwitz," she explained.

"I'm very sorry for the tragedy your family has suffered. It's terrible . . . But tell me, do you know what happened to my parents?"

"What I have to tell you is very sad, Samuel, but that's why I've come here. I don't want you to have to live your life not knowing, that's worse than grief . . . Your father was taken from the hospital, still badly wounded, two or three days after Kristallnacht . . ." Heidi paused, unsure of how to continue.

"Go on, please, I need to know. What happened to him?"

"The last thing my father learned, from people in touch with other prisoners, was that he died shortly after arriving at Dachau, of a brain contusion."

"So that means my mother was already a widow when she sent me to England, although she didn't know it," said Samuel, a sob lodged in his chest.

"I'm afraid so."

"And my mother? What happened to her?"

"She didn't have much better luck, I'm afraid. Because she was waiting for your father, she missed her opportunity to emigrate. Your neighbor, Theobald Volker was his name, a retired military officer, hid her for a while, then she moved in with us. The colonel sheltered her for as long as he could, but when he fell seriously ill, my father made space for her in the back room of the pharmacy. In the basement under the back room, actually; she hid there for a long while. But the SS discovered her when they raided the pharmacy and arrested my father. There wasn't enough time to warn her."

"And what happened to her?"

"Forgive me for being the bearer of all this bad news, Samuel . . . They took her to Ravensbrück."

"The women's concentration camp?"

"Yes. Over thirty thousand female prisoners died there, Samuel. Your mother and your aunt Leah among them."

HAVE SOME FUN, SAMUEL, *try to enjoy yourself. You have to live the lives your parents didn't get to,* Lidia Evans once told him. But he had always been a serious person and learning the truth of his parents' tragic fate only made him more taciturn. He didn't even know how to have fun, as Lidia suggested.

His first job was with the London Philharmonic Orchestra, already very prestigious even though it had been around for only twenty years, very little for an institution of that kind. He knew at first glance that an orchestra was a prime example of teamwork, but in reality each musician was an island. This suited his solitary nature perfectly.

The orchestra was his refuge and music was the only thing he truly enjoyed. Nothing could compare to the experience of diving into an orchestral piece as if it were an ocean, sailing effortlessly over the waves and currents, adding his violin to the formidable chorus of other instruments, each one with its distinctive voice. In those moments, the past was erased and he felt that he disintegrated, his body dissolved, and his spirit, free and exultant, rose up with each note. When a performance was over, he was always surprised by the strident applause, pulling him brusquely back to the theater. Afterward, as other members of the orchestra went out to unwind over drinks, he walked to the flat he rented in a neighborhood of Caribbean immigrants. He covered his violin case in plastic to protect it from the rain and fog, and he hummed the pieces he'd just played. That hour and a half strolling slowly through the dark streets was the closest thing to fun that Samuel knew.

On the days that he didn't have a concert, he tried to go walking in the countryside or rowing down the Thames. On more than one occasion he got lost in the hills or was overtaken by a fog so dense that it took him several hours to return to his starting point. Solitary exercise in the fresh air was like music to him: It gave him peace. He visited the Evanses often. He didn't have any friends his own age and he laughed at Lidia's efforts to find him a girlfriend. Luke laughed about it too. "Leave him alone, Lidia, he's still young," he would say. But Samuel feared he would never find a woman capable of loving him.

Everything changed for him at twenty-five, when he decided to travel to the United States. He wanted to study jazz, which he considered to be the most original thing that had emerged in Western music since the nineteenth century. He was fascinated by the freedom and energy of it, the bold incorporation of different styles, and the chance for reinvention with each new execution. He was awed by the unfettered creativity of the musicians, who played in an altered state of consciousness, in ecstasy, and the genius of stars such as Miles Davis, Louis Armstrong, Ella Fitzgerald, Billie Holiday, Ray Charles, and countless others, whose records he obsessively listened to over and over. He needed to hear jazz live, to get lost in its syncopated rhythms, its melancholic blues, the irresistible force of the instruments conversing among themselves, calling out to him. And to do this he had to go to the place it had all started: New Orleans.

LETICIA

EL MOZOTE & BERKELEY, 1981–2000

L eticia had a U.S. passport and citizenship, but anyone could tell by looking at her that she was originally from somewhere else, with her caramel skin, black hair, and indigenous features. She was sometimes asked if she was Native American because she spoke English without an accent. She had no roots left in any other land; they were firmly planted in California. She knew she had relatives back in El Salvador, but she wasn't in touch with any of them. Of her immediate family, only she and her father remained.

She'd entered the United States clinging to the back of her father, Edgar Cordero, as he swam across the Rio Grande. That had been in early January 1982, twenty-four days after the El Mozote massacre. She rarely spoke of that time. She had never even talked to her father about it because he held his pain in the sealed box of memory, believing that only silence would keep the hurt intact. Words dilute and deform memories, and he didn't want to forget anything. Leticia had never spoken about it to her American friends either, because in her new country no one had ever heard of El Mozote and if she told them, they wouldn't have believed her. In truth, very few of them could even pick out El Salvador on a map, and the tragedies of that country, so close geographically, would've been to them like something out of ancient history from some far-flung land. The immigrants who came from Central America all looked the same to them, dark-skinned and poor, people from another planet who simply turned up at the border out of nowhere, laden with problems.

She remembered little from her childhood before the border crossing, just the smell of the wood-burning stove, the dense vegetation, the taste of ripe corn, the chorus of birds, warm tortillas for breakfast, her grandmother's prayers, her brothers' and sisters' cries and laughter. She never forgot her mother and treasured the single surviving photograph of her, taken in a town square when she was pregnant with her first child. Leticia saved the picture, her only heirloom, in a small box that served as a portable altar, where she also kept a few photos of her father, the license from her third marriage—the only one that counted, her daughter's first loose tooth, and other sacred items. What she remembered most clearly from that time was the massacre, even though she hadn't been there. She'd compiled images of the event throughout her life, trying to understand what had happened. And from so much research, it was as if she'd witnessed it.

For many generations, her family had lived in the Salvadoran village of El Mozote, made up of some twenty-five houses, with a small church, a rectory, and a school. Her home, like almost all the others, was a tiny clapboard structure with a packed-earth floor consisting of two rooms shared by her parents, the children, and a grandmother. The radio was always set to a station that played news and popular music; there was a portrait of her mother and father on their wedding day, tense and solemn, and a little plaster statue of Our Lady of Peace, the patron saint of El Salvador. The Corderos, like the rest of the inhabitants of that small village, were evangelicals, unlike most of the people in the overwhelmingly Catholic region, but that didn't lessen their devotion to the Virgin of Peace.

Leticia slept with two of her siblings on a pallet on the floor, the grandmother shared her bed with one of the children, who couldn't walk because he was born with an illness that affected his bones, and her parents slept in another bed with the two youngest kids. They had chickens, dogs, cats, and a pig who all roamed free, as did the children; no one felt the need to monitor them as they played in the mountain caves, ran through the underbrush, or swam in the ponds. From a young age, the children participated in farming and domestic chores. Leticia helped her mother wash clothes in the river, scrubbing them with soap and beating them against the rocks after soaking them all night in ashy water. The girl walked to school carrying her single pair of shoes in her hands—so as not to wear them out—and put them on when she arrived. She had many friends among the kids from the neighboring villages who came to study at the one-room schoolhouse. There, a single teacher taught them from books yellowed with age. The woman earned the children's respect by rewarding them with candies for good behavior or punishing them with blows of the ruler to the palms of their hands.

Leticia's father was a farmer, like the rest of the men in the area, cultivating corn, yuca, and avocado on a small parcel of land in conjunction with his neighbors. He always said that they were poor, but less poor than others, because they didn't have to break their backs on the coffee plantations owned by the large landholders. And they never went hungry.

Sunday service was the social event of the week. On their only day of rest, they put on their best clothes to sing hymns and pray for the harvest to be free of pests, for the animals to breed, for the guerillas and the soldiers to leave them in peace, to become closer to Jesus. The Corderos also prayed for Leticia, who had been suffering stomach pains for months; the teas of anise seed, mint, and parsley did nothing to alleviate her ailment.

The most important day of every year was when the eight-year-old children were baptized. The day was celebrated with a morning procession to the river where the children were submerged, followed by music, dancing, and food at night. Leticia's grandmother was already sewing her a new white dress to wear the following year.

But the girl's pain worsened week by week. She was bloated and had no appetite. She dozed off all the time and wandered around like a sleepwalker. She seemed so weak that they excused her from washing clothes with her mother or helping her grandmother in the kitchen, but they wouldn't let her miss school. One day she vomited at recess. That afternoon, the teacher walked her home and spoke with her father.

"Excuse me, don Edgar, but your daughter is spitting up blood. That's very serious."

"She throws up sometimes. The government doctor saw her when he was through here some four or five weeks back, if I recall."

"What did he say?"

"That she had indigestion and anemia. He gave her some drops to take and told her to eat more meat and beans, but everything makes her sick. I'd say she's getting worse."

"She needs to get to a hospital."

"That'd be a very expensive trip."

"Let's see what we can do," said the teacher.

That Sunday, the itinerant pastor explained Leticia's situation to the parishioners, and as they always did when called upon to help in an emergency, everyone contributed as much as they could to the collection, which went entirely to the purchase of two bus tickets and a little extra for travel expenses. Leticia's grandmother packed a bag with the girl's best clothes, so that she would look decent when she arrived in the capital, and a basket with bread, cheese, and half a grilled chicken. Her mother wasn't able to help with the preparations because she'd just gone through a long and difficult birth that left her exhausted, but she accompanied her husband and daughter to the bus stop. Several neighbors, the pastor, and the teacher were there to bid them a safe journey. After saying a brief prayer for them, the pastor gave Leticia a small plastic cross and explained that it glowed in the dark, just as Jesus's love shone in times of darkness.

The bus was packed with men, women, children, live hens, and all kinds of bags and parcels as it bumped along twisting, turning roads. The journey would have been arduous for Leticia if not for the bottle of valerian extract she'd been given by her teacher, who took it for insomnia. Thanks to those drops, the girl slept for hours leaning against her father, and another dose permitted her to keep sleeping later in the city, when they had to spend the night on a park bench.

At the hospital, they were informed that they could get an appointment to see a doctor in two months' time. Just as Edgar Cordero was filling out the paperwork, the jostle of the bus had its delayed effect and his daughter fell to her knees, vomiting blood at the receptionist's feet. The girl was rushed away on a stretcher and her father watched her disappear behind a door.

Many hours later he learned that Leticia had a ruptured ulcer in her stomach and had undergone an emergency operation. They explained that she'd lost a lot of blood and required a transfusion. She would have to remain in the hospital until her condition stabilized, but he wasn't allowed to stay with her and was instructed to call in a few days to find out when she would be released so he could come back for her. They allowed him to see her for a few minutes, but the girl was still under the effects of the anesthesia and all he could do was plant a kiss on her forehead and ask Jesus to protect her.

Edgar Cordero hitchhiked back to his village, saving his bus ticket for his return trip with Leticia.

.　　　.　　　.

TWO DAYS AFTER THE operation, Leticia had a bandage around her stomach and her arms were covered in bruises from the hypodermic needles and tubes, but she was beginning to eat purees and navigate the halls with the help of a walker several times a day to strengthen her legs. At first she was dizzy and her knees felt like gelatin, but she kept trying because she was determined to get well and return to her family as quickly as possible; she couldn't wait to hold her newborn brother in her arms.

The public hospital provided medical services to a broad area of low-income families. It had too many patients and too few resources, the doctors were always in a rush, and the nurses, exhausted and underpaid, could barely keep up. The paint was peeling from the damp walls, rust stained the bathrooms, the trash cans were overflowing, and the sheets—so thin they'd become transparent—were in such short supply that some beds only had a plastic tarp covering the mattress. Nevertheless, the medical attention was good.

Leticia was the only child on an adult ward where there was never a moment of silence as hospital staff constantly paraded past. It was as bustling as a market, but Leticia felt that she was all alone, like in the caves where she played hide-and-seek with the other kids from her village. She was used to sleeping with her siblings, to the presence of her family, to the limits of her home and her town. She missed her mother, and she was afraid something might happen to her father that would keep him from coming to get her. She wanted to see if her little plastic cross truly glowed in the dark, but it never turned to night on that hospital ward, where the lights were left on at all times. She cried often, silently so that no one could hear.

On the fifth day, she was released from the hospital. She sat waiting for her father with her bag packed, freshly bathed, her hair in two long braids like always, and, in place of the bothersome bandage, only a small patch on her stomach. She'd said her goodbyes to the hospital staff and the other patients, and she was anxious to leave.

When her father arrived, she hardly recognized him. He looked like a filthy beggar, with dark stubble and the terrified expression of a man who had walked through hell and back.

The attending nurse on her ward paused her comings and goings for a moment to give Edgar Cordero the necessary instructions about his daughter's care. She informed him that the recovery had gone very smoothly and that in a couple of weeks Leticia would be like new, as long as she ate well and rested. She needed to be careful not to exert herself to ensure her stitches did not open.

"It doesn't hurt at all anymore, Papa. I can eat and I don't throw up after," the girl added.

Edgar simply gripped her hand, threw her bag over his shoulder, and walked her out into the blinding midday sunlight.

"Are we going back on the bus, Papa?"

"We're not ever going back, Lety," her father replied, and a deep sob drowned out his voice.

YEARS LATER, LETICIA TRIED to find out as much as possible about that terrible December in 1981 that had forever marked the course of her life. Over a decade would pass before the truth was revealed little by little, because neither the government of El Salvador nor the United States wanted the world to learn the details of what had happened in El Mozote and other villages of the region. They denied the massacre, impeded investigations into the events, and assured the impunity of the murderers. The bloodbath had been perpetrated by a military operative trained by the CIA at the infamous School of the Americas, in Panama, to combat insurgents from the Farabundo Martí National Liberation Front. For years, the United States intervened in Latin American politics to defend their economic interests in the region, facilitating cruel repression. In reality, it was a war against the poor, just as had happened in other countries during the Cold

War. It was a systematic attempt to root out any and all leftist move-ments, especially the guerillas.

There were no guerillas in El Mozote, only farmworkers from the village and surrounding areas who flocked there in search of safety when the soldiers flooded in. But there was no safety to be had. That day, December 10, the soldiers of the Atlacatl Battalion arrived in the remote region by helicopter and occupied several villages in a matter of minutes; the objective was to terrorize the rural population to keep the people from supporting the insurgents. The following morning the soldiers began by separating the men to one side of the village and women to the other; the children were sent to the rectory, which they called "the convent." They tortured everyone, including the chil-dren, trying to glean any information; they raped the women and murdered every living soul. Some were shot, others were stabbed with knives or machetes, some were burned alive. The children were run through with bayonets or slaughtered with machine guns, and then the convent was burned to the ground. The little charred bodies trapped inside were unrecognizable. With the blood of a murdered child they wrote a message on the wall of the school: *One dead child, one less guerilla*. They also killed the animals and set fire to the houses and fields. Then they left, leaving only blazing coals and bodies strewn across the ground. They fulfilled their mission of scaring the locals into submission by annihilating more than eight hundred peo-ple, half of them children, with an average age of six.

There were many operations similar to this one in the eighties. The civil war left more than seventy-five thousand dead, almost all civilians, almost all of them murdered by their own country's mili-tary.

EDGAR CORDERO HAD ARRIVED back at his village two days after the massacre, which had taken place while he and Leticia were in the city. By then, the military had already abandoned the area and all that was left were piles of bodies rotting in the sun amid hordes of flies. That's how he learned what had happened. Leticia didn't know if he'd been able to find and bury her mother, siblings, and grandmother, because he refused to speak about what he saw that day. "It's best you don't know" was his answer whenever she asked.

When she was released from the hospital, the only explanation Leticia received from her father was that the military had passed through their village and their family no longer existed. They would have to go somewhere far away to start a new life. The girl didn't understand the magnitude of the tragedy, but she felt it as an immense void in the center of her chest. She wasn't in any condition to undertake the journey that her father had planned, so they waited in the city for two weeks, with no money and no friends. They were taken in by an evangelical church, which provided them with a place to sleep at night and a breakfast of coffee and bread, but they weren't able to stay there during the day. Each morning, Edgar left his daughter in the shade of the trees at the park and went out in search of any work to be had, earning barely enough to buy food. Sitting beneath the trees, alone and hungry, Leticia gathered enough strength to begin walking to the North.

THEY MADE A LARGE part of the journey on foot, hitchhiking or perched atop cargo trains whenever possible, because they didn't have money for transportation. They ate thanks to the charity of kind people and the shelters that aided migrants along the route. Sometimes they were allowed to sleep for a night or two in the courtyard of a church, where they were given a hot meal and a hose to wash themselves; other times they spent the night curled up together in the open air alongside other travelers like themselves, huddled close to protect one another from thieves, gangs, and police harassment. Since they didn't have a guide—a coyote—to show them the way, they simply followed the flow of migrants, other men, women, and children hoping to reach the North. They advanced more slowly than most because Leticia was still weak; her father hoisted her on his back and carried her for long stretches, driven by pain and rage. One of Leticia's worst memories was the crossing of the Rio Grande at night, tied to her father with a rope as he gripped a tire tube in both hands for flotation. The current took her prized glow-in-the-dark cross.

Ever after, she'd sometimes wake in the night, terrified by a vivid sensation of cold, terror, darkness, silence, whispered prayers, and the river's powerful pull.

Their early days in the United States were very difficult. Edgar Cordero got sporadic work picking fruit, making bricks, or loading grain sacks; none of the jobs lasted long and he and Leticia were forced to move around a lot. They stayed with other migrant families or in dismal rented rooms, never stopping in one place for long enough to call it home. The one constant was that Leticia always went to school. Her father got angry with her only if she received bad grades, and the only time he ever hit her was when she stole lip gloss from the supermarket.

The evangelical churches of the Latin community provided a support system. These were itinerant temples—migratory just as their undocumented congregation was, always on the move in search of work. Leticia's father found solace among people who shared his faith; he would attend services several times a week and diligently study the Bible in Spanish. Those religious services were their only social outlet, where they were not alone but part of a community. Members of the congregation helped one another out, organized sporting events for the kids, sewing classes, bingo for seniors, Sunday breakfasts of doughnuts and hot chocolate, AA meetings, and other activities. The pastor would greet them at the door of the church, everyone said hello to one another, many knew their names and asked if they needed anything. Leticia could still remember the hymns, which they sang with fervor. The pastors said that God loved everyone, no matter the color of their skin, but rejected sinners. At the end of each service, anyone who needed to forgive or ask for forgiveness was invited to come forward. Half the congregation would move to the front of the church, hugging one another or sometimes falling into states of trance, overcome with emotion. Edgar cried, because he knew he could never forgive the men who murdered his family.

LETICIA'S FATHER COULD GET only the worst jobs because he was undocumented and didn't speak English. She, on the other hand, picked up the language very quickly and would translate for him. The man had only a few years of elementary education but he hoped his daughter might go to college, praying that with Jesus's help she would get a scholarship.

In their times of deepest poverty, they happened to meet Cruz Torres, who had been in the United States for many years making a living in construction with an entire team of Latin workers under him. Cruz knew how to work with cement, brick, wood, and stone; he knew plumbing and electricity; he could replace a roof or put in a swimming pool. He took pity on Edgar Cordero—that sad, silent man who had lost everything except his daughter and held on to her like a life preserver. He could tell that Leticia was the only reason the man had to go on living. With Torres's help, Cordero's situation improved. Since his small construction company was based in Northern California, he convinced Edgar to move there and promised he'd never again lack for work. Cruz found them two rooms for a steal in a rent-controlled building in Berkeley. The place was in a dilapidated slum, but for Edgar and his daughter it felt like a palace.

Instead of going to college as her father dreamed, Leticia ran off with her first love before finishing high school. Despite the trauma, displacement, and poverty she'd suffered all her life, she was a lively girl who could start up a conversation with any stranger on the street, and she was always up for a good time. She had rhythm in her blood. She fell in love, in the passionate, all-consuming manner of a sixteen-year-old girl, with a young American man, blond and athletic, as good at partying as she was. In fact, the couple met at a bar, where the girl should never have set foot in the first place, because she was underage and her father would've had a heart attack if he'd known. Edgar was very strict and followed all of the moral precepts of his religion to the letter, condemning alcohol, pop music, dancing of any kind, provocative clothing, and even public swimming pools.

"A young virgin like you could get pregnant in a pool with strange men," he warned her.

"Ay, Papa! That pool has so much chlorine that none of their little sperms would be able to survive," Leticia replied, though she wasn't sure it was true.

Her boyfriend, plumber by trade and alcoholic by vocation, got Leticia a fake birth certificate that said she was two years older, so that they could marry. That fraudulent start to the marriage turned out to be beneficial, because they were later able to separate without the trouble of divorce papers. The marriage was never valid, but Leticia didn't realize that until much later, when her patience finally ran out.

The girl broke her father's heart when she dropped out of school and ran away with her boyfriend, also abandoning the evangelical church. "Even if you leave Jesus, he'll never leave you," he would say, and he prayed daily for his daughter's salvation. But Leticia argued that religion was a matter of faith, and she simply didn't have it; she had too many doubts. She believed, nonetheless, in the power of Saint Jude, the patron saint of lost causes, and in Saint Christopher, the patron saint of travelers, whose picture she carried in her purse to ward off traffic accidents. She left the church because she couldn't stand a pastor telling her how to think, how to live, and even who to vote for. One of those preachers tried to convince her to stay with the plumber, who had become abusive, saying that God would not accept fickle and arrogant women who thought they were equal to men, since the Bible was very clear on the matter: Eve was created from the rib of Adam and therefore owed him submission. With men, the pastor was more tolerant.

The young couple's burning passion quickly turned to aggression; they fought over jealousy, money, his drinking. She was tired of flipping burgers at McDonald's, of living constantly in debt, while he blew his salary on partying. Any conversation could devolve into insults, shouts, and blows. The plumber had had a brief wrestling career, which left him with a broken nose, several menacing tattoos of demons and dragons, and a strong tendency toward violence. The relationship didn't last very long, because Leticia soon understood that she was living with two different people. The one everyone else saw was a happy, attentive, and generous man, who earned good money as a skilled laborer but couldn't seem to save because he was all too willing to splurge on frivolous items, gamble it away, or loan it to friends. She fell in love with that version of the man, the life of the party. But inside, he carried around a monster lying in wait, ready to rear its ugly head as soon as he got drunk. It wasn't obvious that he drank as much as he did; he could sometimes fulfill his duties for several days at a time even though he was always intoxicated, but when he got lost at the bottom of a bottle, it was terrifying.

Alcohol would light the fuse of the pent-up aggression that had served the man so well in the wrestling ring. In his normal life he had no outlet for it, and so it built up in his veins with mounting pressure. Leticia was always looking for the signs of danger. If she wasn't able to get out of the way in time, she'd have to suffer the consequences. She put up with the man for a couple of years, forever hoping that he would change, as he promised he would after each reconciliation. But one night her patience ran out. He tried to hit her but was slow with drink, and she charged at him with the fury of a bull in the ring, butting him in the chest. Taken by surprise, the man lost his balance and fell backward, smashing his head against the granite countertop. Leticia left him lying inert in a puddle of blood and walked the twenty-two blocks to her father's apartment in long strides. It never occurred to her to call an ambulance. She walked into her father's home, her shoes stained with blood, and calmly explained that she'd killed her husband.

It turned out he wasn't dead, just unconscious. From that day onward, her husband respected her. When she announced that she was leaving him, he didn't dare to stand in her way. Leticia never saw him again and she never again allowed anyone to intimidate her.

The plumber was eventually replaced by another man, whom she met in a restaurant where they both worked as waitstaff. He seemed like a nice guy, but just a few months after she married him, he took up with another woman, whom Leticia classified as a vulgar trollop on the rare occasion she had cause to mention her. That second marriage left her with so few memories that later in her life, she often forgot the man's name.

LETICIA KNEW VERY LITTLE about El Salvador beyond what she'd been taught by the teacher at the rural school in El Mozote, but she was able to rediscover her homeland at the public library. There, through the internet, books, and magazines, she'd seen hundreds of images of the tropical vegetation, clear streams, fruits and flowers of every color, mountains and volcanoes, the bright blue Pacific Ocean. She diligently studied a book of tropical birds whose cover showed a torogoz, the national bird of El Salvador, with brilliant plumage and a long tail. She had many friends in the Bay Area Salvadoran community who helped her maintain her original accent in Spanish and stay connected to the traditions, music, and food. She did not, however, share in any nostalgia for their country. Many returned to visit every year, but she had been back only once. "Why would I go back?" she would respond when they asked her. She no longer had any family or acquaintances there and had heard it was dangerous. After the peace agreements between the government and the guerillas had been signed in 1992, the civil war came to an end officially, but the violence never ceased. Criminals and narcos, fully tattooed, packed the prisons but were protected by membership in the maras, the ruthless gangs that no government had been able to dismantle.

At twenty-two, between her marriages to the alcoholic plumber and the waiter who ran off with the trollop, Leticia traveled to El Salvador. Her father refused to join her because he'd vowed never to set foot on the land stained with the blood of his family. Leticia had hoped to get in touch with some distant cousins but didn't have enough information to locate them. So she went directly to El Mozote to face her memories and nightmares.

She found a guide willing to take her to her family's tiny village, but not before warning her that there was nothing left to see. For over ten years, the government had denied the massacre, destroying all evidence and silencing reports from the few fearful survivors, but with the end of the civil war the truth finally came to light. Everyone in the region remembered the horrific events. Leticia and the guide reached the area by bus and then had to continue on foot. She recognized the landscape, even though the vegetation was overgrown and the temperature much hotter than she remembered. They advanced slowly, cutting their way through the jungle in some stretches where the path had been taken over by plants, but the guide knew the route from memory. He told her that he had been ten years old when the massacre occurred and he survived by hiding in the hills, where the people of his village had learned to take refuge during the years of the civil war. The soldiers would come every few months on one of their sinister missions and then the villagers would escape to the caves. That had been his life growing up, constantly fleeing, and, he said, to that day he had trouble sitting still. Like Leticia, his entire family had been massacred that December day in 1981. The soldiers had orders to sow terror but since those poor farmers' lives were of little value and no one was keeping count, they went overboard.

"Why did they kill the children? Even the most savage beast in the jungle isn't that brutal. And these crimes were committed by men just like the victims, people from the country, poor people," he said.

In El Mozote, Leticia found no traces of her past. No record that her mother, brothers and sisters, or grandmother had ever existed. In the spot where her small village once stood, all that remained were some bones hidden in weeds and the ruins of a few shacks. Not a single person stirred. The air was filled with the buzz of insects and the whisper of lost souls. Leticia almost thought she could hear the faint cries of the children, though it might've just been the wind in the reeds.

AFTER SEEING LETICIA HAPPILY married to Bill Hahn, her third husband, Edgar Cordero died. He never got to meet his granddaughter, whose arrival he'd been anxiously awaiting; Leticia told him that the baby would be named Alicia, just like her mother. They found him sitting in a chair, his head resting on the Bible laid open on the table. He wasn't sick or old, but the life simply left his body, a peaceful transition. The pastor said that he'd flown to heaven in the arms of Jesus, Our Lord. Cruz Torres took care of the funeral arrangements, paying for everything from the coffin to the flowers, and then invited the small group of mourners to eat at a Mexican restaurant.

Leticia, gripping her husband's hand tightly and seven months pregnant, attended with her face puffy from crying.

"Now that don Edgar has left us, remember that I'm like a godfa-

ther to you, Leticia. You can always come to me if you need anything."

"Thank you, don Cruz, but she's my wife and I can take care of
her," Bill Hahn interrupted respectfully.

"Of course, but you never know what might happen. I hope you'll
always stay in touch, Leticia."

Bill Hahn had descended from pioneers who'd crossed the North
American continent on foot in 1849 with hopes of striking gold. His
great-grandparents lived a dire existence chasing a slippery fortune
that they never obtained. Some of their descendants passed through
brief periods of prosperity, but the family seemed destined to a life of
hard work and little compensation. Bill, proud of his lineage, had
studied the California Gold Rush, going as far as to compile the letters and documents of his ancestors. That curiosity for history earned
him a post at the Oakland Museum and a modest salary. It was enough
to support his wife. He didn't want her to have to work while she was
pregnant or immediately after, while trying to care for a newborn. He
was an introverted man with deep emotions, who'd fallen in love with
Leticia at first sight in the museum hall. He was disarmed by her
looks, her self-assurance, and the wide smile she flashed to thank him
for directing her to the cafeteria. She'd made such a strong impression that he abandoned his duties to follow her and, overcoming his
ingrained shyness, asked permission to sit down at her table. He decided that he had to win this woman's heart and worked methodically
toward his goal until he achieved it.

They'd been married a little over two years and she was as content
as she had ever been. That man, so unassuming, possessed an inexhaustible reserve of tenderness and a surprising sense of humor.

Nevertheless, one never knew what might happen, as Cruz Torres
had wisely predicted on the day of her father's funeral. Bill had been
suffering a severe headache for several weeks, which he kept at bay
with painkillers. This was accompanied by blurred vision and a stiff

neck, but he put off a visit to the doctor with the hope that his symptoms would disappear in time. But that afternoon, when the museum had closed and he was checking that everything was in order for the night watchmen, an aneurysm burst in his brain. He was blinded by a flare of pain and fell to the floor, where he was discovered two hours later.

Leticia heard the news from a police officer, who showed up to take her to identify the body. She felt as if an abyss was opening at her feet. She arrived at the station bathed in tears, hugging her baby girl to her body, and trudged into the freezing room where her husband had been laid out. She planted a long kiss on his lips and repeated the promise they'd made to each other so many times: They'd always be together.

At first, the young widow stayed shut inside the small apartment she'd shared with her husband, clutching her daughter, barely daring to venture beyond her front door. She didn't want to see anyone, but her neighbors insisted on bringing food and condolences. Bill had been kind and she was friendly, happy, and generous; the time had come for her to be on the receiving end. But eventually her friends and neighbors returned to their own lives and she felt the tremendous weight of loneliness. She'd gotten used to depending on Bill and his constant attention, sleeping next to him in bed with their daughter between them. She hadn't worked in over two years and had very little savings left in the bank, so she decided it was time to set aside her grief, for little Alicia's sake. She couldn't afford the luxury of crying forever.

That was the year 2000. She was twenty-seven years old, with an eighteen-month-old daughter, and her life in shambles. And then Cruz Torres reappeared, like a gift sent from heaven. He took one look at her, hopeless, sad, and poor, and immediately lent her money, paying one year's rent in a decent room where she could live until she got back on her feet. At that time he had a contract to remodel an old house in the hills of Berkeley, a long-term project that involved a lot of work. He introduced Leticia to the owner of the house, who needed someone to help with the cleaning and other domestic chores.

The woman hired her without asking any questions. Cruz's word was all she needed. The good man also helped Leticia find other clients for cleaning homes and offices, setting her on the path to what would become her main occupation.

SELENA

SAN FRANCISCO & NOGALES, 2019

O n December 23, Selena showed up at the law offices of Larson, Montaigne & Lambert. The firm occupied the top three floors of a skyscraper on Montgomery Street, the heart of San Francisco's financial district, with a spectacular view of the city. Steel, concrete, and glass, furniture made of leather and aluminum, live plants, neutral colors, photographs of sand dunes and clouds. From the moment she passed through the glass double doors with the names of the senior partners in gold lettering, Selena could feel that authority, efficacy, hurry, and hierarchy reigned there. The receptionist told Selena to wait without offering her a seat, and dialed an internal line. Selena smiled, amused, inferring that the icy courtesy, bordering on hostility, was designed to intimidate visitors. She, however, was not easily discouraged.

She stood waiting for fifteen minutes, examining the framed sand dunes and clouds, as she watched people carrying covered trays down a hallway. Finally, a middle-aged woman, who looked uncomfortable in her high-heeled shoes and skirt suit with a too-tight jacket, came to greet her.

"Selena Durán? Good morning. I'm Mr. Lambert's assistant."

"I have a meeting with him," said Selena.

"Yes, of course. Follow me, please. Excuse the chaos. Today's the last day of work before the Christmas holiday. We have the end-of-year party this afternoon."

Selena thought of the covered trays, imagining shrimp, ribs, and steak on little sticks. She'd had a cup of coffee and a couple pieces of toast at five o'clock that morning, before taking the first flight from Tucson to San Francisco at seven-fifteen. It was now nearing noon and she was hungry. The assistant led her down a wide hallway to a set of double doors at the end and rapped softly with her knuckles. A few seconds later, Ralph Lambert opened the door. Selena recognized him from his pictures in the media; he was the face of the law firm, which had a reputation for winning cases for celebrity clients willing to pay exorbitant fees. He was sixty-something, shorter and slimmer than she'd supposed from his photographs.

"Welcome, we're ready for you," he said.

Selena stepped into a large conference room with one entire wall of windows. There were a dozen people sitting around a long table and several others standing against the back wall. She assumed they were junior associates.

"Ms. Selena Durán, from the Magnolia Project," Lambert announced, pointing Selena toward a chair.

She dropped her enormous handwoven bag from Guatemala on the floor beside the door, tucked a strand of hair behind her ear, and ignored the chair as she stood at the head of the table to face the group.

Selena knew that for occasions such as this one, she had to take greater care with how she presented herself, as her grandmother constantly reminded her. In her everyday work, comfort was more important than looks, which was why she always wore blue jeans, T-shirts, and sneakers. But that morning she'd made an effort to make her grandmother proud, pulling her hair back into a sleek ponytail, putting on lipstick, and wearing the black suit she referred to as her "begging outfit" because she used it only when she had to ask for donations of money and time. She thought it made her look like a serious professional.

Sitting at the table, a short distance away, was Frank Angileri, the firm's young star lawyer, whom his coworkers called "the favorite" behind his back. They gossiped jealously that Lambert was grooming him as a protégé, which explained why Frank always landed the biggest clients; he'd just been assigned the Alperstein case.

Frank considered himself an expert in sizing people up at first glance, a skill that served him well in the courtroom, but this woman was unclassifiable. Based on her name, he guessed she was Latin, but she didn't fit the stereotype; she was tall and light-skinned. He found himself attracted to her even though she was a few pounds heavier than what he generally considered appealing. The woman seemed to have made very little effort to impress them with her appearance. And what the hell was this project?

"Good morning. I'm here today to talk to you about the Magnolia Project for Refugees and Immigrants," the young woman began. "As you know, there is currently a serious humanitarian crisis at our border with Mexico. The U.S. government has implemented a policy of zero tolerance on immigration and ordered the separation of all families who come here seeking asylum. It was already common practice, unofficially, even before the presidential order went into effect. Thousands of children have been taken from their parents; there are even cases of infants being pulled from their mothers' breasts. I recently had to accompany a one-year-old before a judge, without his parents. He was in a stroller, sleeping."

The border separations had been public knowledge since May of the previous year, when the press began to cover them. There was a fierce national and international outcry against the policy; it was hard to remain indifferent to images of children being kept in cages, curled up on the ground, dirty and crying. Finally, the government was forced to give in to public pressure and rescind the order, but by that point thousands of children had already been separated from their parents. Selena explained that in actuality families were still being separated under different pretexts and that hundreds of children were being held in detention centers because officials hadn't bothered to keep accurate records, and now their parents couldn't be located. No one had enough foresight to consider the need for later reunification. Thousands and thousands of minors had also been arrested after reaching the border alone. More continued to arrive.

"The Magnolia Project is trying to help these kids," Selena continued. "We're not the only organization involved; there are almost forty thousand lawyers and law students working pro bono to aid the crisis. A serial killer has the right to a lawyer in this country, but that right does not extend to immigrants and refugees. Almost without exception, a child who goes before a judge without the proper legal representation will simply be deported, regardless of the situation they were fleeing in their country and without knowing if their parents are even there to receive them. But when there's a lawyer present to defend the child and explain their case, they are often granted asylum."

"Ms. Durán needs our firm's help, and of course, we're stepping up to the plate," Ralph Lambert added.

Frank inferred that this was all part of the PR campaign aimed at improving the firm's image. The firm had long held a reputation for successfully defending criminals who were clearly guilty but prepared to pay a fortune to get off the hook. In the past, this was almost a point of pride. But the winds of society were changing and it was time for a rebranding. Total impunity for the super-wealthy was not tolerated as it had once been. Hence the sudden gestures of philan-thropy, the appointment of women to key roles, and the hiring of professionals of color. White males still dominated the pristine of-fices, but not as completely as before.

Immigration was a hot-button topic, and engaging with it might bring a lot of headaches, but Frank knew that Lambert would've weighed the risks. He was impressed by the young woman's calm elo-quence and felt embarrassed that he hadn't paid more attention to the tragic fiasco playing out at the border.

SELENA ASKED LAMBERT IF she could share a brief PowerPoint pre-sentation. He gave the order for his assistant to press a button on the wall and the window shades silently lowered. Another person placed a projector on the table facing a screen and Selena connected it to her laptop. She'd given this presentation many times and knew that the most important thing was to keep the viewers' attention. The images appeared in rapid succession: Central American families making the dangerous pilgrimage to the U.S. border; hundreds of people riding on the roofs of cargo trains, walking through the desert, or swimming across the river; border guards and armed vigilantes who granted themselves the right to impose the law with deadly force; the deten-tion cells called iceboxes, where people from warm climates were subjected to freezing temperatures; heartrending scenes of border agents dragging screaming children away as their mothers and fa-thers pleaded desperately. Selena explained that these separations were just as prevalent as before, but now carried out secretly, at night.

No one stirred. A thick silence blanketed the room. Many people had been openly affected by the slideshow; a few wiped away tears.

"How can we help?" one of the women asked.

"We need lawyers who are willing to volunteer to defend these children and to help put an end to this form of torture for good. Never again, never again," said Selena Durán.

"I don't know anything about immigration law . . ."

"That's not a problem. We'll provide you with the necessary training," Selena told her.

"Count me in, then."

"What's your name?"

"Rose Simmons. But I'm not sure how much I'll be able to help; I don't speak Spanish."

"Don't worry, we have interpreters. Thank you, Rose."

"The firm will give you some flexibility with your hours, Mrs. Simmons, but you can't neglect your obligations here; the extra work is to be done on your own time," Lambert said.

"I understand, sir."

"You won't regret it, Rose. I assure you," Selena said. She looked around the room.

Frank blushed as he suddenly felt that Selena Durán was staring at him, singling him out in the crowd, judging him.

"There's no money or glory in this work, which is why our team is made up almost entirely of women. Care for the children in the detention centers and the social and psychological assistance they receive are in female hands as well," Selena said.

In a spontaneous impulse, Frank raised his hand and announced that he would like to help. The gesture was met with collective shock. No one had expected that from the favorite, busiest, most ambitious member of the firm.

Lambert gestured for Frank to follow him out into the hall and closed the door behind them.

"Don't you think you have enough on your plate already, Angileri? I expect you to give two hundred percent to the Alperstein case."

"I can do the pro bono stuff in my free time."

"You don't have any free time. Or vacation days either."

"For Christmas, I'm only going to my parents' in Brooklyn for two days and I'm taking the Alperstein file with me. But I'm not a miracle worker; any jury he gets is going to skewer him. One of the victims, who was drugged and raped, was only fourteen years old."

"That's why I'm counting on you to keep this from going to trial, no matter what, Angileri. One misstep here and your career is as good as over."

"Don't worry. I got this."

WHEN THE MEETING WAS over, Selena Durán put away her laptop and her notes, then proceeded to take down contact information for Rose Simmons and Frank Angileri as she explained the responsibilities they'd have at the Magnolia Project. First, they would complete an online introductory course on immigration law, and then they'd be assigned one or two cases to start. They would meet the children they were representing, spread out across several detention centers, prepare their defense, and attend hearings to explain each child's case when it was their turn to appear before the judge. It often took a long time to get a hearing, she told them, because the courts were overwhelmed with thousands and thousands of backlogged cases.

"I have to warn you that once you get involved in this project, it's hard to step away," she added with a complicit wink.

"Well, since you've trapped us, Ms. Durán . . ." said Frank.

"Call me Selena."

"Selena. The least you could do is have lunch with us," Frank suggested.

"I can't," Rose apologized. "My in-laws are coming in from Missouri to spend Christmas with us."

"And I'm leaving for Los Angeles this afternoon," said Selena.

"Do you live there?" Frank asked.

"I live in Arizona, but my family is in Los Angeles. I'm going to spend Christmas Eve with them and then fly back for work the next day."

Frank silently thanked the heavens that Rose had to leave, then convinced Selena that she had more than enough time for lunch before her flight. He took her to Boulevard, one of the expensive restaurants where his bosses popped bottles of Dom Pérignon over lunch. The young woman, with her worn boots, a coat that looked like it came from a secondhand shop, and the brightly colored bag that passed for her luggage, was the opposite of the sophisticated women he was used to being seen with in public. He greeted the maître d' by name, trying to impress Selena, but she was on her cellphone, having a conversation in Spanish. They were shown to a table in the back by the window, and the manager, who had a good memory for generous tippers, brought them each a glass of prosecco before handing them the menus.

"This is a sparkling wine from northern Italy, the Veneto region," Frank instructed Selena.

She drank it all in one gulp. "Not bad," she said.

Frank realized that a nice bottle might be wasted on this woman, who clearly didn't know the difference between a Quintessa and a cooking sherry.

He began to think it had been a mistake to volunteer for extra responsibilities and another mistake to ask this woman out to lunch, but he was now locked into both decisions. He'd acted on impulse, spurred by his sexual attraction to Selena, hoping to show her he was a generous man of principles. Inviting her to lunch, he'd hoped, would lay the groundwork for a more intimate encounter in the near future, when he returned from Brooklyn. *I'm an idiot,* he thought, more amused than annoyed. But after a few minutes of conversation his doubts faded.

Over a bottle of Quintessa, Frank dominated the conversation and Selena listened distractedly as the lawyer continued to expound on the challenges of his important cases, the firm's prestige, and his exemplary court record, making passing mentions of his time at Yale, without a single question about the pro bono work he'd volunteered to do. She decided not to rush things: There would be time enough for this conceited guy to have a reality check, she thought, amused.

Selena ordered filet mignon with French fries. Frank's knee-jerk reaction was to comment on the calories and cholesterol, but he stopped himself. He opted for steamed turbot; he was watching his figure. The women he dated were normally vegetarians who would carefully pick at a plate of lettuce; he couldn't remember the last time he'd been with a woman like Selena Durán, who ate the bread and poured creamy dressing all over her salad.

THE LUNCH RAN LONG and as they ordered dessert, Frank decided he would skip the hellacious office party. Instead, he would take Selena to the airport so he could spend an extra half hour with her. The fact that he would have to return later that night to take his own flight did not discourage him.

Selena ate her profiteroles with chocolate sauce without offering Frank a single bite and with the pleasure of someone who hadn't eaten in hours, as he told her all about Christmas in Brooklyn, where his family had lived ever since his grandparents emigrated from Sicily. The holidays were his only chance all year to see his entire extended family, who always gathered at his parents' house. None of the Angileris ever missed it: his two grandparents, their children and partners, the grandchildren, some cousins, an unmarried neighbor who had been an opera singer, and his crazy uncle Luca.

"He walks around with a huge old pistol from Garibaldi-era Italy and claims he fought with the International Brigades during the

Spanish Civil War. For that to be true, he'd have to be at least a hundred and three years old, but he doesn't look a day over ninety," Frank explained.

"Tell me about your parents," Selena asked, so that she wouldn't have to talk and could concentrate on her food.

"They own the best Italian deli in the city. I don't think my father has ever read a book, but he wanted all of his children to get college degrees. My mother is a force of nature. She's usually very sweet, but when she gets mad, you better stay out of her way. When we misbehaved as kids she would spank us with a wooden spoon. And she once banged me on the head with the lid of a spaghetti pot. I wasn't hurt, but I'm still scared to go near her when she's cooking pasta. She wanted us to be bilingual so, when I was growing up, she never spoke to us in English. In my family we still fight in Italian and make up in Italian."

"In my family we do it in Spanish. But it's great you speak Italian, that'll help you with the kids since it's fairly similar to Spanish."

"I studied Spanish in high school and college, but I'm pretty rusty."

"The children you'll be representing are grateful for a smile or a kind tone, Frank, they can make do with few words. My Spanish isn't perfect either, but it's improved a lot through this work," Selena explained.

"At least you can speak it."

"That's thanks to my great-grandmother, who always spoke to me in Spanish."

"Very few people get to meet their great-grandmothers," Frank commented.

"I come from a long line of immortal women," she said. "Men come and go, or they die on us, but they never last very long, which is why we all use the name Durán, passed down from my great-grandmother. She was born in Mexico, like my grandmother, who's clairvoyant, but my mother was born here just like me and my sister, and now her two kids."

"Did you say clairvoyant?"

"Yes, she's psychic. She was born with the gift. She can communicate with the dead. They even appear to her sometimes."

"You're joking!"

"She's very famous actually. You've never heard of Dora Durán? She's been on TV several times. And she participated in the Chapman University research program on paranormal phenomena. The police and people from all over consult her."

"What about?"

"It depends."

"Okay, just give me one example," said Frank, holding back laughter.

"Well, one of the most recent cases was a nine-year-old boy who went missing. My grandmother helped them locate his body, inside a well."

"Wow. Was she able to identify the murderer?"

"He wasn't murdered, he just fell in."

"How did your grandmother know? Did she see it in a dream?"

"Sometimes it comes to her in a dream, yes, or other times it's a very strong intuition or premonition. From time to time a lost soul will visit her. That's what happened with the boy. She'd gone to pick up my sister's kids at school and was waiting on a bench in the park when the boy appeared beside her. My grandmother suddenly felt freezing cold and her heart started pounding. The boy told her where he was and then he disappeared."

"It must be terrifying to grow up surrounded by dead people."

"I've never seen them or heard them myself, so it's never bothered me."

The lunch crowd had dispersed by the time they left the restaurant. They walked slowly to Frank's car and he drove Selena to the airport. They agreed to meet after Christmas in Arizona and in the meantime she'd send him the immigration law material he would need to begin studying. She explained that the judges had no time, so to speed the cases along, they had to make everything as simple as possible. A strong legal argument was essential, but it was even more important to elicit emotion. It all came down to the judge, some were empathetic and understanding, others were total assholes. The newly appointed ones fell into that second category.

Frank walked with Selena as far as he could in the airport and then waited as she went through security. He'd expected the woman to turn around and wave a final goodbye, a minimum courtesy after he'd dedicated so much time to her, but she just kept on walking without so much as a backward glance.

SELENA DURÁN SHARED AN apartment with another social worker in Nogales, Arizona, ten minutes from Nogales, Mexico, across the border in the state of Sonora. What had started as a temporary arrangement had gone on for two years. According to her fiancé, Milosz Dudek, it was time to make more permanent plans. Like finally getting married, for example, and moving back to be near her family in Los Angeles, where her future husband waited impatiently and ever more frustrated over her delayed return. He'd lost count of how many years she'd been finding excuses to put off the wedding.

The Durán family widely considered Milosz to be a great catch; he was young and healthy, with no known vices, and as a truck driver he earned better money than some doctors, transporting heavy cargo across the country, a task that required emotional stability and physical endurance. He could offer Selena a stable life, and a love that had been tested over the years but always triumphed. He wanted kids, a cozy home, a happy wife waiting for him when he returned from his long trips in the big, slow trucks. According to the Durán women, Selena didn't know how lucky she was. Where else would she find another man she could control with a mere glance, who was also gone most of the time? No reasonable woman wanted a full-time husband. Milosz had loved Selena since she was a teenager; they'd almost married on two different occasions, but then broke up, went their separate ways, got back together, and started the process all over again. Now he was sick of this endless cycle. He'd had plenty of opportunities to be with other women, and sometimes took advantage of them, but he never even remembered the women's names. Selena was the only love he'd ever known.

Before the Magnolia Project, Selena had been employed by the California Health and Human Services Agency, where she had acquired the administrative and organizational experience needed to manage funds and programs. The new job paid less than half of what she'd made before, but she felt she'd finally found her place in the world. When she first learned about the families being separated at the border, she joined the ranks of outraged people and decided to take the three weeks of vacation time she'd accrued at her state job and volunteer to help. She had heard about the Magnolia Project, which had been in existence for almost thirty years, and she reached out to them, despite the objections of her fiancé and her family. After just one week working with those children, she quit her administrative job for good. A short while later she became a full-time member of the Magnolia team.

Since then, she had returned to Los Angeles only for brief visits because she was busy working all day and attending virtual courses on law and psychology at night. She dreamed that once the crisis at the border was resolved, she might be able to go to law school. It would add to her already sizable student debt, but it would be worth it.

.   .   .

FRANK HAD ARRANGED WITH Selena to arrive in Tucson on December 25. He planned to meet with her and the girl he'd been assigned to represent first thing the following morning.

When he boarded his flight, he had not yet recovered from the culinary orgy that his mother had begun preparing a week in advance of the holiday: manicotti, shrimp scampi, lobster, breaded fried eel, octopus salad, spinach and rice pie, beef Wellington, and for dessert, cannelloni, almond nougat, and an obscene array of cookies. The Christmas Eve meal would begin around four in the afternoon and continue until it was time to file out for Midnight Mass, a tradition they all upheld even though half the family was agnostic. To make sure that no one went home hungry, there was always gnocchi in red sauce after Mass and Mrs. Angileri was offended if anything was left over. Frank was the only member of this family who could be called fit; the rest knew how to enjoy life. Sometimes his mother's eyes would well up when she thought of her poor little boy, alone, hungry, and brokenhearted in San Francisco, that depraved city of heathens, grifters, drug addicts, and homosexuals. To make sure he stayed well fed, she sent him frozen meatballs by express mail twice a month.

On the flight to Arizona, with a connection in Denver, Frank had seven hours to study the firm's case on Alperstein, a business magnate close to the president, accused of trafficking minors, embezzlement of public funds, and money laundering. When Frank appeared on the national news, standing behind this despicable man, his mother almost fainted. He tried to explain over the phone that everyone has the right to a legal defense and his client was innocent until proven guilty, but she interrupted him, shouting: "Mi spezza il cuore! Che peccato! Un mio figlio che difende un pedofilo!" And she hung up the phone. She was right, Alperstein was repulsive. Frank sent his mother a card and a box of chocolates as a gesture of reconciliation.

He was exhausted from the overnight flight from California followed by that excess of food at his parents' house and lack of sleep, but he couldn't afford to waste any time. Seeing Selena again was the real motivation behind this whirlwind trip, since he could've probably gathered enough information about his first migrant case without being there in person. He'd been thinking about Selena more than he was comfortable with, given that she was far from his ideal woman. And, judging by her indifferent body language, she wasn't even particularly interested in him. He found this baffling, but thought that maybe she just had an unusual way of flirting. He would give her another chance.

He rented a car at the Tucson airport and decided to drive straight to Nogales without stopping to check in to his hotel. The town was nestled in the foothills, deep in the desert, separated from its sister city in Mexico by the long dark snake of the border wall. He'd expected it to be hot, but the temperature at that time of year was cool and much more pleasant than the icy New York December. The Magnolia Project's offices were closed but since Frank was eager to get a head start on the work, Selena had offered to meet him at her apartment, which he took as a good sign. He was worn out, but planned to invite her to dinner after washing up. It was still early since they were three hours behind East Coast time.

The apartment building was a cement block, identical to several others on the street, which counted not a single tree. The elevator didn't work, so he walked up a stairway of questionable cleanliness and found himself in front of a green door. A woman opened it, introducing herself as Selena's roommate; she offered him a glass of water, and picked a cat up off the couch so he could sit down. Frank was allergic to cats.

The apartment consisted of a living-dining room separated from a small kitchen by a countertop, a hallway with two doors, which Frank supposed led to the bedrooms, and a bathroom. Every wall was painted a different color: sky blue, terra-cotta, cinnamon, moss, stone, the colors of the desert, supposedly. The effect was exhausting and the plaid sofa, clearly second- or thirdhand, did nothing to improve the décor. Frank felt nostalgic for his own apartment: white, naked, orderly, simple, masculine.

The roommate informed him that Selena would be back soon and then said goodbye, because she had a date. Half an hour later, when Selena arrived, Frank was spread across the couch, snoring softly with the cat lying on his chest. He was sleeping so soundly that she didn't have the heart to wake him. She simply covered him with a blanket, because the temperature dropped sharply at night, and took the cat into her room.

FRANK WAS AWAKENED AT six o'clock the next morning by blinding sunlight and the smell of coffee. It took him a few seconds to remember where he was. His mouth was dry, the shadow of a two-day beard darkened his face, and he was foul-smelling and sticky with sweat. Selena Durán, dressed in blue jeans and with wet hair, placed a cup of coffee in front of him.

"Rise and shine, young man; we have a lot to do and we start early here."

"I need a shower. I have a clean shirt in my suitcase."

She pointed him to the bathroom, fed the cat, and began to fry bacon and chop vegetables for an omelet. Breakfast was the only meal she ever made at home; the rest of the day was fueled by sandwiches and sodas. Half an hour later Frank Angileri emerged from the bathroom a new man. He was meticulous in his grooming, liked long, hot showers, and always traveled with half a dozen of his own products, refusing to touch the sample-size bottles at even the nicest hotels. His aftershave lotion and his cologne both had delicate hints of musk, which he'd read was an aphrodisiac. By the time he sat down to breakfast, his omelet had gotten cold and Selena was talking on her cellphone in Spanish. Frank imagined she was on her daily call to the clairvoyant grandmother she'd mentioned. After hanging up, she pulled out a folder and spread its contents across the table.

"Your first client is Anita Díaz, seven years old," Selena explained. "She was separated from her mother, Marisol Díaz, in late October and has spent the past eight weeks in a group home for children. Her mother was detained and taken to a private prison in a remote part of Texas, a huge fortress surrounded by barbed wire, which has had multiple reports of abuse and mistreatment. Shortly after that, she was moved again, apparently due to a health issue related to a gunshot wound she received in her country, which may have reopened on her journey here. It's unclear where she was sent from there, but our best guess is that she was deported."

"Where to?"

"We don't know. The family is Salvadoran, but I can't find any record of Marisol being sent back to her country. Usually, they just drop them across the border, in Mexico. We haven't been able to locate her."

"How did she and her daughter end up here?" he asked.

"In mid-October they presented themselves at a port of entry here in Nogales seeking asylum. They were denied and were not allowed to cross the border. There's a presidential order blocking anyone from entering. Ten days later, Marisol crossed illegally near Nogales, where she was detained in the desert along with her daughter. When an immigration officer interviewed her, she showed him the recent gunshot wound in her chest and explained that she and her daughter were fleeing the man who had tried to kill her; she knew him to be corrupt and dangerous and she feared for their lives because he was still after them. It's all in the official report. What's not part of the report is the officer's response, which Marisol told me when we spoke on the phone. He said: 'I don't believe you. You people all say the same thing; it's my job to keep you from getting into this country.'"

"Our country is required by law to consider every request for asylum," said Frank.

"In theory, but in practice all migrants are treated like criminals. Nobody wants them. The zero-tolerance policy and inhumane tactics, like separating children from their parents, are meant to discourage people from coming."

"So what's going to happen to the daughter, Anita?"

"As I said, she's at a youth home. She was able to speak with her mother twice before we lost all trace of Marisol Díaz."

"How could something like this happen!"

"Disorganization, laziness, negligence, zero accountability. No one is going to pay for any of this since the orders come straight from the White House," Selena said.

"Is there a date set for the girl's hearing?"

"Not yet. That's your job, Frank. You have to convince the judge not to deport her and try to buy us enough time to find her mother or some other relative in the United States willing to take her in. They're trying to pressure Anita into requesting a voluntary deportation even though her mother was convinced the girl's life would be in danger if she returned home."

"How could a seven-year-old be allowed to make that decision?" Frank exclaimed.

"That's the policy and it's followed blindly. I just saw the most ridiculous case yet. The judge looked straight at my client and asked if he wanted to be voluntarily deported back to his country. The client was one year old! He hadn't even said his first word. How did they expect the baby to respond? But Anita is very sharp. She refuses to return to El Salvador without her mother."

Selena told Frank that in one of her brief telephone conversations with Marisol, she learned that the mother and daughter had been forced to spend three days in a so-called icebox. Women and children, even some babies under two years old, were kept there, shivering in the glacial cold, huddled together on the concrete floor, with only a Mylar blanket for warmth. Detainees were meant to occupy those icy cells for only a matter of hours before being interrogated and moved, but in reality they often ended up trapped in the iceboxes for three or four days. Along with Anita and Marisol was a five-year-old boy all on his own because he had been separated from his father, for whom he cried constantly as the women tried in vain to console him. The conditions were very bad: barely any food, lack of basic sanitary conditions, lights left on all night, verbal abuse. Anita had said she was thirsty and a guard told her that if she wanted water she should go back to her country.

The little boy there on his own, begging for his father, made Marisol suspect that she and Anita might be separated. She had tried to prepare her daughter, explaining that they might have to stay in different places for a few days, not to be afraid, that she would be taken care of and they'd be back together again soon. She asked Anita to be patient and brave; it was one more trial they had to face, but after that they'd be able to build a new life together in the United States.

"Marisol was taken away in shackles to be interrogated by an asylum officer and when they brought her back to the cell, Anita was gone. She never saw her again. Like so many other mothers, she wasn't even allowed to say goodbye to her child," Selena explained. "The officers lack the training necessary for a crisis of this scale and they're completely overwhelmed. Many of them have put in transfer requests because they don't have the stomach for carrying out their orders."

Frank Angileri placed his head in his hands. He'd heard terrible stories in his years as a lawyer, but nothing that compared to the institutionalized cruelty that Selena was recounting. "I think I may be in over my head here, Selena. I'm used to representing large corporations and wealthy clients like Alperstein, who can pay to circumvent justice. I don't know if I have what it takes to help Anita."

"What matters most is that you're willing to try and that the judge can't trip you up on any technical detail. They'll use any excuse they can find to reject the entire case."

"I don't know anything about immigration law."

"You'll have to study a little, Frank. I'll help you."

THE YOUTH SHELTER THAT Selena drove Frank to was one of the best in the country. Group homes normally housed between one hundred and four hundred children, but this one had only ninety-two. The children were all assigned a number, because the staff was often unable to pronounce their names or remember them, but for Selena it was a point of pride to call each and every child by their name.

"They've lost so much, it's terrible to think they have to lose their identities too," she told Frank. "And the homes can be horrible. A reporter described one center as a chaotic scene of filth and disease, the children and their clothes unwashed, many of the kids sick, and there were shortages of beds, baths, soap, and toothbrushes, the foul stench perceptible even before entering. I suppose that's why they don't let the press in anymore. But you won't see any of that here, the place is decent."

The home was exclusively for younger children, the smallest only eleven months. Anita was the oldest. The compound consisted of ten little houses facing a central courtyard. Eight to ten kids lived in each unit along with their "house parents," who worked and lived there.

"The kids should be in these shelters for as little time as possible," said Selena. "If there's no close relative or sponsor willing to take them in, they get placed in foster care. Sometimes the relatives won't step forward to claim them if they're undocumented because they're afraid they'll be arrested and deported. Anita's situation is unusual; she's been here for longer than normal because of an administrative issue."

Selena told Frank that some of the institutions for older kids, who often arrived at the border alone, were actual prisons, like the juvenile detention center that had been improvised out of a gigantic supermarket warehouse in Texas or the former military base that had been hastily converted in Florida. Some were run by private companies interested in retaining as many children for as long as possible, since the potential profits were enormous. The fee they charged the government for caring for each child was very high. The conditions in these places were such that human rights organizations and the press were not allowed to enter; even members of Congress had been kept out.

"My job is to manage all the cases I'm given. But we social workers are overwhelmed; there are too many kids."

Her tasks included determining how the separation occurred, procuring any social or legal services available to the child as they tried to locate their families, and, if possible, obtaining psychological support for them. It was often hard to get any clear information if the child was very small and didn't remember, or was simply too young or too traumatized to speak.

"There are hundreds of children like Anita, stuck in limbo because nothing was done to maintain a paper trail connecting them to their parents," Selena explained. "It's going to take years to track down all of these minors' relatives and reunite them with their families. In some cases it might be impossible. It's a total nightmare."

"Knowing that they could have their children taken from them, I don't understand why parents would risk the border crossing," said Frank.

Selena described for Frank the situations these families were fleeing. The majority came from Guatemala, El Salvador, and Honduras, the infamous Northern Triangle of Central America, one of the most dangerous regions in the world. There, people often died from conditions of extreme poverty and starvation; domestic abuse was the number one killer of women; gangs, narcos, and criminal organizations murdered with impunity; and government corruption was rampant. It was no surprise to her that refugees would choose to risk being separated from their children here over watching them die at home.

"They imagine that no matter how inhumane U.S. bureaucracy may be, it's still better than the situation they're trying so desperately to escape," she said.

"But we can't just open the floodgates and let millions of immigrants and refugees in. What's the solution, Selena?"

"Well, putting up walls and building new prisons has not helped at all. And ripping children away from their parents is clearly not the solution, Frank. The immigration system could use a total overhaul and we need to address the factors forcing people to leave their home countries in the first place. No one wants to abandon everything they know and run away; they only do it out of total desperation."

"Well, that's not the American government's problem."

"It is, actually, because the American government is at least somewhat responsible for the mess these countries are in. During the Cold War, the United States tried to end all leftist movements in Central and South America by arming, indoctrinating, and training brutal militaries; they knowingly financed government repression. Here, we justified it as the 'expansion of democracy,' but it did exactly the opposite. The U.S. government overthrew democratically elected leaders and imposed vicious dictators; the only thing they were actually defending was the business interests of American companies and the super wealthy."

"Are you a Communist, Selena?"

"Don't be so naïve, Frank. Hardly anyone is a Communist, unless maybe you're talking about China or North Korea. This isn't about left, right, or any other direction. It's about finding practical solutions to real problems."

Selena led Frank into one of the little residences. The people who ran it tried hard to make it look as much like a real home as possible. It consisted of a shared living space, two bedrooms with four bunks each, a bathroom, and a kitchenette used to make baby bottles and heat up snacks. In one corner sat an artificial Christmas tree, and the walls were decorated with children's drawings and Mexican paper cuttings. Selena explained that the food wasn't bad, the group home provided the children with clean clothes because they arrived with nothing more than what they were wearing, and they had recreation hours when they could watch TV and play. The kids had a rigid, structured schedule. Some centers had been accused of abusing, even raping minors, and a few children had even died of neglect, but Selena hadn't seen anything like that in her cases. The kids were all clean, dressed in pants and T-shirts, but Frank immediately noticed the silence in the room. From what Selena had described, he'd been expecting inconsolable sobbing from the kids, but instead they were calmly drawing with crayons, so absorbed that none of them looked up when he and Selena entered. Selena gestured to the only child who was not participating in the activity, sitting alone, holding a rag doll.

"Anita! It's me," she called out in Spanish.

The girl immediately jumped up and rushed to hug Selena, who had crouched down to greet her. Anita was very thin and short for her age, with golden-brown skin, delicate features, and black hair chopped very short. Selena had told Frank that the kids were rarely in one place long enough to build a trusting relationship with caregivers before being transferred elsewhere, but she'd been working with Anita since she first arrived and had formed a bond.

"This is my friend Frank, say hello to him."

The girl froze. Selena had warned Frank that Anita was distrustful of men in general, even the few male social workers at the shelter, either due to her experience with the border guard or because of someone in her past. Frank knelt down to her height.

"Don't be scared, Frank is nice. He's going to help you get back together with your mama," Selena reassured the girl.

After a pause, which to Frank seemed eternal, Anita tentatively held out her hand and Frank shook it. That's when he first noticed that the girl was blind.

THE NEXT DAY FRANK flew back to San Francisco. He'd spent many hours at the youth shelter, first playing with Anita until she felt comfortable with him and then interviewing her in the tiny office that Selena had lent him. They shared a lunch of microwaved burritos and after an endless day taking notes, his mind reeling from everything he'd witnessed, he crashed at Selena's apartment on a bed she made up for him on the sagging couch. He could've driven into Tucson, where he'd reserved a room at a hotel near the airport, but he was exhausted and didn't hesitate when she offered to let him stay another night at her place instead of making the drive. By then he'd already put any plans to seduce Selena on hold, indefinitely. He was now firmly committed to a cause much more important than the fling he'd envisioned, and he understood that any insinuation on his part would be out of line and offensive. Getting romantically involved with her had been a misguided idea to begin with, a bad habit that he needed to kick. He also considered the possibility that Selena might laugh at the notion. Somehow, she still didn't seem that impressed with him.

He had two and a half hours in the air to go over the Alperstein file that he would need to discuss with Lambert as soon as he arrived, but instead, he studied his notes on Anita. The girl was very mature for her age, possibly because of everything she'd experienced on her journey and the trauma of being separated from her mother. Circumstances had required her to take care of herself. She was almost completely blind, but thanks to the sharp memory and powers of observation that she had always had, nothing escaped her. It was as if she had antennae that allowed her to pick up everything around her. Aside from the fact that she never let go of her doll Didi, and whispered to her frequently, she behaved as if she were several years older, which contrasted with her fragile appearance. Selena served as interpreter so that Frank could communicate with her, but he was pleased to find that he understood almost everything the girl said; his high school Spanish hadn't vanished completely.

Anita confirmed what Selena had told him about her previous life and their journey from El Salvador to Guatemala and then through Mexico to the U.S. border. She missed her mother and fought back tears when she talked about her.

"I heard that you weren't born blind, Anita," Frank said.

"When I was little I had an accident. If there's a lot of light, I can see some. I used to go to school and I learned how to read, but I think I'm forgetting how. My school from before wasn't for blind kids," Anita clarified.

Selena explained that there was apparently a cousin or aunt of the family who lived in the United States, but Marisol could only tell her that the woman was named Lety; Anita didn't know her last name or any way of locating her. Lety could have been a relative of the girl's father, Rutilio Díaz, who had died when Anita was three.

"Who did you live with before, in your country, Anita?" Frank asked the girl.

"With my Tita Edu. She's my abuela. And with my abuelo, but he's sick and always stays in bed. My mama came to stay with us on Saturdays and Sundays."

"We know that you made a very difficult trip with your mother. It took a whole month and you even rode on the roof of a train," Frank said.

"Yes, with a bunch of other people. I was the littlest."

"Do you know why you made that trip?"

"Because there was a man who was going to kill my mama. He

shot her. Tita Edu took me to see her at the hospital and I was very scared because I thought that she was going to die, but we prayed a lot and we lit candles at church and she didn't die. After she got a little bit better, she came to get me and we left. Tita Edu and my mama cried a lot, but I didn't cry because I promised my mama I would be a good girl."

"Who was the man that shot her?"

"Tío Carlos. He wears a uniform and he always has a gun."

"Do you know his last name?"

"Gómez. He sometimes came to Tita Edu's house, but she didn't like him. My mama didn't either."

"Tell me about your granny. What's her name?"

"Eduvigis Cordero de Díaz," the girl responded without hesitation.

"We assume it's Marisol's mother-in-law, the mother of her late husband, Rutilio Díaz," Selena explained. "Marisol's maiden name is Andrade and her married name is Marisol Andrade de Díaz but they put her down as Marisol Díaz in her immigration file."

"Tita Edu is very nice. She took care of me when my mama had to work. She works too," said Anita.

"What's her job?"

"She works at the indigo factory. She knows everything about indigo and she explains it to visitors and tourists."

That night, at Selena's apartment, Frank completed his notes with the details that she filled in for him, and he planned the girl's legal strategy. Then they had pizza for dinner and stayed up late talking and listening to Latin music. It was past midnight when Selena suggested Frank should just stay the night instead of making the drive into Tucson. She went to her room and he lay down on the couch covered in cat hair. Selena fell asleep as soon as her head hit the pillow, the cat curled up beside her, never for a moment suspecting that Frank was tossing and turning in the next room. As a teenager, when she realized the effect her appearance could have, she harnessed this power and for a brief time made the most of it. But shortly thereafter Milosz Dudek appeared in her life and she had fewer occasions to use her charms. Mostly she deployed them when required to ask a favor of a man in relation to the children she defended.

Separated from Selena by a thin wall, Frank couldn't stop thinking about her, as if he were drawn by some mysterious force that defied reason. He made a mental list of their many differences and her obvious defects: her sloppy clothes, her lack of flirtatiousness or refinement, her bad taste—clear from her apartment. He could go on and on, but all of this was overshadowed by the image of her generous body, her kind eyes, her firm, rhythmic voice, the happy, carefree way she embraced life even in the midst of so much suffering. He was also kept awake by thoughts of defending the little Díaz girl. He was certain that this would be the most important case of his life, one he'd never forget. If he made any missteps in the Alperstein case it would be the end of his career, as Lambert had warned him, but if he made any mistakes with Anita, his soul would never again be at peace.

ANITA

NOGALES, NOVEMBER–DECEMBER 2019

I think Mama is close, that's how it sounded when we got to talk to her on the phone. What do you think, Claudia? Don't you think she sounded close? I didn't cry when we talked to her, even though I wanted to. Well, I cried a little, but she didn't notice, because I didn't make any noise. If Mama could come get us, she would, but she can't right now. Mama was crying too, so that's why I told her we were good in this place, we have other kids to play with in the yard and sometimes they give us ice cream. It's not like it was in the hielera. I didn't want to tell her that we don't eat because we don't like the food. It's not yummy like what Tita Edu makes. It's better for Mama not to know about that. Miss Selena told me that she's going to try to call her again soon, but it's hard, because they moved her somewhere else. Crying won't do any good, it will just make Mama sadder. If we start crying so hard we can't talk, I'll put Didi on the phone to talk to her.

Of course I remember when they took Mama away in shackles,

94 · ISABEL ALLENDE

but that's what they always do to the people in the hielera. It's just for a little while, then they take them off. It's nothing to cry about, Claudia. I could hardly see anything, but I heard the officers and the sound of the chains and how Mama and the other women in the hielera with us started to shout and ask why the officers were treating them like that, that they were decent people, mothers with children, not narcos or criminals. But they wouldn't listen to them. They took her. She shouted for me not to be afraid, that she'd be back soon. I don't know if she went back there, Claudia, because right after they took her away, they put us on that bus.

Miss Selena said that we're only here for a little while, just until they work out Mama's papers, and then they'll take us to wherever she is. We're fine here. We're super fine, that's what we have to tell Mama next time we talk to her. You get it, Claudia? We don't want Mama to worry. We don't need to tell her that we're sad and scared, or to ask her why she brought us to the North. She knows what she's doing. In El Salvador we were fine until Carlos started showing up and Mama got so scared. I want everything to be back the way it was before so we can go back to Tita Edu's house, and we don't have to live with people we don't know who don't even talk the same way we do. But we can't have everything we want in life.

When you feel like crying, Claudia, do like me. You can think about nice things: about Mama when she was happy and we all slept together, about Tita Edu playing with the dogs and feeding the birds; about school where you painted with your fingers, jumped rope, and played games; about the street parties with all the neighbors and balloons and firecrackers; and about the picnics at the beach. It was so nice to live there, in our country! Do you remember any songs? I do! We can sing "Pin Pon." Not that one? Then we can sing "Arroz con Leche," you always liked that one. Arroz con leche me quiero casar, con una niñita de la capital . . . When I feel like crying I just think about Tita Edu's pupusas on Fridays and how she let me help her in the kitchen. I got good at kneading the dough. I don't have to see to do that. We would put flowers from the garden on the table and wait for Mama, who got home late, on the eight o'clock bus, but she always came home. Tita Edu wouldn't let her do anything to help, because she'd been working all week, and it was time for her to rest. On Friday night I would rub Mama's feet while we watched TV. That would make her fall asleep and then we'd have to explain everything she'd missed on the telenovela. On Saturdays she wouldn't be so tired anymore and she'd get up early to help Tita Edu give Abuelo his bath and do things around the house. Then we'd go out for a walk. I don't want you to forget any of this, Claudia, that's why I'm telling you again, even though you already know.

I also like to think about the storybooks at school and that book with fairies and magical creatures that Tita Edu had. She would read that book to us, do you remember? I could read it too, but not very fast, only little by little. My favorite thing was to start a book, read only one page, then keep going with another book and then another, mixing up the pages, so the story would change every time and it would never end. It was my favorite way to read before the accident. Now I have to read using just the thoughts in my head until I can get a huge magnifying glass, like the one Tita Edu had. That helped me a lot at school. One of these days I'm going to ask Miss Selena if she can get me one; I hope it won't be too expensive.

I've already told you about Azabahar, the enchanted kingdom where you and me are princesses and Mama is queen and Tita Edu is the fairy godmother. It's a star where the people and the animals all live happily, and it's even better than heaven, because you don't have to die to go there. There are no saints or martyrs there, only Our Lady of Peace, who is the one in charge. There are people from that planet and also visitors from other planets and all kinds of animals, some that we already know about and other ones that don't exist here on Earth. Of course, there are a lot of guardian angels, both boy angels and girl angels, because they live there, that's their country. There are some dead kids there, but not too many, and you can't tell because it's just like they were alive. Azabahar is on a faraway star. Tonight, when it gets dark and everyone is asleep, we're going to go outside and look for the brightest star of them all. That's Azabahar.

WE SHOULDN'T CRY BECAUSE we'll scare Didi and they don't like kids who cry here. It would make Mama sad if she knew that we were crying and that we don't want to eat. We promised her we would be brave. Don't be scared, the teachers here are nice, they don't hit us or anything like that; the kids are nice too, most of them. We're not going to play with Rony or Luisito, they're not nice; but I'm bigger and I'm not going to let them bother us; if anyone tries to take Didi away I'll punch them real hard and I don't even care if I get punished for it. Rony is grosser than Luisito. He's a caca worm, that's his name, Gusano de Caca. We're not going to bother him, but if he bothers us we'll spit at him. And stupid Luisito's name is Vómito de Iguana, because he pukes so much.

Listen, Claudia, last night, when you were sleeping, I saw my guardian angel. She's real little. I always thought that angels were very tall people who wore nightgowns and had big wings with feathers, like at church, but they're not like that at all. They're more or less the size of a parakeet. My angel has little wings that are clear like a window, you have to look real careful to see them. And she doesn't have a golden halo, she has an antenna on her head with one feather on the end, like the torogoz's tail, and that's what she uses to talk, because she doesn't have a mouth. I could see her in my head, because you don't see angels with your eyes, only in your head, so it doesn't matter that I'm a little bit blind, I could still see her perfectly. She was right beside my bed, all white, even her hair, like a cloud. I remember clouds, I haven't forgotten them. I was scared at first, but when she told me she was my angel I wasn't scared anymore. She talked to me with quiet words, words in my head, that's why no one heard her; the other kids were all asleep and you were too.

She told me that everybody, absolutely everybody, has their own guardian angel. You have one too. That's why we have to pray every night, it's like saying hello to them: *Guardian Angel, made of light, do not leave me, day or night.* If you're a girl, you have a girl angel; if you're a boy, you have a boy one. The boy ones aren't like at church either, no big wings and all that, they're just like the girl angels but blue, or sometimes green, it depends.

My angel is going to take us to visit Azabahar. Mama is definitely going to come get us here, but if she takes too long, we can meet her in Azabahar. The next time we go, she'll be waiting for us. She might be invisible, that happens sometimes, but it doesn't matter because we'll be able to feel her and talk to her. Yes, we can take Didi. But this is a secret for the two of us, don't even think about telling anyone, because the angel will get mad and she won't take us anywhere. No, she won't go away forever, Claudia, don't be silly. Guardian angels have to stay with their kid, it's their job, she can't just leave whenever she feels like it. Your angel will stay with you even if she's mad, but if you can keep a secret, she'll be so happy.

ALMOST EVERYONE HERE WETS the bed, you see how many kids do it, even Gusano de Caca; that's what the plastic under the sheets is for, so that the bed doesn't get ruined. I don't know why that happens here in the North; back home with Tita Edu we never wet the bed. But they're not going to punish us for it. Miss Selena told me that they can't punish us for that, it's an accident, it's not the same as having a fight or throwing a tantrum. So I'm not mad that you had an accident in my bed, it's not a big deal. That's life.

The Christmas party was fun, I liked the music and the presents. I got colored pencils, but since I can't use them, they changed them out for some modeling clay. I'm going to use it to make some little mice for you and Didi to play with, okay? All the kids were happy, no one cried or got into fights. You wanted there to be a Nativity scene, but they don't have those here. I miss the one we had in El Salvador, even though the little people were so tiny you couldn't tell which one was Joseph and which ones were the shepherds. It's our first Christmas we've ever spent without Mama and Tita Edu. Do you remember how Mama didn't have to work on Christmas and New Year's? She always had those days off. We would go to the beach to see Tío Genaro. When we get back to El Salvador I'm going to ask Tío Genaro to teach me how to surf. I don't think it matters that I'm blind. It made me sad to spend Christmas without Mama and Tita Edu, but I felt better when Frank came and told me he was going to try to get me and Mama back together as soon as possible. I liked Frank a lot, even though he talks funny. He doesn't know very much Spanish. I think he's nice, because he's Miss Selena's friend. I hope he does what he said he was going to do.

SAMUEL

NEW ORLEANS, LONDON, & BERKELEY, 1958–1970

F or someone like Samuel Adler, who lived a highly structured existence in London, New Orleans was a mesmerizing place. That year, 1958, was a memorable one for the city because in February it snowed for the first time in twenty years and in March Elvis Presley came to town to film a movie. Such large, enthusiastic crowds gathered outside his hotel that he was forced to come and go using the fire escape. When Samuel arrived, months later, Elvis was still the main topic of conversation among the younger crowds, even as critics picked him apart and the old folks repeated Frank Sinatra's damning opinion that "Rock 'n' roll is the most brutal, ugly, desperate, vicious form of expression it has been my misfortune to hear." But Samuel wasn't interested in the rock star with his uncontrollable hips; he'd come to New Orleans for jazz.

Perhaps if Samuel had ever explored the Caribbean neighborhood near his home in London, the contrast might not have been so sharp, but the only reason he rented in that area was the price; he couldn't afford anything else. At home, he floated like a ghost through the loud and colorful crowds without speaking to anyone, then shut himself inside his flat to practice his violin, tuning out the sounds of the steel drums on the street and the tropical rhythms blaring from his neighbors' radios. At the market he purchased only the bare minimum to keep himself fed, always the same few items, oblivious to the exotic fruits and vegetables, the birds shrieking from elaborate cages, the hens and pigs awaiting execution, the baskets overflowing with seafood, the brightly colored flowers, and the handmade crafts, all just a few rows deeper into the market. All this foreign culture hit him in New Orleans like a slap in the face. He couldn't understand the Cajun French spoken on the street and found it hard to decipher the drawling Southern-accented English as well. The city forced Samuel out of his comfort zone; there was no room for squeamishness or shyness among the crowds of revelers. If he wanted to learn about jazz, he would have to dive headlong into the chaos of the French Quarter at night.

He had ten days and his goal was to focus solely on the music, not wanting to waste any time exploring the sights or lingering in restaurants. His plan would've surely been successful, if fate hadn't set Nadine LeBlanc squarely in his path on his first night out.

The bar, one of many lining Bourbon Street, hadn't been redecorated since the turn of the century, but it was dark and bursting with jazz, which was all Samuel cared about. It was packed with people, many standing, as waiters weaved their way between the tables, all full, balancing trays of cocktails. The smell of smoke, sweat, and perfume was suffocating, as if a gloved hand were gripping his neck, making him cough. The African American musicians experimented on their instruments, improvising solos and harmonizing, all without missing a beat. From time to time a soloist would rocket off to another galaxy on the piano or saxophone, then return to the arrangement as another musician blasted into the stratosphere, the bass marking the relentless rhythm, calling them back to Earth. Samuel was amazed. He knew that they used signals to indicate each soloist's entrance and exit or to mark the end of a performance, but they were so seamless he wasn't able to identify the gestures.

He was fully absorbed in the music, following the rhythm, not even noticing that he was dancing in his seat when someone sat down beside him and blew cigarette smoke in his face. Samuel recoiled, annoyed at the interruption, but as the smoke cleared he saw not some drunken tart, as he'd expected, but a beautiful young woman, leaning across his table.

"Hello, Humphrey," she boomed, making herself heard over the music.

"My name isn't Humphrey," he clarified.

"Has anyone ever told you that you look exactly like Humphrey Bogart? You could be twins. Have you ever acted? Bogart is my hero."

"Didn't he die recently?"

"He's still my hero. This place is too loud, we can't talk. Come with me, Mr. Bogart." Grabbing him by the hand, the girl pulled Samuel out of his seat. He fumblingly dropped a bill on the table and followed.

They stepped outside, where partygoers of all ages, appearances, and races filed past, drinking and laughing, out for a good time on the town. Music spilled from every bar and restaurant, mingling with the din of the crowds and the conversations shouted from one balcony to another.

"Is it Mardi Gras?" asked Samuel.

"No, silly, carnival is in February. This is just a humdrum Friday night. Tomorrow should be livelier," she explained.

"I'm Samuel Adler, pleased to meet you."

"My name's Nadine," she said, and turning to a group of well-dressed young people, she introduced him as her new friend, Mr. Bogart.

NADINE LEBLANC BELONGED TO an old New Orleans family and had just debuted in society that season after twelve years at a strict Catholic boarding school, where she'd learned to speak perfect French, lie like an expert, smoke like a chimney, curse like a sailor in two languages, and drop from a second-floor window in the middle of the night without ruffling her dress. As she explained to Samuel, she was reveling in every minute of her newfound freedom, much to her parents' chagrin.

"I'm an independent woman," she declared. But in reality she was far from it. She was, in fact, entirely dependent on her family's money, but unwilling to ask their permission for anything. After completing school, girls of her social standing were presented to society—at dances, concerts, picnics, horse-drawn carriage rides around town, or steamboat trips down the river—where they could be observed and evaluated for marriage potential. Families made monumental efforts to show off their influence, connections, and assets, as the debutantes modeled fashionable new dresses, feigning virtue and modesty that they did not truly possess in a cutthroat race to hook the best husband. After all, a girl had to be married off before age twenty-five to avoid being labeled an old spinster.

Nadine was unlike other Southern belles. In her younger years, she had delighted in scandalizing first her family, then the nuns at school. The season she was presented to society, she set out to scandalize the entire town. The last thing she wanted was to play the part of aristocratic virgin only to trap a man like her father or her brothers, who would shackle her to a boring life as a wife and mother. She enjoyed stirring up gossip with her "wild ways," as her parents described her behavior, and she knew she could be forgiven almost anything thanks to her irresistible charm. She stayed out drinking till all hours in bars, smoked with a long cigarette holder, drank too much, and danced in states of rapture, barefoot, shaking her hair loose, ignoring the mixture of revulsion and envy that she inspired in the other girls and boys of her standing. To her family's horror, she bragged about having a great-grandmother who was Black, such a shocking admission in that racist society that it ended up being reported in the papers. But none of Nadine's boastful claims of defiance and irreverence intimidated Samuel.

Samuel was spellbound. The young woman was his polar opposite. Eager to break the mold of what was considered appropriate, she challenged him and tempted him. Even her beauty was an unconventional one, her body thin and flat as a boy's; she had an expressive, unusual face, thick eyebrows, curly black hair, tanned skin, and an easy, crooked smile, painted red. Her most memorable feature was her bright hazelnut eyes, which reminded Samuel of a panther's. Despite her youth, she had a natural talent for seduction, which she wielded like an expert.

"I'm going to take you to hear the best jazz in New Orleans," she declared when Samuel explained the reason for his visit.

But their nights didn't end when the shows were over. He joined Nadine's group of friends, all wealthy, uncultured, arrogant, and younger than Samuel, as she gave him a tour of the good life, taking him to parties. One night they went on a ride down the Mississippi on the steamboat that had served as a casino for over a hundred years, to smoke hash and drink moonshine whiskey on an island in the delta called The Temple, where the pirates of the Caribbean had once auctioned enslaved Africans and other booty from their plunders. She organized a nighttime visit to an area of abandoned houses said to be haunted by zombies, ghosts, and vampires, where, as the other girls shrieked in terror, Nadine had her photo taken with a skeleton. She also took Samuel to a run-down shack in an old neighborhood where formerly enslaved people used to live to consult a Haitian witch doctor, a large, imposing woman wearing a turban and strings of multi-colored beads, who dealt in enchantments, fortune-telling, good-luck talismans, love charms, and amulets said to bring death. The sorceress splattered Samuel with the blood of a sacrificed hen, blew tobacco smoke over his body, read his future in some seashells, and sold him—for a reasonable price—a handful of herbs and tiny bones wrapped in a rag to ward off the evil eye.

"You can ask me one question, that's included in the reading," she told him. But Samuel, dizzy from the alcohol, couldn't think of anything to say.

"Tell us if we're going to be married," Nadine demanded.

"Of course you will, my lovely."

After four days and nights living it up all over town, Nadine stopped planning group outings. She wanted to be alone with Samuel. She was extremely attracted to the musician with the smoldering good looks of a Hollywood heartthrob. The local boys who had courted her all seemed like babes in diapers compared to this sophisticated European man who dazzled her with his culture and kept her guessing with his brooding silences; she imagined that the Englishman guarded untold secrets, and she even went as far as to speculate that he was an international spy using a passion for jazz as a convenient cover.

For his part, Samuel quickly deduced that under that guise of plucky vamp was a spoiled, fickle, naïve girl, but one who was also very generous and intelligent. They fell in love with the urgent passion of young romance.

Then after ten days, Samuel had to say goodbye and return to England. Before leaving he begged her to marry him.

·   ·   ·

SAMUEL AND NADINE SPENT almost two years apart. Her parents refused to give their consent for her betrothal to a groom who lacked any fortune or social standing to speak of—who was in fact a complete stranger. She wasn't mature enough to decide for herself and might never be, they decreed. Nadine continued going to parties and flirting with her many admirers, but the day of her twenty-first birthday she announced that she was moving to England to be with her true love. Her parents made a huge scene over her plans to shack up with a man before marrying him but she simply bid them a cheerful goodbye and marched off in a bright periwinkle dress and matching hat that set off her golden skin tone, with no luggage besides a small suitcase.

The young couple was married in a private civil ceremony in London. The lone witnesses were the Evanses, whom Samuel introduced to his bride as his parents in spirit. That's when Nadine learned that her husband had been orphaned in childhood, he had no living relatives, and the Quaker couple were the only family he could remember. She also discovered that her husband wasn't English, but an Austrian Jew. She was thrilled at the scandal this news would cause among her racist relatives when they found out.

In married life, Nadine LeBlanc proved to be much more mature than anyone who'd known her would've ever guessed. Her husband pieced together a living for them playing in the orchestra and giving music lessons, the two jobs together providing barely enough for an existence free of luxuries. She'd left her wedding trousseau behind in New Orleans, even though she'd been preparing it since age fifteen like all the other girls from wealthy families: embroidering sheets, towels, and tablecloths and accumulating undergarments of silk and lace, Baccarat crystal, Christofle silver, Limoges porcelain, and other items considered absolutely essential to any refined household. Her sisters could have it, she wasn't interested. She left her past behind without so much as a backward glance and, against her family's most pessimistic predictions, she missed nothing and no one from her former life. She was determined to be happy with Samuel Adler and so she was.

From one day to the next, "the feral one," as her siblings had dubbed her and as she even described herself half in jest, half seriously, transformed into another person. Back home in New Orleans, she had been a member of a large clan, a network of family and social connections that provided support and protection. She'd never had to think about money, because she'd always had it. She could get away with being irreverent and even rude, because the privileges of her class afforded her impunity. But upon marrying that poor musician in a foreign land, she was forced to face the difficult reality of the other immigrants who lived all around her. She walked proudly into this new life without a hint of regret over all she'd lost.

She first set out to turn Samuel's run-down flat on the fourth floor of a walk-up building into a cozy home. She hung cheerful wallpaper to hide the flaking paint, bought colorful blankets to cover the decrepit sofa and to liven up the bedroom, made paper lanterns, and placed potted plants in every corner. She became as much a part of the local Caribbean community as anyone who'd come straight from Jamaica, learning to cook with the unfamiliar spices and dance to the tropical rhythms in local bars and restaurants where people gathered in the evenings. Shortly after arriving, she joined a protest against police brutality. It turned out that the British bobbies were just as racist as the American cops. In a confrontation between police and protestors, Nadine received a blow to the back that sent her flying into a line of trash cans. She was found by stragglers from the protest who were returning home hoarse from shouting and bruised by the police. They helped her up and led her to the local coffee shop, which at night was converted into a bar with a dance floor, and they called a local doctor. The man, born in Trinidad, possessed the knowledge conferred by his profession combined with the wisdom of a shaman.

He quickly determined that she had not broken any bones and prescribed rest, ice, and aspirin. "This woman is very brave. And also pregnant," he announced to the crowd of onlookers that had formed. That night Nadine won the respect of her neighbors and went on to make many friends, whereas Samuel, who had lived in the area for years, hadn't known a soul before his wife introduced him to the surrounding community.

IN A SHORT TIME, Nadine changed Samuel's life and softened his temperament. He learned that he should never try to control her because she would only slip through his fingers like sand. He tried, at first, to keep pace with her, but that proved impossible. In the end he resigned himself to trailing behind, admiring the elliptical arc of her life, so different from his own. She was much quicker than he was, unpredictable, explosive, and passionate. She possessed an intuitive intelligence and assurance that allowed her to reach a decision in a matter of seconds, while Samuel could take weeks vacillating and planning. She was gregarious, curious, and bold, striking up conversations with strangers, adopting animals, and disappearing on mysterious excursions, which in time were revealed to be charity missions. Her joy tempered her husband's tendency toward melancholy; her free spirit provided balance to his extreme cautiousness. Samuel was certain that he loved and needed Nadine much more than she loved or needed him; this gave her a tremendous power over him.

Samuel would always remember her as a new wife in London, her belly round with child, wearing a cotton sundress and sandals, a bag of vegetables on her arm, and that proud, defiant gait. There, on those streets so colorful they didn't belong to London, among her dark-skinned neighbors, the smell of coffee and the sounds of honking horns, voices, and music in the air, Nadine reinvented herself. She was determined to soak up all the art and culture that London had to offer. With her husband's help, she learned to appreciate classical music, visited museums, and attended the theater when their budget permitted or thanks to her sporadic work painting sets.

Their daughter, Camille, was born in 1961, at the local hospital in the Caribbean neighborhood of London where Nadine shared the experience of childbirth alongside a woman from the island of Saint Thomas, a descendant of formerly enslaved people. While Nadine moaned and shouted the French swear words she'd learned at the nuns' school, the other woman sang Christian hymns between contractions. Afterward, both women, each with a newborn daughter in her arms, agreed to call their babies Camille in honor of the impressionist painter Camille Pissarro, whom Nadine admired almost as much as Van Gogh. The other woman had heard the name on the island, but until then thought it was a remedy for intestinal worms.

Nadine's Camille grew up as an extension of her mother. Nadine took the baby everywhere in a wrap on her back or tagging along behind as she grew older. The girl learned from a young age to behave like a well-trained pet, spending hours sitting quietly in a corner entertaining herself with make-believe games or reading. As a father, Samuel played a passive role. He never once prepared a bottle or changed a diaper, taking it for granted, as did everyone at the time, that the husband should provide and the wife should look after the children. This arrangement fit his solitary nature; he had always found it difficult to connect with people, and his daughter was no exception. Nadine was the only one who'd ever managed to penetrate his emotional walls. He began to interact more with Camille when she turned three or four, once she'd developed a sense of humor and could begin to reason. She was the perfect daughter for a couple busy with their own interests; she never bothered them and was practically self-sufficient.

The love of art that would end up leading Nadine down the road to fame began in a humble community center near their London apartment, hung with dozens of Haitian paintings. She spent hours studying them, photographing them, and trying to copy them, fascinated by the themes and colors. She wanted to paint in that style, but the results always turned out strident and fake. You had to be from Haiti to paint like that. When Camille started school, Nadine signed up for an arts and crafts workshop where she saw a loom for the first time. She quickly mastered the basics and began creating increasingly elaborate textiles inspired by the colors of Haiti. In time they would become valuable pieces of art.

Samuel was not a man inclined to poetry, but he always thought that weaving was a beautiful metaphor for his wife's personality. She went through life collecting and weaving together stories and people, just as she collected and weaved the threads of many colors for her tapestries.

IN 1968, WHEN CAMILLE was seven years old, Samuel was offered a chair in the San Francisco Symphony Orchestra. The couple didn't have to think too hard about it, given that the salary was a major improvement and they were itching for a change of scenery. They landed in California the same day that Robert Kennedy was killed in Los Angeles and two months after the assassination of Martin Luther King, Jr., in Memphis, as the country was being shaken by major upheaval. They settled temporarily at a boardinghouse in the hippie mecca of Haight-Ashbury.

Shortly after joining the San Francisco Symphony, Samuel had the idea to offer a talk to the audience before each concert to provide information on the pieces that they were about to hear, with the notion that if the public understood a little more about the music and its composer, they could better appreciate the performance. At first only thirty or forty people, most of them with white hair, turned up early to hear Samuel's talks, but as word got around, more audience members, including younger ones, began to attend. In time half the house would be filled before the concert, eager to hear Samuel speak. These talks, casual but very informative, became so popular that Samuel's name acquired a certain prestige. He was asked to host a weekly radio program on classical music and shortly thereafter he was hired by the University of California at Berkeley. The recordings of his conferences and a few books on the evolution of Western classical music would become his most steady source of income in the years ahead. But even the university position did not allow him to explore his greatest passion. The course he'd proposed on the history of jazz was given to an African American scholar from Louisiana. As they politely explained to Samuel, a white British professor would not be the best match for that particular course. He consoled himself by regularly attending shows at his favorite clubs, where they sometimes allowed him to get onstage and improvise on piano. Those moments were utter joy. Nadine would occasionally accompany him, but she was mostly absorbed with other interests.

While Samuel, with his rational and solitary nature, concentrated on his work, not paying much attention to his surroundings, Nadine walked the streets, soaking in the turbulent energy. It was the time of the civil rights movement and the Vietnam War and the draft, which sent hundreds of thousands of young men to fight and die for a cause that many didn't believe in. The college town reverberated with the sounds of the students' revolution, demanding freedom of expression, shaking the foundations of the university before extending out from there. Berkeley was the young, passionate soul of the country. Nadine was fascinated by the progressive, rebellious, multiracial, and artistic culture of the city, which fit her like a glove. She would drop off Camille at school and take the bus to the university campus, the backdrop to everything that interested her. She spent her days there, having lunch in the cheap Indian restaurants where she relished the spicy food she'd learned to enjoy among her Caribbean friends in

London. She attended conferences, stood shoulder to shoulder with students in the protest marches or in the audience at spontaneous rock concerts and plays. She sat in on classes, painted posters for various causes, from César Chavez and the migrant farmworkers to the Black Panthers, and she chatted with the artisans, beggars, and addicts on Telegraph Avenue.

Right around that time, Nadine's father died in New Orleans and she received an unexpected inheritance. It turned out that the LeBlanc family was much wealthier than she'd ever known. Without asking her husband for permission, she began to look for a house in Berkeley. She found one she thought was perfect and she convinced Samuel they should buy it, with the argument that it had a historic past: The house was a former brothel and was said to be haunted by long-dead ladies of the night. Samuel wasn't overly impressed by its pedigree, but he liked the location, near the university, and the price, a steal since it was in such disrepair. In its better days it had been a mansion perched on a hill and surrounded by a large garden with panoramic views of the bay; now it was blocked by the overgrown trees and shrubs.

THE ADLER HOUSE HAD been built at the turn of the century. It was made of redwood shingles in the Queen Anne style, similar to the other mansions in town, with two turrets, multiple columns, balustrades and carved wainscoting, original beveled-glass windows that leaked when it rained, and five worn steps leading to the front door. The home's past splendor was evident in its details, from the stained marble in the bathrooms to the checkerboard oak floors, down to the dusty chandeliers on the ground floor, original to the house, dripping with crystal teardrops that were a nightmare to clean. From the outside, it looked like the ideal setting for a horror movie. Nadine christened it "the enchanted mansion."

"How are we ever going to furnish and heat this huge house?" Samuel asked when he saw it.

"We'll take it little by little. For now, we'll just focus on the ground floor," Nadine decided.

They also closed off the dining room and one of the living rooms. Nadine scoured the flea markets of the Bay Area and found second-hand items to furnish the rest of the house. Then, anxious to return to her weaving, which she'd put on hold since the move to California, she chose the room with the best light and placed her looms there.

The empty rooms gradually began to fill up without Samuel noticing. One Sunday morning he woke up early to go jogging, as he did every day. But when he entered the kitchen to make coffee for Nadine, who couldn't function before she'd had a large dose of caffeine, he was terrified to find a huge man standing in front of the refrigerator. A savage howl escaped from Samuel's chest as the man calmly turned around, a milk carton in his hand.

"Peace be with you," he said, raising the carton to his mouth.

"Who the hell are you!" Samuel demanded in a shrill, trembling voice.

"Fetu," the man replied, wiping away a milk mustache.

"Fetus?"

"Fetu, brother. That's my name. Namaste."

"What in bloody hell are you doing in my home? I'm calling the police."

Fetu was Samoan, six foot five and 280 pounds with black hair hanging to the middle of his back and a long thin mustache. He wore a Malcolm X T-shirt that hugged the rolls on his stomach, sandals, and a sarong, which Samuel thought was a skirt. His intimidating appearance contrasted with his calm, peaceful nature. Nadine had met Fetu on Telegraph Avenue, among the many hippies and drifters who panhandled beside the artisans selling their handicrafts. Fetu bragged about never having worked a day in his life, proudly refusing to contribute to the capitalist system, instead earning cash as a small-time dealer of hashish and marijuana. He'd been crashing with other wanderers in an abandoned building, a den of vagrants and addicts, but they'd been turned out when it became infested with rats and the city health department had boarded it up. Nadine considered Fetu a friend and so she invited him to stay at her place for a few days since the winter weather was cold and rainy.

Fetu didn't bother them much, spending his time either out on the street or asleep. He had no urgent desire to find another roof over his head, because the Adlers' enchanted mansion was very comfortable. So comfortable, in fact, that he moved in one of his girlfriends, a small, ethereal woman who had a daughter Camille's age. She believed her child to be the reincarnation of a Celtic goddess, dressing the girl in white tunics and weaving crowns of flowers into her hair. The girl, however, seemed fairly normal.

"How long are they going to stay here?" Samuel asked Nadine.

"Why do you ask?"

"This isn't a hotel. I don't like having people camped out in the living room, devouring everything in the fridge."

"You're such a square, Mr. Bogart! If you don't want them downstairs with us, we can give them one of the rooms upstairs, okay?" she suggested.

That's how the hippie takeover began. They slowly started to come from beyond Telegraph Avenue in Berkeley, with more than one person moving over from San Francisco. Some stayed longer than others, but there were never fewer than ten guests in the home, not counting the children. It was like an improvised commune, with no rules of any kind, made up of bohemians, frustrated artists, aspiring rock stars, and simple wanderers, almost all young and broke. Since none of them could contribute to the expenses and Nadine only sold an occasional weaving, Samuel was stuck with the task of supporting them all.

The situation went on for months. Very soon Samuel and Nadine began to have such nasty fights that he tried to spend as little time at home as possible. Everything irritated him, from the constant parade of strangers, the filth and disorder, the smell of incense and marijuana, the guitars and tambourines, to the Ganesh altar that had been erected in the foyer. The night he walked in to see a threesome frolicking in his living room, Samuel's patience ran out.

"Is this the kind of example you want to set for Camille? I want all these depraved hippies out of here, now!" he exploded.

"I can't just turn them out on the street, Mr. Bogart! They don't have anywhere to go. We have to give them some warning at least."

"I want this place totally empty by tomorrow or I'm calling the police to have them evicted!"

"This is my house. I bought it. Remember?"

"Fine. Then I'll leave."

"Do whatever you want. This marriage isn't working anyway, all we do is fight; neither one of us is happy."

"What are you trying to say?"

"Leave and don't come back."

Samuel moved to a bed-and-breakfast to wait for things to cool off, convinced that Nadine would soon see reason. A couple of weeks later he received a message that she'd filed for divorce, a possibility he hadn't even considered.

Samuel set aside his pride and anger and returned to the enchanted mansion prepared to work out some solution. He found the house empty. There was a note from Nadine on the telephone table: *I took Camille to Bolivia. You can keep the house.*

SAMUEL HAD ALWAYS DREAMED of a relationship like the one between Luke and Lidia Evans, his adoptive parents. The two had met very young in the London Quaker community and dedicated themselves for years to serving others, especially children in times of war. For as long as Lidia was able, wherever there was armed conflict, they traveled to help, without making a fuss, driven by faith and their love for each other. They always walked hand in hand and Samuel never saw one without the other. When Lidia's illness worsened, Luke cared for her devotedly; in her final years he bathed her, dressed her, fed her, pushed her wheelchair. She died of Parkinson's and Luke took his own life the day after burying his wife. Samuel would've liked to share a love of that caliber with Nadine, but neither of them possessed the capacity for it.

That ideal set by the Evanses was impossible to emulate. Nadine's sudden disappearance and the divorce dealt the fatal blows to that dream of perfect love and consolidated the loneliness that Samuel had always felt. He tried to go out with other women, but he was incapable of carrying on any conversation that did not lead directly to Nadine. He had plenty of opportunity at the university; although it was tacitly understood that it was better not to get involved with students, it would be years before it became law. Young women openly offered themselves to professors, some wishing to obtain favors, others simply testing out their power, and others still out of sheer infatuation. Samuel knew it happened, had even noted some attempts, but he never fell into the trap; more than being afraid of a scandal, he wanted to avoid looking ridiculous. He'd witnessed certain colleagues succumb to their own vanity, convinced that they deserved the love of girls half their age. Out of caution, he always met students with his office door wide open and avoided all familiarity, which sealed his reputation as a cold, stuffy Englishman. Without Nadine, his social life was reduced to almost nothing, since she'd been the one to cultivate friendships. He had merely tagged along, sitting silently with his impeccable grooming and manners, his distinguished air, and his talent for listening.

He had a few very brief affairs, purely sexual and completely unsatisfying, but they dragged on for much longer than he wished them to because he didn't know how to end things without offending the other party. These flings only served to confirm his suspicions that he was merely a mediocre lover; the pleasure he'd shared with Nadine was all thanks to her.

A short while later he finally received news of Nadine. She informed him that they were no longer in Bolivia and had moved on to Guatemala, where there was an incredible weaving tradition. She included several photos of Camille, looking skinny, suntanned, disheveled, and happy. She didn't need to be in school because she was learning so much in her contact with nature and the locals of Lake Atitlán, Nadine maintained. There was also a photo of Nadine surrounded by women in typical Guatemalan dresses and another in which she was holding the hand of a man wearing shorts. On the back of the photo she'd written his name: Orlando, Argentine anthropologist.

Samuel put in a request for a sabbatical at the university and at the symphony. He packed his suitcase, closed up the enchanted mansion, bid farewell to the tortured souls that haunted the place, and took off for Guatemala.

ANITA

You haven't been able to see your little guardian angel because you're always asleep when she comes. I wake up because I hear her wings flapping. It sounds like someone cleaning windows. I see my angel almost every night; we're starting to be friends.

Did I tell you that she's as white as a cloud? What I remember about clouds is that they change shape in the sky, sometimes they look like an animal, or a train, or like the cotton candy they sell at the circus. You probably don't remember the circus, Claudia, because you were so little when we went. That was before the accident. There were clowns smashing pies in each other's faces and spraying each other with water guns, trapeze artists flying up high like birds, and a bunch of little doggies that danced on two legs. Mama said that they had even better circuses here in the North. One day she's going to take us to the biggest circus of all, where they even have elephants. Maybe by the time she takes us to that circus, I'll be able to see a little better. The angels change shape too, like clouds; sometimes they look like tiny little ladies and other times they look like chickens or sails on a boat, but I can always recognize them by their voices, which I hear in my head.

I think it's a good idea to take Miss Selena with us when we go to Azabahar, but I'm not going to say anything to her yet, I have to wait for my angel to get permission. I'm not going to invite Frank; first he has to do what he said he would do, he has to get us back together with Mama. Azabahar is very far away, but the girl and boy angels just close their eyes, say some magic words, and when they open their eyes, they're there. That's how they'll take us. We have to start eating, Claudia. I know we don't like the food here but today is pizza and Miss Selena said there's not a single kid in the world who doesn't like pizza. They don't have pupusas here, but when they give us Mexican food I sometimes eat it. The quesadillas are okay. I'm going to ask my angel if there are pupusas in Azabahar; I'm sure there are.

I hope that in Azabahar there are plants and trees; that's even more important than the pupusas. I remember green. It's the best color, because it connects everything, Mama says. Here the only trees they have are cactuses, which don't give any shade and have spines that sting like bees, we have to stay away from them. Miss Selena told me that there are amazing mountains here, red as strawberries, purple as beets, orange as mangoes. I wish I could see them. She's going to bring me the kind of big magnifying glass I need, and I don't have to pay her anything for it; she's also going to let me borrow a book about Arizona and the Grand Canyon, which is one of the wonders of the world. With the magnifying glass I should be able to see a little of it. Miss Selena is nice to us—she's even nice to Didi. She wants to make her a new dress and some hair, because Didi is almost bald, but I told her you won't let go of her even for a second. We have to at least give her a bath, Claudia, she smells bad. We can't take her to Azabahar like that, the angels will think that we're beggars.

· · ·

YOU SAW WHAT HAPPENED, Claudia. Gusano de Caca attacked me first and I had to defend myself, I wasn't going to let that brat hurt me. He's a bully, always hitting us when no one's looking, but I'm not scared of him. It wasn't my fault that his nose started bleeding. I was trying to kick him in the stomach, but he moved and since I can't see so good, my shoe landed right in the middle of his face. There was a fuss because he was bleeding a lot. It's not fair that they only punished me and just gave him ice for his face and popsicles to get him to stop screaming. Miss Selena came a little while after that and got me out of time-out.

I didn't leave you alone on purpose, Claudia. They took me to the office and made me stand in the corner staring at the wall, which I didn't really mind, because it doesn't matter to me if I look one way or the other, it's all the same. I explained that Worm had started the fight and they told me to be quiet, I was in time-out for being violent. And what about Gusano de Caca? That brat is the violent one. You know I'm not a crybaby, but I threw such a huge fit I could hardly breathe and if Miss Selena hadn't shown up and fixed everything, I'd probably be dead by now. A lot of people drown in the water and die, but people can also drown from swallowing too much air. It took me a long time to calm down. If I'd have had a fit like that at Tita Edu's, she would've stuck my head in a bucket of cold water and that would have been the end of it, that always worked. But luckily that's not allowed here; if someone did that to a kid, they'd take them to jail. I wonder why. It's much worse to make kids stay in the hielera or take them away from their mamas, don't you think, Claudia?

When I was in the office I heard one of the teachers tell another teacher that they were going to send us to a foster home, because we've already stayed here longer than we're supposed to. I didn't dare to ask what a foster home was, because then they would've realized I was listening and they would've probably left me in time-out for even longer. I could always hear good, even before the accident; and here it's helpful to know what people are gossiping about, even though I can't understand so well when they speak in English. Those teachers were speaking in Spanish. I didn't like the sound of the foster-home thing. I don't need anyone to adopt me; I'm not an orphan.

WHAT I WORRY ABOUT most is that you'll forget about Mama; that happens sometimes with the little kids here. I'm going to keep telling you about Mama and if you close your eyes and pay attention to what I say, it's exactly like seeing her. Mama is beautiful. She used to have long hair with blond stripes, very pretty, and I would brush it for her, she liked that a lot, but on the trip she had to cut it all off. She had to cut her hair and mine too, so that it wouldn't get too tangled. Imagine what it would've been like on the train with long hair, or when we were walking through the desert in that terrible heat. It doesn't matter, hair grows. Mine is almost covering my ears now, but it's very uneven. Miss Selena says she's going to take me to her hairdresser one of these days, if they give me permission to leave. I told her that Mama cut her hair off and mine too in Mexico, when we were about to get on the top of the train, so that the men wouldn't notice her and they wouldn't bother us. She told me she was going to call me Son and I had to call her Dad, but I forgot and kept calling her Mama. I'm sure when we see her again she won't be so bald anymore. Mama is always happy, when she smiles you can see the space between her two top teeth, and she laughs all the time, or at least she used to, before the thing happened with Carlos. She likes to play with us and she likes music. Remember how we danced with her all the time—our favorite dance was swish, swish—and sometimes Tita Edu would take off her flip-flops and dance with us, but she only knew how to dance salsa?

SELENA

The Duráns had always been a family of women on their own, from the eldest of the bloodline, who at eighty-four years old, deformed by arthritis and slightly senile, was still the matriarch of her small tribe. The old woman bragged about being one of the warrior women who fought in Pancho Villa's army, but at the time of the Mexican Revolution she had not yet been born. She was a short woman, only four foot seven even in her prime, and had shrunk further over the years. She was inexhaustible, bossy, and foul-mouthed. The true story was that she had arrived in the United States in 1954, crossing the Arizona desert on foot with a baby in her arms, utterly destitute, semi-illiterate, undocumented, and without a word of English. She was eighteen. She started out picking oranges and lettuce in Southern California, with her daughter tied to her back, earning less than one dollar per hour. Like almost all the migrants who worked the land to put food on other people's tables, she went hungry. Ten years later, crippled by chronic back pain from the hard labor and her skin leathered by the sun, she got a job in a canning factory, where she worked until her daughter and granddaughter forced her to retire. As she got older her imagination grew wilder, and by the time Frank Angileri met her she seemed like a fanciful, undernourished eight-year-old child. Beside her, her great-granddaughter Selena looked gigantic.

Frank showed up with a bouquet of flowers and a bottle of the best port he could find, because Selena had told him that her great-grandmother ended each day with a hastily recited Hail Mary and a small glass of the spirit.

"What's your little friend's name?" the old woman asked Selena for the third time.

"You're not senile, Mamagrande. Why do you keep asking the same questions?"

"To pester you, girl." She laughed, chewing the air with the few teeth she had left.

"I thought so. This is Frank Angileri, the lawyer representing the blind girl who was separated from her mother."

"Ah! Anita Díaz, poor thing . . ."

"That's the one, Mamagrande. See how good your memory is?"

"I remember what I want to remember and I don't remember what other people want me to remember. What do you think of this family, young man?" she asked the lawyer.

"I'm very impressed. Four generations of . . ."

"Five. My great-great-grandsons aren't here," the matriarch interrupted. "The first males to be born into the family. I had Dora at eighteen. The Durán women have children young."

"Before they have time to think it through," Selena teased her.

"And you, taking so long to think it through you're going to hit menopause before you have kids," her great-grandmother scolded her.

"Don't worry. I'll tie the knot one of these days," Selena answered.

"Why do you have to get married? I was a virgin when I had Dora."

"Did you just say you were a virgin, Mamagrande?"

"Yes, like the Virgen de Guadalupe and all the other virgins on the saints calendar."

"You know my boyfriend is very traditional; he'd never have kids outside of wedlock," Selena reminded her.

"And what about you, young man, what do you think about having kids?" the elderly woman asked Frank.

"Enough, Mamá, leave the lawyer alone," her daughter, Dora, interrupted from the kitchen, where she and Selena's mother were preparing lunch.

THAT SUNDAY MORNING, FRANK had flown from San Francisco to see Selena and would fly back at six o'clock that evening. Flying to Los Angeles for the day had become routine for him over the past few months, although he generally made the trip in Alperstein's private jet. A limo would be sent to take him to the San Francisco airport and another would meet him at LAX to drive him to the magnate's mansion in Paradise Cove Bluffs, a ten-thousand-square-foot behemoth of a house surrounded by gardens reminiscent of Versailles with a private beach. The Alperstein case had been resolved the week before with a cash settlement, an enormous one. The scoundrel wouldn't have to face a jury or see his final days behind bars, but no one could salvage his reputation; the press had a field day with the details of the scandal. For Frank, this somewhat compensated for the immense displeasure of defending the man, who had once again bought his way out of trouble. Frank had been congratulated by everyone at the firm for his big win as well as receiving the hefty bonus and corner office he'd been promised on the top floor. His mother, on the other hand, once again reprimanded him over the phone for the total lack of scruples it took to defend such a despicable criminal.

Selena was going to be in Los Angeles for a few days with her family and since San Francisco was only an hour away by plane, she suggested Frank come down to meet her psychic grandmother, whom he seemed so fascinated by. He and Selena hadn't seen each other since late December when he met Anita at the Nogales group home, but they spoke often. Since that meeting, they'd developed a friendly working relationship, initially centered around winning asylum for the girl but soon becoming more personal. Frank got along well with women; he knew how to treat them since he'd learned from his sisters growing up. He had a hard time defining what he felt for Selena. He valued her friendship and didn't want to jeopardize it, but he had to admit that his desire to be in permanent contact with her felt a little bit too much like infatuation.

For Selena, who had always moved in almost exclusively female environments, this new friendship with Frank was a novelty. The only man she'd ever known well was her fiancé, whom she was making plans to marry in April. Or, more accurately, Milosz and the Durán women were making plans, while Selena thought of April with a knot in her stomach. She'd been with Milosz for eight years but there were aspects of their lives that they never shared and certain topics that they actively avoided, such as politics, where they had opposite opinions, or immigration, which they couldn't come to an agreement on. While she worked with refugees, he maintained that crossing the border illegally was a crime that should be punished to the full extent of the law, and that building the border wall, as the president insisted, was essential to national security; what sense did it make to carry out wars in remote countries while hordes of illegals were invading at home? Milosz didn't approve of Selena's work and she was not at all interested in his. He also disapproved of her living in Arizona, but imagined it as a temporary situation, only until they were married. He was totally certain of his love for Selena and assumed that she felt exactly the same for him. He didn't seem to notice that every time the upcoming wedding was mentioned, she always managed to change the subject.

Milosz's occupation suited him perfectly. It required attention, discipline, patience, physical stamina, respect of the body's limits, caution, a deep knowledge of mechanics and road maps, and the ability to bear isolation and tedium. A driver with no vices could provide a good life for his family, even save, invest, and retire relatively young. This was his plan for the future; he didn't want to spend the rest of his life behind the wheel. He kept himself entertained by listening to the radio, podcasts, and audiobooks; he was even learning Spanish, at Selena's urging. He never drank and never used stimulants to stay awake, as many of his fellow drivers did. He took good care of himself. He'd been driving for many years and was still as fit as when he'd left the army.

Selena liked his muscular body, his pale eyes, his high cheekbones, tanned skin, large calloused hands, his smell, his voice. She desired him, attracted by what she saw as the best masculine virtues: strength, decency, courage, and responsibility. Their immutable routines offered stability, but still her doubts lingered. These doubts had only deepened since December of the previous year when she met Frank Angileri. Selena knew that for Milosz, a future without her was inconceivable. She also knew that for her, the thought of a future with him was unsettling. She didn't feel at all tempted by the perfect house, children, and comfortable domestic life that Milosz dreamed of; she loved her work and wanted to go to law school. But she had to make a decision soon, because April was just around the corner and Milosz didn't deserve to be strung along until then.

The Durán women all considered the forthcoming union to be the perfect arrangement: plenty of affection, a little passion, and lots of space. Selena feared that this space would disappear once they married.

.   .   .

DORA DURÁN, SELENA'S FAMOUS grandmother, was sixty-six years old and dressed in styles that had been fashionable four decades prior. Out of curiosity, Frank had searched for her on the internet, where he found a web page, interviews, and videos about her incredible psychic abilities. She dyed her hair black and wore an excessive amount of eye makeup; Selena's mother, in contrast, twenty years younger, was dressed in blue jeans, a loose sweater, and no makeup. Dora's imposing presence eclipsed her daughter so completely that Frank couldn't remember her name and Selena had to remind him a few times: Cassandra. Selena's father, much older than his wife, had died when Selena and her sister, Leila, were four and six years old, respectively. Cassandra mourned her husband for a few months, then enrolled in community college, and then university, where she got a degree as a lab technician. Since then she had been the family's main breadwinner. Although she paid the bills and supported her mother and grandmother, the two headstrong women granted her very little decision-making power.

The Duráns—Mamagrande, Dora, Cassandra, and Selena—reminded Frank of his own family, except for the fact that they were all women. They treated one another with the same brusque tenderness as the Angileris, the same unconditional loyalty, total trust, and zero sentimentality. The Duráns, although very different from the Angileri women, shared certain traits: They were strong, practical, direct, and hospitable, just like his mother and sisters. The Durán residence in Los Angeles even looked similar to his parents' home in Brooklyn: small, crammed with furniture and cheap knickknacks, warm and inviting, filled with the smells of cooking and coffee. At that table, sharing homemade dishes, drinking beer and tequila, with everybody talking at the same time, laughing and taunting one another, he felt perfectly at ease among these women: He understood the codes they lived by.

It was Frank who had the idea to go to El Salvador in search of

Marisol Díaz. Although he'd never admit it, he gave great importance to the fact that Dora Durán had not received any signs of Marisol from the Beyond. With the hope that her grandmother could help find Anita's mother, Selena had shown her Marisol's photo from her immigration file as well as others of Anita. Getting nothing from the souls she communicated with, Dora had wanted to meet the girl personally. Her granddaughter flew her to Arizona and managed to get her into the group home, where visitors were generally prohibited, so that she could spend some time with Anita. Dora was very impressed.

"The child has a gift, but it's not like mine. It may manifest itself in the future, when she's a bit older," she informed Selena after the visit.

"What makes you say that, Abuela?"

"Anita can see the invisible, she can picture the future, she can visualize what will come to pass."

"She just lives in her own world. She talks to herself. She has a vivid imagination," Selena explained.

"I think she has the ability to transport herself to another dimension. I felt her power. When I held her hands in mine, she transmitted her force to me."

"Did you get a message from Marisol?"

"No. I hope she never has need to communicate with me. But just in case, I'll remain open to her."

Dora Durán, the baby who at three months made the desert crossing to the United States wrapped in her mother's shawl, had begun to acquire a reputation for clairvoyance around age thirteen. According to Mamagrande, the talent had been prevalent in the women of her bloodline since the times of the Spanish conquistadores in Mexico, but very few had been able to hone the skill. Dora's mother spoke of how she herself lived in constant dialogue with departed souls. But they came only to gossip, she said, not to pester her with their problems.

"With her first menstruation, my little Dora's brain came to a boil," the matriarch told Frank. "They said it was meningitis. She recovered, but her mind had been warmed up. Ever since then, she's had one foot here in this world and one foot in the Beyond."

Frank Angileri couldn't readily understand her, because his high school Spanish didn't include paranormal terminology, but Selena translated for him.

"Mamagrande has several ideas on how our line first acquired their abilities," she added. "For example, she thinks it is possible that a scorpion crawled into my grandma's ear and gave her powers. Or perhaps she ate poisoned mushrooms from a cemetery, and that's why she can talk to the dead."

"What's your preferred theory, ma'am?" Frank asked Dora.

"I have no idea. And I would prefer for the dead to leave me alone," Dora replied.

"Some souls have unresolved issues in this world. They communicate with Dora so that she might help them achieve peace," Selena's great-grandmother added. "That's why the Kennedys appear to her so often."

"She's never mentioned the Kennedys, Mamagrande! Where did you get that?" Selena exclaimed.

"The ones who move on peacefully, they never come to pester us. The thug who killed Kennedy was just a hired hitman, the true assassins never paid for their crimes. The Kennedys want justice," the old woman insisted.

"That was half a century ago, Mamagrande. I think everyone involved must be dead by now."

"Good. May they burn in hell," the elderly woman answered.

"If Marisol Díaz had suffered an accident or a violent death, she wouldn't be at peace, would she?" Frank asked. He blushed as he spoke, because he felt foolish for believing in this nonsense; what would his colleagues say if they heard him?

"Exactly, young man." Mamagrande nodded.

"Well, we can't know for sure," Dora argued, carrying dishes from the kitchen. "If all the troubled souls out there spoke to me, I'd have to be locked up in an insane asylum."

She wasn't crazy and she wasn't a charlatan, like so many so-called psychics. Dora could have made a fortune consoling bereaved relatives with messages from beyond the grave: There were many people who would've paid for her services. But she had an enormous respect for the divine power she'd been blessed with and believed that charging for her talents was a sin. God had granted her this gift to help and serve, not for her own personal gains. She worked for many years as a teacher but since retiring supplemented her meager pension by baking cakes for birthdays, weddings, and quinceañeras, true works of art crowned with sugar figurines identical to the clients. Working from photos, she rendered the brides and grooms or the teenage girls in their princess dresses. They could get the same figurines from China but they weren't as accurate and were made of plaster. Hers were all edible, she explained to Frank.

"Just yesterday I was making a collection of marzipan dogs for a poodle's birthday in Beverly Hills. They're having a party at the Four Seasons with a bunch of mutts. You can't imagine the silly things rich people will waste their money on," she said.

THAT AFTERNOON, WITH THE large lunch of Mexican food sitting in Frank's stomach like a ton of cement, he said goodbye to Selena. They stood in the front yard, surrounded by the fat, floppy-eared bunnies that Mamagrande raised as pets. Frank refrained from mentioning his mother's famous recipe for rabbit with rosemary and mushrooms.

"I'm taking a week off work," he said. "I've earned it after the

Alperstein case. What do you say we go to El Salvador and look for Marisol?"

"You and me?" Selena asked, surprised.

"I can't go alone. You know the case inside out and you speak Spanish. We've already determined that Marisol is not in the refugee camps on the other side of the border. It couldn't hurt to see if she made it back home. It's the most practical thing we can do, Selena. Let's go."

"I don't know, Frank . . ."

"The trip won't cost you a dime. I'll cover all our expenses."

"Why?"

"Because I'm just as invested in helping Anita as you are. In El Salvador, I have a friend at the American embassy; he can help us. Come on, let's go . . ."

Selena wondered how Milosz would react if he found out she'd be going on a trip with another man. She thought it might qualify as one of her professional obligations that he didn't need to know about. She would tell him she had to travel for work, without mentioning Frank, much less the fact that he was paying her way. She didn't plan on telling her family either. She wouldn't be able to count on the Durán family's support in this matter; they'd surely take Milosz's side.

FRANK AND SELENA FLEW to San Salvador on Avianca Airlines the second Monday in February, with return tickets for the following Saturday. They packed light and, armed with a copy of Marisol's immigration report, which Selena had obtained thanks to an ICE officer with a fondness for her, and the information Anita had provided, they set out to locate the missing woman. For Frank it felt like a grand adventure. Before meeting Selena, he'd known almost nothing about Central America; it was merely a spot on the map, as remote and mysterious to him as any. The news coming out of the region was usually bad: revolutions, guerillas, bloody dictatorships, massacres, civil war, corruption, human trafficking, drugs, and, in recent years, the criminal gangs such as the Mara Salvatrucha. He had trouble differentiating between one country and another since they seemed more or less the same to him, except for Costa Rica, where he'd been on vacation, surfing crystalline waves and taking selfies with pelicans and turtles. That country had abolished their armed forces in 1948 and since then had enjoyed seven decades of peace and prosperity; now it was overcrowded with American tourists and retirees. As soon as Frank had taken on Anita Díaz's defense, he began studying the history and politics of the region where the refugees and migrants that Selena worked with had come from.

Apart from his internet searches and what he read in the news, Frank also had Selena's take on the issue and he now understood why so many people undertook that dangerous journey northward to seek asylum in the United States—even going as far as to send their children alone in some cases. The risks on the road and the hostility with which they were met once they reached their destination did little to dissuade them, because the destitution and unchecked violence they were fleeing was much worse.

"No one in this world is ever truly safe, Frank. We could all just as easily find ourselves in similar situations," Selena had said to him, but he couldn't imagine anyone he knew falling into such dire circumstances. When he talked to his mother about it, she reminded him that his grandparents had themselves come to the United States fleeing the Sicilian mafia.

The San Salvador airport was modern, with luxury shops and stores selling handcrafted items. There were so many other travelers arriving that it took a long time to get their passports stamped at customs. The five-hour flight had felt longer and they were tired, but instead of going directly to their hotel, they decided to first quell their hunger with the famous Olocuilta pupusas, which Selena had heard about. The food's strange name did not inspire great confidence in Frank, but he decided to forgo his dietary restrictions for a few days; he didn't want to seem like a wimp in front of Selena. They stepped out of the airport and were immediately overwhelmed by the shocking heat.

"It's like a steam bath!" Frank exclaimed.

"Breathe. You can get used to anything," she answered, panting.

They got in an official taxi and twenty minutes later were standing before a black griddle over an open flame, where two women wearing blue aprons patted out handmade rice and corn tortillas. They ordered pupusas locas, each the size of a dinner plate, filled with cheese, beans, and chicharrón, washing them down with cold beer. It was the perfect introduction to the country.

FRANK HAD INSISTED THAT they stay in a nice hotel and had flown them down in business class. Selena accepted without argument, because it was obvious to both of them that he had much greater resources than she did. They went to bed late, each in their own rooms, each sleeping fitfully. Frank was agitated by Selena's proximity, and Selena was anxious about locating Marisol in only four days. In just a few hours they'd both developed heat rashes and their hands and feet had swollen from the humidity. The air-conditioning in the hotel room was such a sharp contrast to the temperature outside that it left them shivering under the covers.

In preparation for their trip, Anita had been able to tell them more about her grandmother, with whom she'd lived since she was born. But the clues she had provided were vague.

"All we know is the grandmother's name and that she worked at an indigo factory," Frank said the next day as they were having breakfast on the hotel terrace.

"Anita mentioned that she greets visitors and tourists. I think we should start at the Casa Blanca Archaeological Park, there's a museum there and an indigo factory. It's in Chalchuapa," Selena said.

"How far is that from here?"

"I asked the hotel concierge; he said it was an hour and twenty minutes by bus, more or less."

"We're going to need a better way to get around. We have to rent a car," Frank decreed.

"The roads can be hard to navigate, Frank. I think it would be better to hire a pink taxi to drive us for the day. The concierge suggested it."

"A pink taxi?"

"They're taxis driven by women, for women. They're very safe."

They had to show the driver their passports before she agreed to let Frank get in. As a rule, she didn't drive men, but sometimes made exceptions. The car was upholstered in bright pink and had a mirror and beauty products in the back seat for any passengers who might want to check their makeup. Lola, the driver, wore a pristine white uniform. She was short, round, talkative, and friendly, peppering them with a barrage of information. During the drive she gave them a true master class in local politics, the new president, the recent locust plague, the prevalence of gang violence, and the basic precautions they should take as tourists.

"The press talks about crime nonstop. You'd think we all live shaking in fear of the maras and the narcos, but it's exaggerated," Lola told them. "Most of us are peaceful, happy people. Here, any excuse is good for a party. We love to dance and sing, we take care of one another and of our families. Me, for example, I cook for my extended family on Sundays, we are very close. I am sorry that my country gets bad press abroad. We Salvadorans know how to look out for ourselves, we know where we should and shouldn't go and at what hours, we know to avoid dangerous places and suspicious people. You guys are safe with me, I know this place like the palm of my hand."

When she found out that they were interested in indigo, she launched into a lesson on "blue gold," one of the country's greatest artistic traditions, which had been prevalent since the sixteenth century but lost its importance when synthetic dyes were invented. From there she began talking about the pre-Columbian pyramids, which she insisted they had to see. They politely explained that they didn't have time for sightseeing and wanted to go directly to the museum, a colonial building in the middle of the archeological park.

At the indigo workshop, they met the women who made the natural dye using ancient techniques and sold beautiful textiles in deep blue hues. Everyone knew doña Eduvigis, since she'd worked there for thirty years. She wasn't on duty that morning, but someone was able to provide them with her address and Lola quickly located the modest home in a working-class neighborhood of Chalchuapa.

Anita's grandmother spoke to them guardedly from the front yard through a gate crowned with barbed wire and surrounded by several barking dogs, but as soon as Selena explained that she knew her granddaughter and showed her a photo, she opened the gate and eagerly invited them inside. The dogs followed behind, wagging their tails. The woman was as agile and energetic as she'd been in her youth, but her face was lined with suffering. Her life had been one of work and constant hardship. She had been caring for her bedridden husband for many years, had raised five children practically on her own, and had already buried two of them.

"Anita, my sweet girl . . . I haven't had any news of her in months. Where is she?" the woman asked, trembling.

"She's all right, señora. She's in the United States, in Arizona," Selena explained.

"Have you seen her?"

"Yes, I just saw her. I brought you some pictures."

"I miss her so much!"

"She misses you too. Anita adores her Tita Edu."

Eduvigis offered them chairs and served an orange soda she called "cola champagne" in plastic cups. In the car, Lola had warned them not to drink the water here, because it was brought into the neighborhood once a week by truck and wasn't always clean. The home was a low box made of cinder blocks, very simple, tidy, and clean, with linoleum floors and screens on the open windows for air flow. Two large containers of water used for cooking sat beside the stove.

"Anita is going to turn eight without her mama, without her abuela, all alone . . . It's like a knife to my heart," Eduvigis told them through tears.

"We're going to have a birthday party for her, don't worry. She's even going to have a piñata. I asked her what she wants as a gift and she asked for something she can use to listen to music. Frank is going to get it for her."

"She'll like that. Anita knows all the popular songs. She has a very good ear and a lovely voice, that's how she entertained herself after she had the accident, until she was able to return to school. One of the teachers was teaching her how to play the guitar. Have you heard her sing?"

"Not yet, señora, but now that you've told me this, I'll make sure she has more access to music. I'll sing and dance with her," Selena assured the woman.

"Anita is a very special girl; she always has been. At three years old she could already speak like an adult. I taught her how to read when she was five. She was always a good student; I didn't have to keep after her about it. And she took such good care of her little sister! She said that she had to be Claudia's mama when Marisol wasn't here, because she was the oldest. After the accident she became very quiet, she stopped laughing as much as before."

"What kind of accident was that, señora?" asked Selena.

"A head-on collision. A big truck hit the school van," explained the grandmother.

"I am so sorry . . ."

"We have had bad luck for a long time. And now Marisol has gone missing! You don't have any idea where she is? The last time she called me was over three months ago and I haven't heard from her since."

"That's the reason we're here, ma'am," Frank said.

The grandmother apologized for not having any snacks to offer them and said she would run to the market if they wanted to stay for lunch. Then she began telling them about Rutilio, her oldest son who had been the closest to her, the most responsible, who had replaced his sick father as the man of the house and had no vices, not even alcohol, fighting, or women. He lived for his daughters and Marisol, his longtime girlfriend, whom he married when she got pregnant with Anita. Rutilio barely got to know Claudia because he died when she was only three weeks old. He'd worked for a company that made building materials and, in a freak accident, had been buried by a stream of fresh cement. They weren't able to get him out in time. Eduvigis suspected he'd been murdered for being an active union leader, making noise and organizing the other workers. She said he'd been threatened.

"Who threatened him?" Frank asked in his watered-down Spanish.

"I'm sure it was some goons hired by the construction company, but there's no way to prove it."

"It couldn't have been the maras?" Selena suggested.

"Oh, no, Rutilio never had anything to do with the gangs at all. And anyway, the maras kill right out in the open to teach people a lesson; they don't go around faking accidents."

FRANK AND SELENA SPENT several hours with Eduvigis, who insisted on going to buy a "wild chicken"—one raised locally, free-range—because they were very special guests, she said. Lunch consisted of an abundant chicken soup with vegetables, which simmered as they looked at photos, Anita's school notebooks from before the accident that damaged her eyes, and two postcards sent by Marisol on their journey north. They learned that she'd called Eduvigis shortly before arriving at the border and once again from the detention center in Texas, where she got someone to lend her a cellphone. In the few minutes they were able to speak, she managed to tell her mother-in-law that she'd been separated from Anita.

"She told me that it was normal, that Anita was fine and that they'd soon be together again, but I know she was just saying that to put my mind at ease," the grandmother explained. "Here we all know about how they separate families in the North, they show it on TV. Just yesterday, we saw a toddler no more than three hugging his father's legs and crying, poor thing, and then they grabbed his arms and pulled him away. And we also saw about the kids that the coyotes abandon in the desert. Some of them are tiny!"

Frank and Selena learned that Marisol had worked as a maid from Monday to Friday in the home of a politician in the capital. The house, in the Antiguo Cuscatlán neighborhood, was one of only four in a gated community that was guarded day and night. On Fridays Marisol finished her work at six in the evening and took the bus to Chalchuapa to spend the weekend with her family. The rest of the time the grandmother, who had flexible hours at the indigo factory, took care of Anita. At the factory, she worked as a pointer, the person responsible for determining the oxygenation point in the complicated process of transforming the jiquilete seeds into indigo dye paste. She was also in charge of explaining every step of the work to visitors, from the seed to the finished textile.

Since the death of Rutilio, years prior, Marisol had had a few suitors, but had rejected them all; she arrived home exhausted from a week of work and only wanted to spend time with her daughter. She hadn't fully gotten over the loss of her husband and said she'd never find another partner as noble as Rutilio, no one worthy of being stepfather to her child.

"My daughter-in-law is very respectful. She never brought any other man to my house," Eduvigis explained. She added that the only man who came around was Carlos Gómez, who was a security guard at the compound where she worked as a maid. He always showed up uninvited, throwing around the power conferred by his uniform. The first time he came by, Marisol spoke to him briefly on the street. She didn't invite him in, although she knew him. After that first visit it was impossible to shut the door in his face. Gómez would stop by unannounced, at all hours, and insist on seeing Marisol.

"According to Marisol's statement, Carlos Gómez is the man who shot her before she fled the country with Anita," Selena said.

"My daughter-in-law discovered something. Some secret. She never told me what it was, but I heard her talking to Gómez. I wasn't eavesdropping; the walls here are very thin."

"Do you have any idea what it was?"

"No. Marisol promised him that she wasn't going to tell anyone, said it wasn't any of her business, and begged him to leave her alone. Sometimes he threatened her and sometimes he tried to make moves on her, kissing and groping her. She was terrified of him."

The grandmother was scared of Gómez as well, of the way he would sometimes show up in the middle of the week when he knew Marisol was away and demand to see Anita. He made the girl call him Uncle Carlos and he would bring her little gifts of toys and candy.

"I want her to get to know me and love me," he would say. That drove Marisol crazy; she'd left instructions for her mother-in-law to never leave him alone in a room with her daughter under any circumstances.

"But one Friday he picked Anita up from school. That was after the accident. She got in his car without any argument, because he told her I'd sent him. A teacher tried to stop him but he said he was Anita's uncle and he was taking her to a birthday party. The teacher took a picture of his license plate as he drove away."

When Marisol arrived home that night, she found Eduvigis in a state of panic because Anita was missing. She had gone to school to pick up her granddaughter, like she always did, but when she got there the teacher explained about the uncle and the birthday party, and she showed her the photo. Eduvigis recognized the vehicle and understood immediately that the girl had fallen into the hands of Carlos Gómez.

"Why didn't you go to the police?" asked Frank.

"The police? No way! Carlos Gómez was a former police officer himself! He was fired and had to become a security guard, basically a glorified doorman with a uniform and a gun. But he still has friends on the force."

Marisol started calling Carlos nonstop, but he didn't pick up. Finally, around midnight, when everyone on the block knew that the girl had been kidnapped and the mother and grandmother were inconsolable, a car pulled up cheerfully honking its horn. While Anita rushed to her grandmother's arms, Carlos calmly explained to Marisol that he'd simply taken the girl to the beach.

"You have to come with us next time, Marisol, so your daughter can have some fun. I don't like crybabies," he added in a threatening tone. From that day on, aware of her mother and grandmother's fear, Anita would hide whenever Carlos Gómez appeared.

"I think the picture that the teacher took is what saved her. Gómez must have seen her do it as he drove away, so he knew that they could identify him," Eduvigis said. "Still, he didn't stop with his campaign to win us over. He would bring me gifts too, a blender, ham, good coffee, or he would leave things for Marisol. And if I refused them he would get furious. That went on for several months. The threats got more aggressive; he tried to control Marisol, spied on her—he would act jealous, as if they were a couple."

"What did she do?"

"She avoided the devil as best she could! She didn't want to see him!" the grandmother said. "And it went on like that until he shot and almost killed her. That's why she had to leave. What else could she do? I didn't want her to take my granddaughter with her, but Marisol couldn't leave Anita here to the mercy of that man, could she?"

Eduvigis couldn't provide any leads as to where Marisol might be, but she gave them the address of Genaro Andrade, Marisol's brother. Andrade worked as a surf instructor at one of the country's most popular beaches. He was Marisol's only relative in El Salvador; the rest of her family was in Guatemala.

FRANK AND SELENA RETURNED to the capital that night. The next day, Lola drove them to Antiguo Cuscatlán. Selena had made an appointment with Carlos Gómez using the cellphone number Eduvigis provided. She passed herself off as a visitor from Mexico, saying only that a friend had given her his number and she wanted to talk to him.

Selena's heat rash had faded, but Frank was still red and raw. It wasn't the first time Lola had driven a passenger with this problem. She opened the glove box and handed Frank an unlabeled plastic bag with several loose pills and ordered him to swallow one every four hours. Frank obeyed without asking questions.

Large trees threw deep shade onto the wide streets of the genteel neighborhood. From the outside, very little of the property where Carlos Gómez worked was visible, surrounded as it was by a tall wrought-iron fence and an impenetrable wall of vegetation. Frank and Lola waited around the corner in the pink taxi as Selena rang the buzzer and spoke into the intercom. Gómez, who was on duty, asked the other guard to take over while he spoke with the supposed Mexican tourist, and he went out to meet her on the street.

Selena had to admit that the man was imposing in his khaki uniform full of pockets and straps, heavy combat boots, aviator sunglasses, and black beret; he looked like a soldier on active duty. She could tell that from his first glimpse of her he'd begun to let down his guard. Gómez's attitude, initially suspicious, softened as she began to approach, all swinging hair, smiles, tight dress, and that wavy way of walking she had.

"How can I help you, señorita?" he greeted her warmly.

"Could we sit for a minute, Captain? It's hot as hell . . ."

No visitors were allowed onto the property uninvited and Gómez's job, among others, was to enforce that, going as far as to inspect the inside of each vehicle before opening the gate. But he didn't want to look like some subordinate in front of this woman—what a knockout! He generally liked them younger, innocent and undeveloped, but this little lady looked good enough to eat. He gallantly led her through a doorway beside the gate to a bench half hidden among the garden's tropical plants. They sat and Selena admired the dazzling pool and the house in the distance. There was no one in sight, only a pair of German shepherds who growled at her until Gómez ordered them away.

"Now, tell me what I can do for you, pretty girl," the guard said.

"As I told you on the phone, Captain, a friend gave me your number."

"What friend?"

"Marisol Andrade. I met her in Mexico."

"When was this?" the man asked, suddenly alert and defensive.

"Several months ago—it must have been around October of last year? I don't remember exactly."

"I don't know anything about Marisol."

"You do know her, though, right?" Selena pressed.

"She worked in the house. But there are dozens of servants around here."

"But she was special to you. She told me what went on between you two."

"Who are you? What do you want with me?" Gómez exclaimed, standing up.

"Come on, Captain, don't be like that. I know it was an accident." Selena smiled, brushing a strand of hair from her face and crossing her legs, the thin dress revealing half her thighs and her cleavage damp with sweat.

"You have to leave now. You can't be here," Gómez ordered, grabbing her by an arm.

Selena pretended to trip, but the man caught her firmly. They looked into each other's eyes, just a few centimeters apart.

"I just want to talk, Captain. Can we meet up later, when you're off work?" Selena murmured in a sultry tone. "Marisol told me about you and I wanted to meet you because I like strong men who know how to get respect . . ."

CARLOS GÓMEZ AGREED TO meet Selena that night at La Flor de Izote, a dark and dirty bar with a dance floor blasting popular songs in Spanish. He didn't have the budget for someplace more worthy of that fine piece of ass, but he expected that after two or three drinks and a few close dances, she'd appreciate just how much of a man he truly was. He'd win her over. Easily. It always worked like a charm. Marisol had been the only one to ever reject him in his forty years of existence, but that was through no failing of his—she was simply stupid. He still couldn't believe he'd become so obsessed with that skinny, bony woman, who'd already had two kids. He should've moved on right away, before things got so complicated.

Frank and Lola, who had followed Selena in, set themselves up at a nearby table. Lola ordered a beer and Frank a mineral water. Lola had taken off her white smock for the occasion and donned some dangly earrings that looked like Christmas tree ornaments. Frank told her that she looked nice and she warned him with a suppressed giggle not to get any ideas. Unfortunately, she was a married woman.

Selena sat nursing a lukewarm and repugnantly sweet margarita, but Gómez was already on his third beer, had fully let down his guard, and was feeling chatty. The Mexican woman didn't represent any danger, just another horny mamacita like the rest; he knew how to handle her. He was going to make sure the night ended the way he intended it to. They got up to dance and he pressed her close, admiring her pale skin, her smooth rhythm, her smell of sweat and perfume, her full lips, and her long legs and sexy sandals. He ordered a whiskey, feeling generous, friendly, expansive, confident. The woman was gorgeous, she had class, and she hung on his every word, fascinated. Women were attracted to violence, they wanted to be dominated, even if they resisted, kicked, and screamed. All he had to do was show them what a man he was, as he'd done with countless women he'd met on social media. He enjoyed talking to the Mexican woman, she knew how to listen.

"The whole shooting thing was an accident. I'm always armed; I learned to shoot when I was a boy, my father taught me himself, and I always have my gun on me for my job. I can show it to you, if you want. I don't even take it off to dance. I don't even take it off to sleep because I have to defend my bosses. That's what they pay me for, so that no son of a bitch tries to kidnap their kids. The dogs aren't enough protection, someone could easily poison them, with all the degenerates, thieves, and maras around here. That's why they need us security guys around the clock. Six of us work in eight-hour shifts, two at a time. That day—the day of the accident—I was on the night shift, which goes from ten at night to six in the morning. It was cloudy, the middle of rainy season, so it got dark early. The other guard was walking his rounds of the perimeter and I was posted up at the entrance . . . did I already say it was late? It was dark in the garden—after what happened with Marisol they put in motion-sensor lights that turn on if one of the dogs or a bird goes by, so of course it'll light up if there's an intruder. But that night I couldn't see a thing. Do you want another margarita? So then I heard footsteps on the gravel path and naturally I pulled out my gun just in case—you can never be too careful. I asked who was there. No one answered. I shouted again. I shouted like three times and nothing, then I saw someone in the ferns, hiding. I had to defend myself, I ordered the person to come out but he took off running so I fired a shot up into the air, just to scare him, not to kill him. How could I know it was Marisol? She had no business in the garden at that hour; it was almost eleven o'clock at night. The accident was her fault—why didn't she answer me, why did she run? . . . What did you say? That the bullet hit her in the chest, not in the back? Well, I don't remember the details; it's all in the police report. At least it didn't kill her, imagine the mess if— Hey, you, bring me another whiskey!" he ordered the waiter.

"Marisol told me that you asked her to meet you in the garden. You said you had to talk to her about something regarding her daughter," Selena interrupted, improvising.

"That's a lie. It's also a lie that I went to see her at her house, like she told the police. I never liked her. I'd never waste time on a bitch like that. I have plenty of other, hotter women. Why would I even look twice at that skinny, ugly bitch? The only thing she had going for her was her hair, and she chopped it all off, probably because it was infested with lice. She was a crazy bitch who needed to be locked up."

"Why do you talk about her in the past tense, like she's dead?"

"How would I know if she's dead or alive! I don't care one way or the other! She got out of the hospital and then disappeared. Just took off."

"Where to?"

"To hell, I guess. Didn't you meet her in Mexico?"

"She was on her way north, to the United States."

"Ha! Her and a million other idiots. Just to turn right around and get deported."

"They deported her?"

"What do you think, pretty girl, that the gringos welcomed her with open arms?"

"Have you seen her since then?" Selena pressed him.

"No! Who knows where she is? But if she did come back, I'd know about it."

"How would you know?"

"I have my ways, my contacts."

"If she's not here, maybe she's back in Mexico," Selena suggested.

"No, she's not there."

"How can you be so sure?"

"I told you, I have my contacts. But why are we even talking about that bitch? Why do you care so much about her?" Gómez asked, closing an iron grip around Selena's wrist.

"I don't care one way or the other. I just want to know about you . . . Hey, let me go!" she said.

"Be careful, you don't want to make me mad!" he threatened.

"You're hurting me . . ."

Carlos Gómez stared hard at Selena, his eyes red and glassy from the alcohol. She held his gaze for a moment that seemed endless, until he finally released her wrist and leaned back with his glass in his hand.

"You sure you don't want another margarita? Then let's dance."

.　　　.　　　.

WITH THE EXCUSE OF needing to use the bathroom, Selena got up from the table and then snuck out of the bar. Lola and Frank followed, and then the three of them met back at the taxi and went to dinner at a small French restaurant in the Zona Rosa to debrief. Frank wanted to treat them to a place with white tablecloths and a nice wine; he was beginning to feel the effects of the local food. He suggested Lola invite her husband along, but she announced that for once in her life she wanted to have a good time without him. She settled into her seat and before opening the menu, she ordered a Manhattan.

"I don't know what it is, but I saw it in a movie, and I've always wanted to try one," she said.

Lola had thrown herself body and soul into this mission led by the gringos, as she called Frank and Selena. She had several theories on Marisol's whereabouts. After driving them to see Abuela Eduvigis in Chalchuapa, she had searched the internet and found information on Carlos Gómez and the scandal that ended his career with the National Civil Police. He had been accused of raping and brutally beating an eleven-year-old girl, but right before going to trial, the parents dropped the charges. One news article suggested that the police had silenced them with money to avoid yet another scandal, which they had more than enough of to go around, but according to Lola it was more likely that Gómez had threatened them.

"With good reason, Marisol feared for Anita," she commented. "That man is a bad seed, evil. Not surprising, since the apple never falls far from the tree. His father was a military officer during the dictatorship, infamous for his cruelty. He's old and retired now, but everyone knows him for commanding the troops at the El Mozote massacre. They burned people alive there, even the children, can you imagine? That psychopath never had to pay for his crimes and Carlos Gómez won't pay for his either, you can bet."

The food at the restaurant was just as French as the menu had promised, but Lola decreed that the portions were stingy. She vowed to take them to a place tomorrow where they could eat themselves sick for half the price. Around midnight, Lola—two beers, two Manhattans, a glass of wine, and another of champagne in her system—dropped them at their hotel. After promising to pick them up the next morning to go see Marisol's brother at the beach, she drove off in her pink taxi singing to herself.

OVER THE DAYS THEY'D spent together, Frank found every opportunity to casually touch Selena's arm or hand. They tasted each other's food. They drank from the same glasses. They both knew that they would inevitably end up in bed at some point. That night, instead of each retiring to their respective rooms, as they'd done reluctantly the previous evenings, they went out into the hotel garden, empty at that hour. The umbrellas had been taken in, but the reclining chairs were still set out and they each took one, dizzy from the alcohol and the anticipated passion. The heat of the day had given way to a warm breeze, and wafting on the air was the sweet scent of lilies and fresh-cut grass. The still surface of the pool reflected the glow of moonlight. The music and voices from the hotel bar had long ago died down, and only the chirping of crickets penetrated the silence of the night.

Selena felt languid, as if her body were melting into the lounge chair, her bones made of cotton, her eyelids heavy, with sweat under her arms, dampness between her legs, and the invasive fragrance of tropical flowers in her nostrils.

"I drank too much," she murmured, ready to give in to sleep and spend the night beside Frank, without touching, just feeling the vibration of his impatient energy. Frank, by contrast, was gauging how to close the huge distance that separated his body from hers, a two-foot abyss between their chairs.

From the moment they'd met to board the plane at the Los Angeles airport, when he saw her in her faded jeans, her horrendous Frida Kahlo T-shirt, and the misshapen bag from Guatemala that served as her carry-on, he'd accepted, with a sigh of resignation, that he was in love. Now, amid the lilies and crickets, he understood that he'd been in love with her from the day he first met her in San Francisco. He hadn't stopped thinking about her since that December morning when she'd barged into his life and tangled him up in a desperate mission that seemed as impossible as trying to stop the tide.

Anita Díaz had been his first case and shortly after he learned the ropes he'd taken on the defense of two other children. He hadn't mentioned this at work, because, as his boss had made clear, he didn't have the luxury of free time or vacation days. He was stealing hours from the firm. But he was now just as committed to the cause as any of the thousands of pro bono lawyers representing the minors at the border. He'd already accompanied one of these boys before the judge and when he won asylum for the child—readily, thanks to the fact that it was an older justice and not one of the ultra-conservative, anti-immigrant judges that the government had recently appointed—he felt such a relief that his voice began to break. He'd had to go to the bathroom and splash cold water on his face. From there, he called his mother, who congratulated him, almost as moved as he was, and promised to send him more meatballs.

When they met, Selena had told him that she was taking some courses online, but that she wanted to go to law school full-time as soon as she could, to study immigration law. At first he thought it sounded like a terrible idea, so much time and effort only to waste it on such a thankless area. But he'd since changed his thinking on the matter. At that moment he cared much more about protecting Anita and other children like her than the corner office on the top floor that the firm had recently assigned him.

"Selena, I guess you already know I love you," he finally stammered. He'd spent six weeks thinking about how to make his declara-

THE WIND KNOWS MY NAME · 149

tion as moving and poetic as possible, but in the heat of the moment he forgot everything he'd rehearsed and blurted it out like some teenager.

"This isn't love, Frank, it's desire plus opportunity." She smiled from her chair.

"For you, maybe. For me, it's love."

"Are you sure?"

"Yes. And I think you feel something more than friendship toward me, unless I'm so in love with you that I'm becoming delusional," he replied.

"I don't know much about love, Frank; the only love I've ever had is Milosz. We've been together forever. I can't even remember my life without him."

"Do you wish he was here tonight instead of me?"

"No."

"Well, then, let's give desire its opportunity and see what happens."

It was one of the most memorable nights of Frank's life.

SELENA WAS A SENSUAL and passionate woman. Sex for her, like almost everything in her life, was a matter of the heart. Her sexuality had been awakened with Milosz Dudek when she was still a virgin, and she'd only ever really explored it with him. She'd had a few other experiences during the breaks in their long relationship, but they were barely blips. In bed, Milosz was uncomplicated. He knew exactly what to do to pleasure her, something very important to him as he considered it the foundation of a good relationship. He knew Selena's body better than his own, was confident in their mutual attraction to each other and in his own virility; he was certain that she had no complaints in that department, because she would've voiced them. And he was in fact correct. Selena enjoyed herself so naturally with him that she had trouble imagining sex could even happen any other way, as her sister assured her.

Frank encountered a young woman with simple tastes who was eager to please, asked for nothing in return, and gave in to desire with an intensity he found disconcerting. His usual routine involved undressing his companion for the night, slowly or quickly, depending on the circumstances, as he got her in the mood with a variety of strategic caresses. But Selena didn't give him the chance to touch her before she'd ripped off her clothes in three swipes. No modesty, no attempt to seduce him or create the illusion of being seduced. Her naked body looked just like he'd imagined: the wide hips, small breasts, and strong legs that her sundress had revealed, all curves and hills with an alarming lack of muscle, tendons, or bones in sight. *She's on the way to becoming one of Rubens's nymphs,* Frank thought with delight and laughed, enchanted. She kissed him on the mouth and pushed him down onto the wide hotel bed.

Frank wasn't used to tenderness in a first encounter, or hardly ever really, and it disarmed him. For her part, Selena wasn't used to eternal preambles, acrobatics, or dirty talk. Frank's questions about what she liked reminded her of a visit to the gynecologist and far from turning her on, they caused a fit of giggles. Luckily he had enough sense of humor not to get offended and quickly abandoned the tactic. He was surprised to find that his vast knowledge and experience did not seem to impress Selena, but once he stopped trying so hard, he was finally able to give himself over to her. She hadn't gone to Frank's room to participate in a circus of erotic skill, but to make love. And so that's what they did that night and the other two they shared. They simply loved each other.

ON THURSDAY MORNING, LOLA turned up at the hotel refreshed and with no visible signs of a hangover. She first drove them to the U.S.

Embassy, where Frank had a meeting with Phil Doherty, a senior diplomat whom he counted among his closest friends. They'd known each other since high school and Frank had been the best man at his wedding. Frank couldn't come to town without stopping by to see him.

From outside, the building looked like a military compound, completely surrounded by an impenetrable wall that had been painted with cheerful frescoes to make it seem less imposing. Phil was waiting for them at a side door, where he hugged his friend and walked them inside, jumping the long line at security. Lola, meanwhile, drove around the neighborhood, ready to return when they called, since there was no parking on any of the adjacent streets, which were patrolled by security vehicles.

Phil, Frank, and Selena spent a pleasant hour in one of the rooms reserved for important visitors, drinking fresh pineapple juice. The two friends brought each other up to speed on their lives, talked U.S. politics, the new Salvadoran president—a young populist who had already had a confrontation with the Americans—and the unavoidable topic of the massive northward migration of Salvadorans.

"People leave because there's a lack of opportunity here, sure, but mostly because it's such a dangerous place to live. The country has a reputation for being one of the most violent places in the world. They haven't been able to do anything to rein in the gangs, human traffickers, or narcos," said Doherty.

"Well, that's why we're here, Phil. I'm representing a girl who arrived in Arizona in October seeking asylum," Frank said, then proceeded to sum up Anita's case and their efforts to find her mother.

"Why are you two so invested in this one case when there are thousands of minors in the same situation?" the man asked.

"I've been working with Anita since she was first separated from her mother and brought to the shelter. I have a lot of other cases and I love all my kids, but she's been with me the longest and she's completely won me over," Selena answered.

"Because she's blind?"

"That's part of it, yes, but even if she weren't . . ."

"Was her mother deported?"

"We don't know. She's not at any of the camps on the Mexican side of the border."

"What happens to the girl if you don't find her mother?"

"Eventually Anita could be declared an abandoned minor and granted a special visa. But that takes a long time."

"You can count on my help, if there's anything I can do," Phil offered.

Selena hadn't spoken much during the meeting, but Phil was impressed by her nonetheless. As they were leaving he pulled Frank aside, and quietly told him this was a woman he could not let get away.

AFTER THE EMBASSY VISIT, Lola drove Frank and Selena to El Tunco beach, where Marisol's brother worked as a surfing instructor. The trip took two hours because of traffic, but all the hassle and the intense heat faded away when they reached the wide expanse of gray beach and roaring waves. Even on a weekday it was crowded with people, half of them tourists, weaving their way between the bars and restaurants, surf rental shops, and stalls of local crafts. Lola explained that international surfing teams trained there for the Olympics.

Genaro Andrade sat waiting for them in one of the rustic restaurants. As soon as they arrived he ordered cold beers and shrimp in garlic and cilantro sauce. He was a young man, broad-shouldered, tanned, and muscular, with half his body tattooed, his hair bleached by the sun, and a crooked smile. He was aware of the harassment Marisol had received from Carlos Gómez, whom he went to speak with on one occasion, demanding that he leave his sister in peace, but the man merely threatened him too. The guy was dangerous, Genaro told them. Gómez was up to his neck in corruption and shady business dealings, just as his father had been before him. Genaro hadn't heard any news from Marisol for months. The last time he saw her was after she was released from the hospital, when she came to his house to lay low until she healed enough to collect Anita and make the trip north.

He told them what he knew about Gómez, who, after being fired from the police force, got a job at a private security company, where he worked for a few years. But then that company folded after a criminal investigation exposed it as a front for an operation that trafficked people and weapons. Gómez was then hired by a similar agency, which lent its services to the gated community where Marisol worked.

"No one thought to check his references?" Frank scoffed.

"The clients only deal with the agency; they don't ask for references on every guard."

"What do you mean by trafficking people, Genaro?"

"Migrants will pay coyotes up to ten thousand dollars and sometimes more to be taken illegally into the United States. Some are fairly trustworthy, but others will abandon them halfway there or extort them for more money. When they or their families can't pay, many of them simply disappear. Marisol couldn't afford the amount they were asking so she had to go alone."

"She managed to cross Guatemala and Mexico without their help," Selena said.

"Women face a lot of danger on the road—they can be raped, kidnapped, killed. No one investigates the crimes, as if these women were simply disposable. I warned my sister what it would be like."

"Her intention was to ask for asylum, but she was stopped before crossing over into the United States. That's what they're doing with everyone now. So she crossed illegally through the desert," Selena explained.

"That was a crazy thing to do with Anita. I don't know if I'll ever see my sister or my niece again."

"Do you have any idea where your sister is now?"

"She hasn't contacted me."

"We think it's strange that Marisol hasn't tried to find out what happened to her daughter," Selena said.

"It's not like her at all," said Genaro. "She loves that girl more than anything."

"Do you know why Gómez shot her?" asked Frank.

"It was no accident. My sister found out by chance that Gómez was involved with some high-ranking military officers who were selling weapons to the maras. That's how far corruption goes here. He wanted to make sure she didn't talk."

Since they'd come all that way, Genaro insisted on taking Frank surfing, and he lent him a bathing suit. The lawyer had surfed many beaches, but few like this one and never with an instructor as daring as Genaro, who had been defying the waves since he was a boy. Lola and Selena chose to watch from the shade, enjoying coconut ice cream.

"I was really hoping we'd get more information by coming here," Selena said to Lola. "Our volunteers with the Magnolia Project couldn't find Marisol in the refugee camps on the other side of the Mexican border. There are thousands and thousands of people waiting there for the chance to request asylum but the conditions are terrible. The maras do whatever they want, and the police don't intervene."

"Why do you think that Marisol would be at one of those camps?"

"Because that's what usually happens. They round migrants up and drop them on the other side of the border without a care for where they came from. If she had been officially deported, her name would've been registered, but I can't find any record of her. The immigration officials aren't forthcoming with information."

"Oh! Why didn't I think of it before?" Lola exclaimed. "If she was deported back here she would've come by plane and her entry would be registered. My husband works at the airport; he could check the passenger lists for us," she said, pulling out her cellphone.

By six o'clock that evening, after a lunch of red-mouthed fish with fried yuca and salad, they were back in the capital. At ten o'clock that night Lola's husband informed them that Marisol Andrade de Díaz's name did not figure among the deportees who had been officially sent back to the country in the last six months.

ANITA

TUCSON, MARCH 2020

Miss Selena was gone for a few days because she went to El Salvador. She brought back pictures of Mama that Tita Edu gave her and other ones she took of our abuela, the dogs, and even the parakeets; they're all doing good. Miss Selena described the photos to me and I have them in my backpack so that everyone knows we have a family and no one can adopt us. She went there by plane with Frank. The trip here with Mama was super long, but by plane you can get there real quick, it's as fast as going to Azabahar with the angels; in the blink of an eye we'll be there. It must be cool to fly on a plane.

Tita Edu was sad because we hadn't called her. Now she has Miss Selena's cellphone number and we're going to get to talk to her every week. Tita Edu can go buy a phone card and then she'll be able to call us too. Miss Selena is going to arrange it. One day I'm going to have a cellphone. But I have to tell you, Claudia, that if we start crying when Tita calls, it'll be like a knife in her heart. We have to promise that we're not going to cry or else I'll have to tell Miss Selena it would be better not to call her.

Frank is very busy with the papers he has to get so that we can see Mama again, that's why he hasn't come, but at least we can talk to him on the phone. I think I understood almost everything he said about the judge. We don't know if it will be a woman or a man judge but it would be better if it's a woman. Frank is going to explain how my English isn't very good so that they'll hopefully let me speak in Spanish; they have interpreters, which is what they call people who can think really fast in English and Spanish. I shouldn't throw a fit; I can cry, but without making too much noise. I know what I have to say, just tell the truth about what Carlos did to Mama, the hospital, and the whole trip: the part when we had to walk for so long and we were very tired, the trucks full of people, and riding on the roof of the train, which was the scariest part because it shook so much and if you fall from up there you get run over by the wheels and die or at least get your legs cut off for sure. Frank knows that we had to leave because of Carlos. He told me not to call him Tío Carlos because an uncle is someone you love and he's not my uncle; he's bad and he hurt us. The judge won't understand if I call him uncle because here you don't call people that unless they really are your uncle; you just call them mister or miss.

EVER SINCE THEY BROUGHT us to this foster home I haven't seen my angel once, because there's so much noise and they have the TV on all the time; I can't get the racket out of my head for long enough to hear her. But I know she's around, that's her job: She has to protect me. As soon as I see her again I'm going to ask her to take us away from this place to wait for Mama somewhere else. No, Claudia, don't be silly, you can't call an angel on the phone. Have you ever seen an angel with a cellphone in church? Well, guardian angels don't have phones either. We could maybe write her a letter, but my handwriting is hard to read. I used to have the best handwriting of every-one in the whole class but now I can't even read what I write. That's life.

Miss Selena told me not to worry, that we're not going to stay in this foster home forever. We have our own family, we're not orphans. This is just a place for us to stay until we can go to our real home. It doesn't matter what they call it, I don't like it here at all. It's supposed to be like a family, with a mom, dad, sisters, and brothers, but I don't want a different mom, I already have a mama named Marisol and a papa who died, and I don't want any more brothers or sisters. I said this a bunch of times but I think I probably shouldn't say it anymore, because they might get mad and kick us out.

They want me to call the lady in charge of this foster home Mom, but I explained that I'm not going to call anyone that except for my own mama. I said I can call her Señora María, but she didn't like that. She also didn't like when I told her she can't adopt me. I think she got kinda mad, because I heard her tell Miss Selena that I was stubborn and rude. It's not true. No one has ever called me stubborn or rude before in my whole life, they can go ask Tita Edu and my teachers at school from before. At least Señora María speaks Spanish; she's Mex-ican, I think, because she calls us chamacos. That's what they call kids in Mexico, you remember when we went through Mexico? The only good thing about this foster home is that we don't have to put up with Gusano de Caca and Vómito de Iguana. The other kids here are all littler and they don't bother us.

I FIGURED OUT HOW I can send a message to my guardian angel. It's easy. I just have to find a hole in a tree or in the ground, or it could even be a hole in a rock. I'll say the message into the hole and it'll stay there until my angel picks it up. It's the same way you can talk to fair-ies, gnomes, elves, and all the other magical creatures of the forests and water. It's better to leave a written message in the hole, but they'll still understand if you just say it. I'm going to tell the angel that I'm tired of waiting here in the North, but we can't go back to El Salvador without Mama—no way—and also that the whole foster home thing isn't a good idea. Couldn't they find us somewhere else to live? It would be great to go stay with Miss Selena at her house. I know she'd like it too, she told me so, but it's not allowed. I have to think about what to say in the message because you can't ask for too much. The most important thing is to get Mama back.

Tonight we're going to go to a party in Azabahar, but it's rude to give my angel the message there, I'll have to do it later. All the people, animals, and magical creatures that we already know about are going to get dressed up in costumes for the party, because it's a carnival. They're going to give us costumes to wear too, yours is a butterfly, so you can fly, and mine is a hummingbird, so I can fly with you. I wanted a mermaid costume to swim in the sea with the dolphins and seals, but I have to stay with you. You need to pay attention, Claudia, because this is our first party there and we have to make a good impression so they'll invite us back. Remember to say hello to everyone and please and thank you.

I'm going to have to give Didi a bath because we can't take her anywhere all dirty like that, they won't even let her into Azabahar. I'm going to wash her in the sink outside, so we don't get the bathtub all dirty. I put a little bit of shampoo in my toothbrush cup and it's going to clean her up good and new, even better than soap. Then I'm going to put her in the sun. That's what Tita Edu does when she washes clothes, and since Didi is made of cloth, we can do the same thing with her. If she doesn't dry in time, we'll just take her wet.

AFTER EVERYONE GOES TO bed and turns off the TV and the lights, I'll wake you up and we can go real quiet out to the backyard. You have to be careful not to make any noise, do you understand, Claudia? My angel will be waiting, but she might be invisible. It doesn't matter. If she says she's going to be there, she will. Angels can't lie, it's against the rules; if they do they'll get fired from their job. That would be terrible for them.

We have to scrunch up between the bushes and the fence and close our eyes. You can't open them, Claudia, because you'll get too scared and ruin everything. It's very tricky, you have to follow directions. Just like when we took the bus with Tita Edu and she would repeat the rules over and over; if we didn't follow them she would pinch us. I'm going to tell you all about Azabahar; I can see perfectly there, like before the accident. I told you that we can be princesses and Mama will be a queen and Tita Edu a fairy godmother, but I was wrong. I didn't understand my guardian angel right. There, human people, magical creatures, and animals are all the same, so everyone bows to everyone else, like I showed you. I'm going to tell you about the palm trees and the beaches, the bright colors, the crystal city, the horchata waterfalls and rivers of hibiscus tea; the rainbows and the sky, which isn't blue, it's pink, and sometimes yellow. There are swimming pools filled with ice cream where we can eat as much as we want, for free, because everything is free there. All of the animals are nice, because no one bothers them and they never get hungry; there's lots of music and a big circus where we can swing on the trapeze and ride on the elephants and no one is ever afraid, because if you fall off the trapeze you just float in the air like a balloon.

NO ONE IS EVER going to take Didi away ever again, I promise you, Claudia. Señora María got mad for no good reason, because wetting the bed is an accident and it's not anybody's fault, like Miss Selena told us at the shelter; and here in this foster home it's the same. It wasn't fair for Señora María to take Didi away, I told her so, and I told her that if she didn't give her back I was going to call Frank, my lawyer. She almost hit me, she was about to, but then she changed her mind and just locked me in the closet instead. It was only for a little while and I wasn't scared. The closet smells bad, because there are stinky old shoes in there. But besides the stinky smell I didn't mind. You know I'm not scared of the dark, Claudia, because I can't see anyway, but I was mad that she wouldn't give Didi back. I told her next time she better punish us both together. Señora María didn't like when I said that, she thought I was making fun of her.

Miss Selena talked to Señora María about the closet and I heard everything, even though they closed the door and tried to talk quiet. Señora María said she'd been doing this for a long time and she'd never had a chamaca as rude as me, that I wasn't only blind but I also had mental problems, and that I wasn't normal. Miss Selena told her that there was nothing normal about my life. She's right about that. Then Miss Selena asked me to make an effort to be more respectful to Señora María, who has a lot of work to do taking care of so many kids. Also, because of the virus everywhere, she doesn't have anyone to help her, she can't send the kids to daycare or school, she can't even take them to the park, because everything's all closed up. That's why she gets so mad, but she's not a bad person. That's what Miss Selena said anyway, but she doesn't know her.

I also heard them say they're going to take me to a psychologist. I know what that is, because I went to a psychologist after we had the accident. It's more like a teacher than a doctor, they're not going to examine me or give me any shots. I'm going to go with Miss Selena and I can take Didi; you can come with us too, Claudia. But no crying. We have to be good. No, we're not lost. The wind knows my name. And yours too. Everyone knows where we are. I'm here with you and I know where you are and you know where I am. See? There's nothing to be scared about. Mama will be able to find us, she just has to call and ask Miss Selena or Tita Edu. We don't have to worry about the guardian angel either. She always knows where we are and she never goes too far away.

LETICIA

As she did every morning except Sunday, Leticia stopped by the Brunelli bakery to buy a cappuccino for herself and another for Mr. Bogart. She reminded the barista that one of them needed to be decaf; she'd made this decision without consulting her boss, because caffeine gave him heart palpitations. She was certain that, without her care, the old man would already be dead and buried. When his wife first passed, he'd resigned himself to wither away of heartbreak; he didn't want to eat, would barely touch the organic pureed vegetables and chicken soups Leticia prepared for him. In those early days, Nadine, his late wife, would appear to Mr. Bogart on the stairway landing, and he would sometimes see women dressed in old-fashioned clothes, the ladies of the night who'd worked in his house many, many years ago. Mr. Bogart described them to Leticia so convincingly and in such detail that she almost began to see them herself, even though she didn't believe in ghosts. If spirits of the departed could in fact appear to the living, she'd have an entire village of phantoms visiting her.

It was easy to imagine that Mr. Bogart's house was haunted; it was huge and dark, with many closed-off rooms, lots of wood, and little light; it groaned as if its joints ached and sometimes, when the water pressure changed, the pipes would wail. Leticia had been working as housekeeper there for twenty years and knew the place better than anyone; her broom and feather duster had touched every corner, except the attic. She'd initially found the place hideous, but over time she'd grown to love it. If it were up to her, it would be painted in bright colors, to give it a more youthful vibe, and she'd throw out half the furniture, most of it as shabby as the house itself, starting with the threadbare rugs, which according to her boss were very valuable antiques. He'd purchased them on a trip to Turkey. Leticia was convinced they'd swindled him. It was inexplicable to her how anyone could be talked into buying dirty old rugs when they sold brand-new ones everywhere.

Nadine and the good-time gals vanished when Mr. Bogart was prescribed an antidepressant, which renewed his interest in the world of the living, but he wasn't fully back to his old self until Paco rescued him. Leticia had found the dog digging in the trash in a back alley near her house, so skinny and mangy it was a miracle he was still alive. He looked like a mix of a half-dozen mutts, with a face like a hyena, but he was gentle by nature, a regular Gandhi; nothing could perturb him. Leticia took him home and cleaned him up and as soon as his scabs healed she gifted him to the elderly widower to help him in his grief. The man and the dog were soon inseparable.

Mr. Bogart had been married to his wife for more than fifty years and her decline was so sudden that he hadn't had time to even imagine life without her. He was very guarded with his emotions, but based on the fact that he started seeing Nadine, Leticia imagined that the pair had been madly in love. She'd heard it said that ghosts often surrounded the senile, but her boss was fully lucid. Leticia had worked for a time in a geriatric facility, which is where she learned that at the end of life, when loneliness begins to weigh heavily on a person, the dead often come calling. The dead were lonely as well, she supposed. But she believed that Mr. Bogart saw images of his wife out of love more than loneliness. She'd learned that desire can blossom at any age, proven by the ninety-year-old lovebirds who'd met on her watch when she'd worked at the geriatric home. They would spend all day gazing into each other's eyes, wordlessly happy. They couldn't marry because the woman's children didn't approve, wanting to avoid complications with her sizable estate. Seeing their situation, Leticia improvised a wedding ceremony so that the pair could be married at least in spirit: She dressed in black and pretended to be a justice of the peace. Everyone teared up at her solemn speech, the elderly couple were overjoyed, and their children never found out.

Not only caffeine but also the news gave Mr. Bogart heart palpitations, which was why Leticia always made sure he had his medication before turning on the TV. Ever since the current president had moved into the White House, her boss had been furious. He wasn't the only one; almost everyone in Berkeley seemed to feel the same way. She was an exception, because she didn't care about politics one way or the other; no matter who was in charge at the top, nothing would change for people like her, struggling to earn a living on the bottom. For much of her life, she'd managed to barely scrape by, washing dishes in cheap restaurants, taking care of children or the elderly, washing dogs, selling eggs and cheese door-to-door, and other, more grueling jobs. Now she was finally able to pick and choose her clients and charge by the hour for her cleaning services.

At seven-thirty every morning, Mr. Bogart woke to the sound of Paco snoring at his feet. Before Leticia got there, he always opened the window, even in winter, to air out the doggy smell, he said, although she thought it was more likely old-man smell, because Paco didn't stink. The bedroom was dark and gloomy, like the rest of the house, which would've been a dreary cave if Leticia hadn't insisted on putting out vases of fresh flowers all the time. She would sit in an armchair as worn out as the rest of the furniture while they had their coffee, watching the morning news. Mr. Bogart could still shower and dress without any help and was mortified at the thought of anyone even seeing him shirtless. Leticia had suggested more than once that he should get over that fear, because she'd probably be wiping his butt before too long. "Don't doubt for a moment that I'll take my own life before I let that day come" was her boss's answer.

Except for his mild heart palpitations and high blood pressure, the man was healthy and handsome for his eighty-six years, still with a full head of curly hair. He was meticulous with his grooming, always clean-shaven and well dressed, as if ready for a photo shoot; he had the manners and habits of an old-fashioned gentleman. He stayed active, going to the gym, kayaking on the bay, or riding his bike. Leticia worried he would fall and break something and begged him to set up a stationary bike in one of the empty rooms, but he ignored her.

After the news, they didn't see each other until the following morning. He'd begin his exercise routine, go out on some errand, or prepare his symphony talks and radio program. Meanwhile Leticia did the cleaning and then moved on to her next client.

ONE MORNING, LETICIA SAW a notice on the door of the coffee shop. "Starting tomorrow, Brunelli will be closed until further notice due to Covid-19." For several days, the virus had been the main topic on the news, but until that moment, she hadn't really taken it seriously.

"These are the last Brunelli cappuccinos for a while, Mr. Bogart," she announced. "You're going to have to get a coffeemaker."

They turned on the TV and learned that the state of California

had imposed a lockdown order starting at midnight; no one was allowed to leave their house unless their job had been deemed essential,
everyone else would have to work from home. The virus had started
in China and spread quickly across the globe, leaving a trail of critically ill patients and cadavers in its wake. Almost immediately Leticia's cellphone started ringing and, one after the other, her clients let
her know that they would be suspending her cleaning service. If
things went on this way for very long, she'd be forced to dip into her
meager savings. Also her daughter, Alicia, called her. She lived on a
military base in Southern California, where she worked as a nursing
assistant and her husband was a lieutenant in the navy. Alicia told her
not to worry because there everybody followed the rules, so it was
probably the safest place to be in a pandemic.

The lockdown order was a heavy blow to Mr. Bogart, accustomed
as he was to his immutable routines; he would no longer be able to go
to the gym, give his talks at the symphony, or rehearse with his quartet, as he did every week. He wouldn't be able to visit the jazz clubs
of San Francisco to hear new talent and maybe even get invited onstage. His age hadn't taken away an ounce of his energy when it came
to sitting in on a jam session at the piano. The only thing he could do
from home was record his program for the classical radio station.

"I hope you're not planning to abandon me," he said to Leticia.

"I'm not sure I should keep coming, Mr. Bogart. Imagine if I get
the virus and I give it to you; it would be fatal at your age."

"Everyone has to die of something."

"All my other clients have canceled out of precaution. This virus
is no joke, sir."

"Well, if we're going to be quarantined, you should stay here with
us."

"In this house?"

"Yes, woman, in this house. It's only for two or three weeks, it can't go on any longer than that. Paco and I would die of boredom locked in here by ourselves. And what would we eat? I don't even know how to cook an egg."

"You know I have other clients too."

"But didn't you just say that they have all canceled? I can pay you a full-time wage and you'll have most of the day free. What do you think?"

"What you really want isn't cooking and cleaning, it's company, isn't it?"

"Well, yes, that too. But you'll be comfortable here. Think what it would be like all alone in your mobile home, like being locked up in a cell."

"Hey, my house may be small, but it's cozy."

"Oh, help a poor old man out, Leticia!"

"Well, I'd have to bring Panchito, my parrot."

"No problem at all. Panchito is quite welcome."

So Leticia went to gather the necessities: Panchito, some clothes, her knitting, her vitamins, and the novel she was reading for her book club. On her way back to Mr. Bogart's, she stopped by the grocery store and filled her trunk with enough food to last two weeks and arrived to find her boss leaving to take the dog for a walk, which was still permitted. He was excited about the prospect of quarantining together and suggested that if the trial run went smoothly, they should make the arrangement permanent.

"And of course we'll adjust your salary accordingly," he repeated.

"You must be crazy" was her response, thinking she wouldn't be able to bear being on call day and night, like being married to an old man but without the advantages, if there were any.

Mr. Bogart was not offended but was prepared to continue trying to persuade her and maybe even twist her arm if necessary. He offered her the best room in the house, his wife's former art studio, which opened onto the garden and had an attached bathroom. Nadine's favorite loom was still set up there along with some of her weavings. Leticia quickly made herself at home, looking forward to long bubble baths and watching TV until late at night in the big bed. She was hooked on a Brazilian soap opera that had 240 episodes all dubbed into Spanish.

MR. BOGART'S DAUGHTER, CAMILLE, called around four o'clock that afternoon, which was seven o'clock for her in Manhattan. She was the editor of a fashion magazine and complained at length about the fact that none of her employees could come into the office because of the pandemic, reciting the complete rosary of her misfortunes: She'd have to mock up the next issue from home, the fundraising gala for the ballet had been canceled, her hair salon was closed as well as all the decent restaurants, eating food from little takeout cartons was too vulgar to keep up for very long, and how would she ever get by without the Filipina woman who cleaned her penthouse. She never once asked her father how he was doing. Their relationship was strained, to say the least. Mr. Bogart wondered how that calm, sweet child had turned into the impatient, opportunistic woman she grew up to be. It was easy to attribute her change to the unscrupulous man she'd married at a young age, but in reality Camille chose a husband she knew could offer the kind of luxuries and social position she longed for. Mr. Bogart blamed himself for never getting to know his daughter better, for having missed the opportunity to raise her properly, to be her guide and mentor, to cultivate affection and trust.

In a moment of frustration, Mr. Bogart had commented to Leticia that Camille cared only about money and social status and he couldn't understand how any daughter of his and Nadine LeBlanc's had turned out that way. He didn't have the highest opinion of Camille's son either, even if the young man was his only grandchild. "He's more fascist than Mussolini," he'd told Leticia once and she'd had to look the name up on the internet. She'd never been overly fond of the grandson, Martin Wendell, either, but she supposed he must have been fairly clever to have landed the job as top presidential advisor at such a young age. To his grandfather, it was an utter disgrace. Leticia had known Martin since he was a boy and had seen him for the last time at Nadine's funeral, when he would've been around twenty-eight. He was already balding, like Mussolini. He hadn't been to visit his grandfather in five years.

Martin's father, who according to Mr. Bogart was a true scoundrel, had made a fortune through questionable business ventures with plenty of vision and little virtue. Their marriage did not last long, but Camille walked away with a tidy sum when he left her. Martin grew up in a building with a doorman in Manhattan and attended the finest private schools and universities, where, from a young age, he stood out for his ultraconservative opinions, which rubbed his teachers and classmates the wrong way. But Martin didn't seem to mind being snubbed and in fact bragged about his innate ability to provoke people. As he rose in the political ranks, he knew he could always count on the support of faithful followers. He relished humiliating his detractors, a game he could always win.

Mr. Bogart often recalled the sweet child Martin had been before becoming radicalized. He'd been intelligent and energetic, a little boy who liked to watch cartoons and play chess with his grandfather. Mr. Bogart taught the boy the game at age five; by seven, Martin could easily beat him. They often did jigsaw puzzles together, Martin matching ten pieces together for every two of his grandfather's. On his summer vacation, when Camille sent her son to spend a few weeks with his grandparents in California, they would fish for turbot and sturgeon together in San Francisco Bay or go for long bike rides in the hills. He was trying to make up for the relationship he'd never had with his daughter. The old man told Leticia about those times, bewildered as to how Martin had changed so dramatically.

She had fond memories of the first time she met Martin, a boy on the threshold of adolescence. At the time, he was still a normal kid, eagerly devouring the stacks of pancakes she made for breakfast. But about when he started high school, he began to transform into a person his grandfather couldn't stand. She could clearly remember the first signs of the pompous man he would grow into. One morning after breakfast, his grandmother Nadine asked him to take his plate to the kitchen. He threw it to the floor and responded arrogantly that that was Leticia's job, since she was the help, wasn't she?

Leticia was sorry that Mr. Bogart had such a small and dysfunctional family. Apart from his quartet, he had few friends because he'd neglected his social relationships after his wife's passing. When Nadine was alive, their home had been an open house, a revolving door of frequent visitors and so many dinner parties that Leticia had become an expert in spicy dishes so that Nadine could brag about her New Orleans roots. Without Nadine, the old house slowly emptied out as their friends drifted away and Mr. Bogart made no effort to keep them close, since he didn't miss them. He was closed up inside himself. Perhaps he had been that way all his life, Leticia thought.

TWO MONTHS OF LOCKDOWN had passed and Leticia was still living in her boss's home. Neither of them could've ever imagined that the quarantine measures would go on for so long. Spring had descended upon them with a riot of flowers and bees who delighted in the overgrowth; the gardeners hadn't been to work in all that time. The warm weather lightened the gloominess that hung in the air but the virus showed no signs of loosening its grip. There were already more than ninety thousand people dead nationwide and hundreds of thousands more across the rest of the world, as laboratories competed in a frenzied race to develop a vaccine. The pandemic was being wielded as a political weapon—some believed it to be a hoax fabricated by opposition to the government and vehemently refused to wear masks, while others followed the recommendations of epidemiological experts to the letter. As the death toll rose and the hospitals filled, the president tried to downplay the severity of the situation or proposed ludicrous cures, such as injecting bleach. Leticia hadn't been able to see her daughter or her granddaughter in person but spoke to them on FaceTime every few days. She had lost all her regular clients indefinitely, but thanks to her increased hours with Mr. Bogart she was able to pay her bills, cover her few expenses, and even help her daughter out. Compared to some, she felt fortunate.

She and her boss had fallen into a comfortable routine. Mr. Bogart insisted from day one that she sit with him at the table for meals and not in the kitchen.

"Leticia, we've known each other for ages and you still call me Mr. Bogart. Are you ever going to start using my actual name?" he asked.

"No, sir. I like to respect hierarchy; too much familiarity between a boss and employee never ends well," she answered.

Nadine had always referred to her husband as Mr. Bogart, although Leticia knew that it was only the nickname she had given him when they first met, because as a young man he looked like Humphrey Bogart, with the same glum expression and tilted hat. The actor was from so long ago that Leticia didn't know who he was, but she grew to know his face well after moving in with her boss. One evening, he invited her to sit and watch *Casablanca* with him. She had agreed, reluctantly, because she didn't like black-and-white movies as a rule, but she was pleasantly surprised. She now suggested they watch the film at least once a week and could recite some of the dialogue by heart with exaggerated melodrama to make the old man laugh. Leticia tried to imagine what Humphrey Bogart would look like at eighty-something; the actor never reached old age, dying at fifty-six from excessive smoking well before she was born. She knew that her boss's real name was Samuel Adler, but he would always be Mr. Bogart to her.

NADINE, MR. BOGART'S WIFE, hadn't believed she was going to die, even though the diagnosis was dire, and so she hadn't prepared for it. Leticia had an abundance of free time now and decided she would use it to organize the chaos the woman had left behind. Before, the widower had been resistant to clearing out his wife's belongings, saying, "When I feel ready, Leticia, I'll let you know." He had forbidden his daughter from touching her mother's things, but Camille had simply taken what she wanted without his knowledge.

"This quarantine has caused me to reevaluate, Leticia. I realize I need to get my life in order before I die, starting with this house," he announced one morning.

"Don't be so grim, sir. With the right care, you'll make it to a hundred."

"And are you going to be the one to take care of me?"

"Who else? But I also think a little romance wouldn't hurt, to keep your spirit young; it's never too late, you know."

"Quit spouting foolishness, woman!" he exclaimed, then let out a loud laugh.

"It's no foolishness. You could meet a nice lady online. I can help you set up a profile. You might be the most eligible eighty-something-year-old bachelor in California, with your health, your looks, your good sense, and your money."

"How do you know how much money I have?" he asked.

"Well, I know you're not poor. There are tons of older women out there looking for a companion and too few old men capable of stringing two sentences together who aren't already in diapers. And the few that are available are probably looking for women thirty years younger. But that wouldn't be the case with you," Leticia said.

"I wouldn't mind a younger woman . . ."

"Don't even think about it, sir. We'll have to screen the candidates carefully, because some of them are only out for money. I had a neighbor who was a veterinarian, he was seventy-five and he owned a few houses he rented out. Then he fell into the clutches of a fifty-something gold digger and was dead within the year. The widow got everything. People say she poisoned him."

"Well, we have to wait for the pandemic to be over, Leticia, before we can start looking for my potential murderer. In the meantime, I want to get this house in order."

"Does that mean I have your permission . . ."

"Yes, you may do as you wish, but don't toss anything out before asking me first."

"I promise," she answered, without the slightest intention of keeping her word.

Leticia sprang into action, surprised by the tremendous imprint a person could make on the world during a single lifetime. In Nadine's closets, she found dresses from the seventies, platform shoes, and Indian skirts sewn with tiny mirrors, from the days when she dressed like a hippie even though she was already mother to Camille and had started to make a name for herself with her weavings. Leticia traced Nadine's life through the moth-eaten clothes she pulled from the closets. By the eighties, there were no signs of her previous bohemian style; at that point she was a famous artist and she dressed like a man. She found photos of the woman in suits, ties, thick-rimmed glasses, and boots. At fifty she had a brief infatuation with miniskirts, tight sweaters, and high heels, maybe in an attempt to impress some new lover, but she eventually seemed to tire of fashion and in the years that followed, up to her death, she opted for faded jeans and T-shirts, which highlighted her youthful appearance. The result was more attractive than the low-cut numbers she'd experimented with around menopause.

Leticia emptied cabinets and drawers filled with expired medication, ancient makeup, and exotic handmade jewelry; Camille had taken all of her mother's valuable pieces the day of the funeral. There were also many diaries and letters, which Leticia planned to read. Mr. Bogart was completely uninterested, perhaps afraid of reading anything that would confirm long-held suspicions.

THE DAYS WERE LONG and they all seemed the same, blending into one another. "Today is just like yesterday and tomorrow's going to be just like today," Leticia often said with a sigh.

Her boss had ordered a cappuccino machine and their mornings started just as they had before, with a cup of coffee and the news on TV. Then Mr. Bogart took Paco out for a walk wearing a mask and latex gloves, as Leticia started in on the cleaning. Her boss liked to drive to the grocery store, although he merely waited in the parking lot while Leticia went in, also wearing a mask and gloves. People in the shops complained that certain items were impossible to find, such as flour, disinfectant, powdered milk, and toilet paper. "These people have clearly never been through hard times," Leticia would mutter under her breath. They would eat a light lunch, usually a salad, and in the afternoon each went off to busy themselves, Mr. Bogart with his music, books, and the stationary bike he'd finally placed in one of the empty bedrooms, while Leticia turned on her Brazilian soap opera and rummaged through Nadine's past. She was becoming obsessed with the amazing life her former employer had led and had the strange inkling that she might even uncover a connection to her own history among Nadine's belongings.

Mr. Bogart liked to have a little more formality at dinnertime, to keep from becoming savages, he joked. The British colonizers had adopted this custom when they traveled to the more remote corners of the empire, dressing in their finery to eat lentils and stewed tiger meat under a canvas tarp, served by native people in white gloves. Too often, however, that had not stopped them from behaving like savages.

Every evening, he put on a suit jacket and Leticia would remove her apron and put on earrings and mascara.

"You're looking lovely this evening, Leticia," he said without fail, as an exercise in gallantry.

"You look very handsome yourself, Mr. Bogart."

Leticia would set the table with a long tablecloth, the good china, and the crystal glasses, and Mr. Bogart put on pop music, since he didn't think Leticia appreciated classical. Before dinner they would have a drink. He always chose the same thing, vodka on the rocks, while she rotated through different cocktails: piña colada, Cuba libre, bloody mariachi, mango margarita, coconut martini, and other concoctions she improvised according to her mood. The bar was still well stocked from the times when the family received regular guests and Leticia set out to empty every bottle, little by little, to keep all that nice liquor from going to waste. At the end of each day, the two of them had time to chat and they slowly got to know each other better. Leticia tried to wheedle information out of her boss, discreetly, because he would clam up whenever she showed too much curiosity. He was a man of few words, but after his second or third vodka he became more talkative and began to open up about his past and his late wife, whom he missed terribly.

"Do you ever think you might be creating a legend around Miss Nadine?"

"We all have the right to make up our own legends."

"I don't need to make mine up, sir."

LETICIA HAD WORKED IN the house for many years but had never set foot in the attic. It was hard to access, through a door in the ceiling of one of the bedrooms that could only be opened by pulling the handle with a metal rod that had a hook at the end. When the door opened, a ladder unfolded. Since Leticia had never even seen anyone go up into the attic, the first time she opened the door she pulled too hard and the ladder fell down on top of her head. It was not easy to climb up, because the rungs were weak and shaky and the attic was dark except for the faint light that filtered in through a few skylights. It took Leticia a long while to find the switch and then change the burnt-out bulbs so she could see. The attic was an enormous, cavernous space, another floor spanning the entire house. It had never been cleaned so dust had piled up on every surface and spiderwebs hung like lace from the rafters. She didn't see any mice but knew they were around because of the little balls of excrement everywhere. It was a universe unto itself, full of treasures and mysteries, where she could've spent months opening boxes, suitcases half rotten with mildew, old dressers, and wardrobes. There were toys left over from Camille's and Martin's childhoods, several artificial Christmas trees, a half-dozen bicycles in various states of disrepair, sports equipment, some of Nadine's old looms, and everything else imaginable. Poking around, she discovered small compartments hidden in the low beams, designed to hide valuables. She found a collection of silver objects still in their original packaging: a full tea service, several trays, candelabras, a set of flatware including lobster crackers and tiny forks for eating snails, ashtrays, which no one used anymore, and picture frames in several different sizes. Mr. Bogart later explained that he and his wife had bought the silver on a trip to Mexico and had had it shipped home, but then they had a falling-out and separated for a time before the shipment arrived. Since he had been living alone in the house when the silver finally got there, he just stuck it all in the attic and forgot about it.

"What are we going to do with all that silver? I don't want to spend the rest of my life polishing fish forks," Leticia said.

"Just leave it where it is. Camille will take it when I die."

For Leticia, the most interesting things in Nadine's trunks were her journals, letters, and photographs. In her free time, which she had plenty of, she began to piece together the life of this fascinating woman. She regretted not having dared to ask Nadine more questions while she was alive, because the woman had enjoyed reminiscing about the past. But at the time Leticia had wanted to keep things strictly professional, proving her efficiency at cleaning, laundry, and cooking without wasting time pestering the lady of the house. Leticia had now been given free rein to dig through the family's past. She'd already uncovered a lot of surprising information even though she'd only opened ten percent of the boxes and trunks.

Nadine's maiden name had been LeBlanc and she never changed it. Leticia imagined that Mr. Bogart must have loved his wife fiercely to put up with her highly unconventional lifestyle. Long-term relationships took a lot of work, as Leticia knew firsthand, but she was of the opinion that if a person was foolish enough to get married, they should adapt to certain conventions, or at least make an attempt to keep up appearances. Nadine openly flaunted conventions and appearances. She was unfaithful by nature and made little effort to hide it, leaving such a clear trail of clues that anyone could've figured it out. She had even hinted as much to Leticia when she was alive, calling herself too passionate for monogamy. Leticia considered passion more of a vice than a virtue. Nadine was already advanced in age by this point; her indiscretions went on well into her older years. Leticia believed that there was a time for everything, and the time to do foolish things out of lust was in youth. After that it was simply indecent, although ultimately it wasn't her place to judge—every person had to be guided by their own conscience.

Nadine had hinted that Mr. Bogart was no stranger to affairs himself, saying that he'd once fallen in love with one of his university students, but that was many years before Leticia began working for them and she had no way of knowing whether it was true. Nadine, on the other hand, had numerous affairs, Leticia was certain, and she'd even met the man who was probably Nadine's last lover: Bruno Brunelli, the owner of the Italian coffee shop and bakery that carried his name. Leticia planned to continue buying coffee there when life returned to normal; she didn't consider it a moral conflict. Brunelli himself had gone to live out his final days in his hometown in Italy, leaving the business to be run by his son.

In one of her diary entries, Nadine wrote: *I waited for him until closing time. He pulled me into the kitchen. He let me taste almond paste and vanilla cream from his mouth, then we made love on the counter. I had powdered sugar all over my clothes when I got home.*

"Oh Mother Mary!" Leticia shrieked when she read those lines. A head full of gray hair wasn't going to stop the woman from having a romp in Bruno Brunelli's pastry kitchen.

IN THE DIARIES SHE found in the attic, Leticia learned of other "trysts," as the author called them. Most of the affairs before Bruno seemed insignificant, because she merely identified the lucky men with initials and a few lines about the locations and circumstances of the encounters, but, judging by the brevity of the descriptions, there were few as interesting as the pastry chef. In one of those notations, Leticia saw the initials CT along with dates that coincided with the period in which Cruz Torres was remodeling the old house.

Leticia had such a strong desire to find something about herself or her father in those diaries that she worried she might be jumping to conclusions with no basis. But beside the initials CT, Nadine had written a brief description that matched the man she knew: *Strong, and intense, with thick, dark hair, long scar on his shoulder, rough working man's hands, he whispered to me in Spanish, I understood a little, we share a similar appetite for love and lust.* She became confident the initials referred to Cruz Torres, who had helped Leticia and her father in their times of need, and to whom she owed her long-term employment with the Adlers.

The renovation of the old house in Berkeley had dragged on for many months, because problems cropped up along the way. If they made a hole in one wall, a pipe might burst on the other side of the house; they changed the drains and several roof tiles became dislodged; they replaced the window frames, and elsewhere the doors fell off their hinges. Nadine made all the design decisions while her husband focused on his classes and his music, without the slightest interest in Cruz Torres and his team, believing, with good reason, that the old house was beyond repair and they should either accept it as it was or bring in a bulldozer to knock it down.

Leticia remembered noticing at the time that her contractor friend and the lady of the house seemed to have a curious friendship, despite their clear differences. Cruz Torres was at least ten years younger than Nadine, of another ethnicity and social class. Leticia often saw them drinking coffee and whispering to each other in the kitchen, going silent or changing the subject whenever she walked in. On one occasion, a few years after the work on the house had been completed, Leticia thought she saw them together through the window of a little restaurant, their hands entwined across the table. When Cruz was deported in 2008, Nadine began to make frequent trips to Mexico.

LETICIA DID THE MATH and inferred that if Nadine LeBlanc and Cruz Torres had been lovers for as long as she suspected, the affair with Bruno Brunelli must've been relatively brief. Nadine was sixty-nine when the Mexican man was sent home and seventy-two when Bruno moved to Italy. Her age wouldn't have stopped her from finding a replacement, if she'd wanted to. She was striking, daring, agile, spontaneous, with wild gray hair, laugh lines, and a loud cackle that could wake the dead. She bragged that she had a mix of French, Spanish, and African blood, called herself a mulatta, and said often that the wealthy Black branch of her family had intermarried with too many poor whites, thus losing their color and their fortune. Leticia remembered her former boss with fondness: Nadine was generous and fun, the opposite of her husband, who walked through life burdened by painful memories and past suffering. With infinite sadness, Leticia watched the vivacious woman rapidly deteriorate and die from an incurable cancer. Since then, the years had passed so quickly that she still sometimes found herself surprised at Nadine's absence.

Leticia had helped Mr. Bogart care for his wife as she was dying. The man dropped everything to be with her, retiring from the university, abandoning his kayaking and cycling to spend day and night beside her. When he couldn't stand to see her in pain any longer, he would escape for a few hours to a jazz club. Before Nadine fell ill, Leticia had cleaned the house twice a week, but at that time she had started coming in daily. They delegated the entire running of the household to her, since Nadine couldn't do anything and her husband was useless when it came to domestic matters; the few times he entered the kitchen to give Leticia some confused instructions, she kicked him out. The housekeeper took care of paying their bills, kept track of the medication schedule and doctors' appointments, and even dealt with Camille, who had an opinion on everything but couldn't take a minute of her time to be with her parents in their darkest moment. Mr. Bogart gave Leticia the money to manage all their monthly expenses without ever asking how she spent it, but she kept meticulous records and saved every receipt, so no one could ever accuse her of misappropriating a single cent.

AS THE ATTIC BEGAN to reveal its secrets to Leticia, she became increasingly curious about the house itself, which had served as a backdrop to most of Nadine LeBlanc's life. She'd long thought she knew the place better than anyone, but suddenly realized she didn't have any idea of its history.

"It was first built by a banker as a summer home back in the days when you had to take the ferry over from San Francisco," Mr. Bogart told her. "After the banker, it was occupied by a woman who ran a gambling parlor and, rumor has it, the upstairs rooms served as a brothel for prominent gentlemen who required discretion."

He went on to explain that the house was later used briefly as a rehab clinic for Hollywood celebrities. And shortly after Nadine bought it, she turned it into something of a shelter for freeloaders she met on the street, since there was so much empty space, until he got sick of supporting the impromptu hippie commune and they divorced.

"Is that true? Did you actually get divorced?" Leticia asked, shocked.

"Yes."

"What happened to Camille?"

"The hippies left once I stopped funding their parties. Then Nadine took off to Bolivia, dragging Camille along with her."

"Why did she go to Bolivia?"

"To study weaving. By then she was already taking her textile art very seriously. She spent a few months in Bolivia and then went to Guatemala. The textiles there are spectacular."

Mr. Bogart explained that his wife fell in love with Central America and maintained contact with people in the villages she had visited, several of whom were devastated not long afterward by a government-ordered military genocide of the Mayan population, which left two hundred thousand people dead, 1.5 million displaced, and more than five hundred villages wiped off the map. The majority of the women who'd taught her their craft were murdered along with their families and communities. In the nineties, Nadine went back to Guatemala and began trying to promote the textiles and weavers from that country, getting their wares into exclusive shops and art galleries, then sending the entirety of the profits back to them.

"After she left me that first time, I flew down to Guatemala to win her back. I was certain that without those freeloaders living on my dime, we could have a fresh start. It worked. We remarried. And it wasn't the last time either."

"Oh, Mr. Bogart, please explain," Leticia begged.

"Nadine and I were married three times in total—the first two times officially, at the courthouse. The last time we simply renewed our vows. On each occasion we agreed on a new set of ground rules for the relationship."

"You never fell in love with other people?" Leticia asked.

"Yes, we did, but we'd invested so much into our relationship that it was always worth saving. People change, Leticia, couples change. Nadine and I went through many different stages together. We fell in love young and formed our family, but that phase ended with the hippies. In our second marriage we both went through existential crises and so decided to try an open relationship; it was a disaster. In our third act Nadine was so focused on her art and I was so distracted by my work that we neglected the relationship. We didn't come to anything resembling a stable partnership until we were much older."

"You must've loved each other very much to keep getting back together, I suppose."

"Nadine was an amazing woman; there was so much love on my part. You remember us that way, don't you?"

"Of course I do. I was there for the renewal ceremony and the party in the garden. Then you guys went on a second honeymoon, or a third maybe, to Argentina. That must've been about fifteen years ago, right?"

"Yes, that was the last time we renewed our commitment to each other."

"If Miss Nadine was still alive, it would probably be about time for you two to get married again, wouldn't it?"

"I'm sure it would, Leticia," he said. "And what about you? I've never asked after your personal life . . ."

"I had three marriages, two divorces, and one great loss. The first two husbands don't count. The third was the true love of my life, the father of my daughter, but fate took him away from me too soon. He died suddenly, at a museum."

"I didn't know you were a widow," Mr. Bogart said.

"I still love that man and I'll love him till the day I die."

IN THE WEEKS THAT followed, as Leticia dug deeper into Nadine's diaries, she found it easier to decipher them. She began to suspect that the letters used repeatedly throughout the last fifteen years of Nadine's life were not the initials of her fleeting lovers, as she'd supposed, but were in fact some kind of code. Her heart skipped a beat when she discovered that Nadine's descriptions of her art contained a code as well: Each color mentioned corresponded to something that had nothing to do with the textile. The initials CT often accompanied the color yellow. Leticia had initially skimmed over Nadine's folders of drawings and wool samples, but when she looked more carefully she found multiple newspaper clippings about illegal immigration. She knew that the issue had interested Nadine, that she donated money to and volunteered with the East Bay Sanctuary, an organization run from a church basement that helped undocumented workers. Leticia imagined that the codes might have something to do with this.

Overcome with curiosity, Leticia called Cruz Torres in Mexico. They hadn't spoken in a few years, but he recognized her voice immediately. He was now seventy and had been back in Mexico for twelve years; he settled in Puebla, where he'd opened a small backpackers' hostel using the money he'd saved over many years of work in the United States. When he emigrated from Mexico as a young man, he'd left behind a wife, whom he'd always supported from a distance and with whom he had three children. He would travel home occasionally, but as the illegal border crossing became more difficult, the visits became less frequent. By the time he was deported back to Mexico for good, his wife had died. Cruz now lived with one of his daughters, who helped him run the hostel.

After they brought each other up to speed on their respective lives, Leticia explained that they were finally going through Nadine LeBlanc's things, five years after her death.

"I hope you won't be offended by what I have to say, don Cruz, but I've found letters and diaries that Señora Nadine left behind, and you're mentioned quite often."

"You know we were friends."

"More than friends, right?"

"That's between Nadine and me. What else do you want to know?"

"I'm interested in her work helping migrants. I talked with the nun in charge of the East Bay Sanctuary; she told me some things. I wasn't able to go in person, but I will as soon as this pandemic ends."

"I'm glad to hear that Sister Maureen is still alive. That Irish-woman is indestructible. What did she tell you?"

"That Miss Nadine helped people come into the country, that she transported migrants from the border, that she hid entire families when there were raids. I think she wrote the initials of these people in her journals and used different colors to indicate the circumstances of each case. Do you know anything about all this?"

"You're probably right, although I never saw her journals," Cruz replied.

"Your initials always appear in yellow."

"I worked with her. I would smuggle people across the border and hand them over near San Diego. Maybe the color indicated the mode of transportation?"

"Don't you think it's strange she used codes? It's as if Señora Nadine were playing spy."

"She had to be very careful, Leticia, because she had the fate of very vulnerable people in her hands."

"Where did you two meet, don Cruz?"

"At the Mexican Museum in San Francisco, during an exhibition on migrants. The artist had hung plastic bags from the ceiling filled with things they'd fished out of the river, left behind by people, including children, who'd crossed it to reach the shores of the United States. Many of them had drowned in the process. Nadine was very moved by a baby shoe floating in some dirty water inside a bag. We started talking . . . That must've been at least a year before she hired me to do the work on her house."

"So, you got her involved with the migrant issue?"

"No. She was already working with Sister Maureen at that point. She recruited me to help. Many of the refugees were Guatemalan women whom Nadine had professional and emotional ties to, through her weaving. She was able to safeguard many families. That's where the profits from her art went."

"This must've gone on for years and years. I don't understand how her husband never knew," said Leticia.

"She thought it best to keep as much as possible from him, so that he couldn't be implicated in what she was doing, which was highly illegal. But I don't think he would've been interested anyway; his thing was music. None so blind as those who will not see, right?" Torres answered.

"I imagine this is how you got deported, don Cruz?"

"No, actually it had nothing to do with the border crossings. I was arrested in a raid. I'd had some problems with the law: a ticket for drunk driving, an electrical installation without the proper permit, tax evasion . . . minor things, but enough to get me booted back across the border, for good. The thing I most regret was not being able to say goodbye to Nadine when she got sick."

"Do you think I should tell my boss what Señora Nadine was doing?" Leticia asked.

"What for? Leave the old man in peace. It might make him sad to know that his wife kept so many secrets from him and never let him into this huge part of her life. I think from the start of their marriage, Nadine accepted that they were totally different and abandoned any hopes of sharing her interests and concerns with him."

"Despite all that, they had a good marriage," Leticia said.

"I'm sure they did, since they stayed together to the end."

LIFE IN LOCKDOWN BECAME more complicated when Mr. Bogart got the notion to climb up to the attic himself and slipped on the second rung of the ladder. He fell, spraining his ankle. He lay on the floor for several seconds, gasping for breath, out of fear more than pain. Worried he might've broken several bones or suffered a heart attack from the scare, Leticia helped him the best she could to the car and drove him to the emergency room, where they were greeted by healthcare workers covered head to toe in green scrubs, gloves, masks, and clear face shields. Leticia wasn't allowed to accompany her boss past the door and could only wave goodbye while they wheeled him away on a stretcher, pale as a sheet. In the six hours that followed, they took X-rays and kept the elderly man under observation, with Leticia waiting in the hospital parking lot, calling frequently until her battery died. In the end, it turned out he'd only twisted his ankle and all his bones were intact. The only cure for it was rest and painkillers, the doctor explained, but Leticia also massaged the patient's ankle with cannabis oil.

"That's what they call marijuana now, how ridiculous. But it helps with the pain and it's legal here; I didn't get it from some drug dealer in a back alley," she explained to her boss.

Given that it all ended well, Leticia wasn't too sorry for what had happened. Now she was free to rummage in the attic without anyone checking in on her.

Mr. Bogart could no longer take Paco on walks, which had been his only excuse to get outside, and he wasn't able to ride his stationary bicycle or drive either. Leticia's duties were therefore expanded to chauffeur and dog walker, in addition to cleaning the house and keeping the old man company.

"We've spent so much time together, it's a miracle we can still stand each other. This is the longest honeymoon of my life," he joked. "At the rate this pandemic is going, I might be locked inside till the day I die. But I can't complain—"

"How's the ankle?" she interrupted.

"Oh, about the same. I forbid you to mention this to Camille. She's got the notion that I should be in a geriatric home. If she finds out I fell, she'll use it as an excuse to get me out of here so she can sell this house; the university made an offer, they want the land and they'll pay a fortune for it. But I'm not leaving this place unless it's in a coffin, do you hear me? You're young and strong and you can take care of me until the end right here in the comfort of my home," he said.

"Well, I'm no match for your daughter. I have no authority over her. It's possible that Camille could have you declared incompetent if she wanted to."

"I don't plan on going senile and spending my final days in a loony bin for the elderly, eating gelatin as I sit waiting for death to come calling," he muttered, and they both burst out laughing. "You know what, Leticia? I think you're the happiest person I've ever known. You can find the humor in any situation; you sing while you cook and rumba while you vacuum."

"That's how we Salvadorans face life. They used to say that El

Salvador was the nation of smiles, but I imagine the smiles have faded some since the civil war."

"You must have a good life if you approach the world that way."

"I live in peace, but that wasn't always the case."

"How long have we known each other?" he asked.

"Twenty years. Cruz Torres got me this job when he was working on the renovations to this house. I was so young when I started working with you and Miss Nadine."

"You still are young."

"I think I look pretty good for forty-seven, don't I? But we age better than you whites," she answered.

"You're certainly aging better than me," he joked, gesturing to his swollen ankle. "What are you doing digging around in that attic, anyway? What are you looking for?"

"Oh, nothing in particular. I just want to get it cleaned out, it's my pet project. You have no idea how much stuff you have; it's an entire universe of junk. I think the ladies of the night have taken over the space. Do you remember when you used to see them?"

"Tell them to come down, no one is going to bother them. And tell them to bring Nadine as well."

ANITA

TUCSON, APRIL–JUNE 2020

The shelter was better. I don't like foster homes. This new one is worse than Señora María's because it's all boys here and they are very rude. They just fight all day and they don't even know how to say please or thank you. They are very nasty, these boys. Tita Edu would set them straight in less than a week, that's for sure. Also, we have to speak English here. I'm tired of English, it's like having a towel in my mouth. You won't even speak in Spanish, and you won't eat. Enough already, Claudia! You're not a baby anymore, you're too big for this. It's your fault Señora María kicked us out. Do you want us to end up begging on the street? Actually Señora María had too little patience. I think she hated me. It wasn't really your fault, Claudia, you're a good girl. It's a good thing we left that place.

The psychologist spoke Spanish and she didn't let Miss Selena go into her office with me. She gave me some dolls to play with, but I explained that they were for little kids and I'm almost eight now. She said in that case we could just talk. She asked me about Didi, about you, about our life before, and about Mama. She also asked me about Señora María's house and about wetting the bed and why Señora María locked me in the closet, although I didn't tell her about that. I don't know how she already knew. I had to tell her about the hielera and about when they took Mama away and they grabbed me and even though I kicked and screamed and cried, they still put me on the bus. I don't like to talk about it, because it makes me want to cry. It's not good to cry when you talk to the psychologist; I learned that from before when I went to see the one at school. It makes them nervous. Then Miss Selena told me not to worry, that they were going to move me to another home.

But I don't like this new place either, even though the lady is nicer than Señora María. She told me we were going to get along very well, that she always wanted to have daughters but God didn't give her any, so I could be like her daughter. I told her that I already have a real mom. I won't call this lady Mom, and I can't call her Auntie either because they don't say that here. She told me it was okay to call her Susan, but it feels strange to me. We call her husband Mr. Rick and we always have to be respectful around him, or else he gets mad. Those rude boys will never be my brothers; I try not to talk to them at all.

I HAVE TO CHEW the pink pills up and swallow them, because they're vitamins. They're not too gross. You just have to close your eyes and imagine that it tastes like a strawberry lollipop or a piece of candy. Susan says I have to eat more and take my vitamins, because I'm very skinny and I need to grow. It's not my fault that the food here tastes weird. Susan said that she's never had a kid who didn't like sandwiches and that she'll look for a pupusa recipe on the internet, but I don't think she will because she doesn't have any time and she doesn't know how to cook, only how to make sandwiches. She said that the vitamins are important but that I don't need any more shots, that was just for when I first got here to the North. She gives me my vitamin and stands there watching until I chew it up and swallow it and I have to open my mouth to show her that I didn't hide it under my tongue. How could I hide it, it's huge.

I have to do what the teachers say on Zoom, because we can't go to school. Because of the virus. The schools are closed and all the kids have to do school in their houses; that's why the boys who aren't my brothers are here all day, causing trouble. Susan can't control them, they do whatever they want, they never listen to their teachers, just play video games and watch TV all day. They only behave when Mr. Rick gets home, because they're scared of him. Mr. Rick is the boss of this house. He pretends to be nice, but he isn't.

I can't see much on Zoom—I can't see anything, actually—but I can hear what the teacher says and that the classes are for little kids. I told Susan that I'm a little bit blind, but I'm not dumb, I can be in a class with kids my same age. I understand a lot of English now. Miss Selena is going to have to do something about this, because right now I'm not learning anything, I'm just wasting my time.

Mr. Rick works for the post office and that's why he still has to go to work every day. Some people are allowed to go out for work, but they have to wear a mask. The post office is like the garbage truck and the ambulance and the hospital, it has to always be open. Mr. Rick has a strange smell. You know that I have always had a good nose but since the accident, I pay more attention. Before, I never noticed people's smells, unless they were very stinky, but now I can recognize anybody by the way they smell. For example, when I'm putting the clothes in the washing machine, I can tell who every shirt belongs to. All the boys here smell bad, but they don't all smell the same, each one of them stinks in a different way. Tita Edu said that my nose is as good as a dog's and I could get a job at the airport catching people who had drugs in their suitcases. Some people smell happy or nice, others smell mean. Susan smells like patience and also like sadness. Mr. Rick smells like something burned in the bottom of a pot. Maybe that's the smell of the post office.

MY GUARDIAN ANGEL TOLD me that she's invisible and sometimes it's too hard for her to make herself visible, but that I don't need to worry, because she's always close by and she knows that I want to be back with Mama. She says she's working on it, just like Frank is. She gave me a very good idea for whenever I'm sad. She told me that instead of crying I could go invisible. It's not easy. You have to concentrate very hard. It's the same thing she does to become visible, but the other way around. I'll teach you, Claudia, and we can practice together when we're alone.

The invisibility trick is very useful, it could help with a lot of things. For example, when those boys who are not our brothers start being mean, instead of fighting them, which isn't a good idea because they're bigger, we can concentrate and become invisible, then they won't be able to bother us. It could also help when we don't want anyone to talk to us, or when we're scared.

But we can never go invisible if Mr. Rick or one of those bigger boys or any man or anyone tries to touch us down there, like Carlos did that one time. No one can touch us. Tita Edu taught me that. If anyone touches me, I have to scream as loud as I can. You too, Claudia. Do you promise me? Mr. Rick doesn't have any business anywhere near my bed. I stay awake as long as I can to watch out, because my guardian angel needs help with that. If I see Mr. Rick or any of those big boys near my bed, I'm going to scream and scream. You have to do the same thing. It's not true that if we scream or we tell someone what happens they'll kick us out. And if they do kick us out we can call Miss Selena. I have her number and I can get a cellphone. I also have Frank's number, but he lives far away and it would take him a long time to get here.

This foster home is so noisy all day long. It drives me crazy. The worst thing that's happened to us here in the North was the hielera, when they took Mama away. And the second worst thing is this foster home. Susan says she can't stand it anymore, she's sick of all the chaos, that her life would be much easier if she had only girls like me who don't make a mess and who help her with the cleaning and washing, but instead she's tired and depressed all the time. I think that's why she spends all day on the couch watching TV and eating; there's no baby inside her big tummy even though it looks like it. The house is such a mess that I'm always tripping over things on the floor, and everything's all sticky. Not to mention the bathroom, the smell is so disgusting it makes me want to throw up. If Tita Edu saw this place she would have a heart attack. The only thing Susan has energy for is fighting with Mr. Rick. She waits for him to get home so she can start shouting at him. She likes me, I think, but she can't protect me. I have to pay attention and make sure none of those big boys try to steal Didi or fight with me, and I have to go invisible as soon as Mr. Rick gets home so he doesn't even know I'm here.

DO YOU SEE, CLAUDIA? The hole worked! That little hole in the wall was just what I needed to leave a message for my guardian angel. She got us out of this foster home like I asked her to. We're finally leaving this place. Miss Selena told me at first it would be just for a little while, but I think we've been here like three months, or maybe three years, I can't remember anymore. I can tell we've been here in the North a long time because look at how the weather's changed. It's even hotter here now than back home in El Salvador, but the air always feels dry. It never rains. Do you remember the sound of the rain? It was louder than the shower. Here they break up the year into spring, summer, fall, and winter, but it's hard to tell which is which. I've been counting the seasons based on the heat: hot when we first got here, more or less cold when we were in the shelter, hot but not too hot at Señora María's, very hot at Susan's. It's been a long time, for sure. But that's life, we have to keep being patient.

We're still waiting for Mama. I think it's strange she hasn't come to get us yet and she hasn't even called. She must not have a phone where she is. When Miss Selena talks to Mama, she's going to tell her where we are. We're not lost, Claudia. You don't have to be afraid, we just got separated is all. At least we can talk to Tita Edu sometimes. We don't need to tell her about Mr. Rick, because she's far away and it would be like a knife in her heart.

What happened with Mr. Rick was actually good in the end, Claudia. I knew it was going to happen, I could feel it right here, in my tummy, like a thought that was stuck there. That's how I always felt whenever he was around and he gave me candy and wanted to touch me. He didn't do that with the boys. He's a bad man, just like Carlos. I know it was very scary, but it turned out all right because now we get to move somewhere else and it's not going to be another foster home like this one or Señora María's. My guardian angel did part of what I asked but she still has to do the most important part, which is to find Mama. Miss Selena has never said that she needs to find Mama but I'm not dumb. I can tell that she doesn't know where Mama is, because if she knew, she would've called her.

Mr. Rick snuck into my room super quiet but I got woken up by the smell of the post office. Before I could say anything, he covered my mouth and got on top of me and started pulling my underwear down with his other hand. He was panting like a dog and telling me to keep quiet and he would give me whatever I wanted, but if not he would strangle me. I couldn't move and I couldn't breathe, I was about to die of suffocation, and he was opening my legs and putting something between them. But then I bit his hand and started to scream as loud as I could, like Tita Edu told me to. *Susan! Susan! Susan! Help! Help!* Mr. Rick jumped off me, but he got tangled up in his pants, I think. And I kept screaming and everyone in the whole house woke up. Susan got there in less than a minute and her husband was still lying on the floor. I told the truth and Susan got madder than ever and Mr. Rick left the house and slammed the door. That's why Miss Selena came very early in the morning; I think Susan called her. You didn't even notice; you're the only one who didn't get woken up by all the shouting.

MR. BOGART

O ver his long life, Samuel Adler had witnessed cities devastated by war, but nothing like the scenes of the pandemic: the streets and buildings of New York, Rome, and Shanghai perfectly intact, but without a soul in sight. It looked like some science fiction catastrophe. In California, drastic measures had been taken to combat the virus, but in other states the directives were confusing; each governor or mayor made decisions based on local political leanings, without consideration for science. Forced to remain in his home in quarantine for many months, Samuel watched his TV screen as, all around the world, life came to a grinding halt. The air that summer was thick with the smell and smoke of nearby fires, which had wiped out millions of acres of forest. Sometimes the ash caused a thick fog that made the sun look like a hazy orange spotlight in the red sky. He told Leticia that they should be prepared to evacuate at a moment's notice if necessary, with their important documents and cash on hand, the car always fueled up and packed with water bottles, food for the dog and the parrot, blankets, and other essentials.

"All these preparations won't do a bit of good if it's our destiny to be roasted to a crisp," she replied.

"Just humor me, woman—don't be so fatalistic."

"I wonder which catastrophe will kill us first, the virus or the fires."

"I'm not afraid of the virus, because we're being careful, but I hate that it's robbing me of the little time I have left in this world. And I'm worried it will leave me senile. I used to have so many challenges that kept my mind active, like my concerts and the talks I gave at the symphony, but that's all stopped. My plans to visit the Galápagos and Easter Island have gone out the window."

"It's probably for the best. You can see turtles and rocks right here. You need to take care of yourself."

Samuel was aware that people of his generation were dying and he had few acquaintances his own age left alive to begin with. Before, death had been something that happened to other people, but in the past months he'd felt it snapping at his heels. Ever since he'd lost his wife, aging seemed to accelerate. He thought a lot about his own inevitable demise, and the fact that it could come at any moment, before he'd had the chance to put his life in order. He didn't want to leave too much of himself behind, as Nadine had, but he worked hardest to rid himself of things only he knew about: sentimental garbage, regret, shame, miserliness. He made a daily exercise of letting go of bitterness and practicing gratitude. He'd learned the technique from Nadine, but only began to make it a habit in recent years, when she was no longer there to take him by the hand. From time to time she would visit him as a sudden gust of wind, and in those moments he would sit perfectly still, not even daring to breathe so as not to frighten her, silently asking his beloved wife to stay with him a little longer.

His ankle hurt and he walked with a limp, but he wore the orthopedic boot and refused to mention his aches and pains. It was annoying when Leticia made too much of a fuss over him. The fall from the ladder was a blow to his confidence, and he now moved more cautiously, didn't dare to drive, and was afraid he'd never be able to ride a real bicycle in the fresh air ever again. Was this the beginning of the end? How much longer could he stave off the inevitable deterioration of his body? And his mind? He sometimes forgot words, a name, an idea, and then he'd be flooded with terror at the horrifying possibility of living without being able to think or remember. If his heart held out and he didn't suffer any major accidents, he might live past ninety; if he did the math, that meant he had around fifteen hundred days left on the calendar. It wasn't a lot; they would fly by and he'd already wasted over one hundred of them locked up inside his home.

"If it weren't for you, the little girl, and Paco, I'd be more lonely and depressed than a man on death row," he said to Leticia.

"Don't forget about Panchito," she replied.

Samuel had little love for Leticia's alcoholic parrot, who would dip his beak into the old man's vodka when he wasn't paying attention and then flap around the house with his feathers standing on end, crashing against the walls.

"The girl's going to need you for at least ten more years, Mr. Bogart, so don't even think about dying on us."

FIRST CAME THE PHONE call for Leticia from a man named Frank Angileri. He introduced himself as a lawyer and explained that he was representing a minor named Anita Díaz. Leticia responded that she didn't know anyone by that name and hung up the phone. The man called back thirty seconds later and once again Leticia hung up on him. He called for a third time and Samuel picked up the phone, asking for an explanation. The man said that he needed to speak with

Leticia Cordero about a family matter, so she got on the line and to-gether she and Samuel listened to what the lawyer had to say.

"I'm calling on behalf of a little girl who's just turned eight. She came from El Salvador with her mother to the border at Nogales, in October of last year. The two were separated and Anita was sent to a residential youth home. Because they haven't been able to reunite her with her mother or any other relatives, she was placed in temporary foster care. But it wasn't a good place for her. She was transferred to another home but—"

"I don't know the girl," Leticia interrupted.

"Just a moment, Leticia. Let's hear the man out," Samuel said.

"We have information that a Ms. Leticia Cordero is first cousin to the girl's father."

"Where is the father?" Samuel asked.

"He died in 2015. His complete name was Rutilio Díaz Cordero. In El Salvador the father's name, Díaz in this case, goes before the mother's, which is rarely used."

"Okay, so you think we're related?"

"Exactly. Do you know a Mr. Rutilio Díaz, Ms. Cordero?" the lawyer asked her.

"I've lived here since I was a little girl, sir. I haven't had any con-tact with my relatives in El Salvador," she explained.

"But do you think that this girl could be a relative of yours?"

"I don't know . . . How did you find me?"

Frank Angileri explained that he'd hired one of the investigators who worked with his law firm, an expert in uncovering buried clues and tracking down witnesses and suspects. The only lead they had to go on was that before they'd lost contact with her, Marisol Díaz had mentioned a cousin named Lety or Leticia, who lived in California. They weren't able to find anyone using Marisol's two last names, An-drade or Díaz. Then the investigator talked to Anita's grandma, Edu-vigis, in El Salvador, and found out that Leticia's last name was

Cordero. He searched for Lety or Leticia Cordero with the hope that she wouldn't be undocumented, because that would've made her impossible to find.

"It took a while, but we finally got lucky," the lawyer concluded.

"No one calls me Lety anymore. That was my nickname as a little girl," Leticia murmured.

"Would you like to meet the girl?"

"I don't know . . ."

"What happened to her mother?" Samuel asked.

"She's disappeared. We think she was deported."

"She disappeared?" Samuel exclaimed.

"No one in El Salvador has seen her. She might've been deported to another country; mix-ups like that have been known to happen. Many are simply sent to Mexico with instructions to wait for the judge to hear their case. But that could take months or even years. There are refugee camps on the other side of the border, tens of thousands of people living in tents, in terrible conditions."

"I know. I read the newspaper."

"The public doesn't know half of what is really happening."

"So in short, Mr. Angileri, at this moment Anita Díaz has neither mother nor father, is that correct?" Samuel asked.

"That's right, sir. While we continue to search for her mother, which is proving difficult, it would be a huge help if Anita could be looked after by a family member. I'm trying to get her permanent asylum with the chance of bringing her mother over to be reunited with her, but it might take a while, especially now with the pandemic. Anita is an extremely bright girl, very polite and respectful."

There was a long pause in the conversation, as Leticia dried her tears and Samuel recalled his own past. The painful memories that had been stored in a secret chamber of his heart came rushing back: the shouts, the smoke, the fear, his mother, so lovely and so sad, bidding him farewell from the station, and also old Colonel Volker in his uniform, pinning a magic medal of courage on his coat. Eighty years later he still carried the medal along with his violin. He had changed the instrument a few times in his career but the medal and his parents' photograph were always taped inside the case. He could not visualize his father, who had been absent during the last days before he was sent to England. Did his father love him, as he was sure that his mother did? Everything before that terrible night of the broken glass was almost gone from his memory. Was he a happy child before that? He wondered if he had consciously erased his first five years or if he was just too young to remember them. Anita was older than he had been when he was separated from his family. She would forget nothing.

"Obviously, I'd prefer to explain all this in person and show you Anita's file and some photos, but thanks to this virus, that's not possible," Frank concluded.

"I think we need a moment. Could you call us back in about ten minutes, please?" Samuel asked.

He spent the next ten minutes persuading Leticia that they had a duty to help that little girl, who had already experienced too much suffering in her short life. Whether she was a relative or not, it didn't matter. Fate had presented them with the opportunity to do something for her and it would be unforgivable to sit comfortably by without doing anything.

"We have plenty of space here. Look at all the empty rooms in this house," he argued.

"And who's going to take care of the little girl? You?" she replied.

"We'll both take care of her."

"You've completely forgotten what it takes to raise a child, Mr. Bogart. And this girl is traumatized—she misses her mother, she's been pulled away from everything she knows, her family, her friends, her school, her community, her language. Can you imagine what that must be like?"

"Perfectly."

"She'll be a handful. The poor thing . . ."

"Exactly, Leticia: the poor thing. We're going to say yes to this lawyer and then we will figure it out somehow."

"Promise me that whatever happens you won't go back on your decision. Once the girl is here, she won't go anywhere else until she's reunited with her mother, okay?"

"I promise."

AND THAT'S HOW THE adventure began. Two days later Angileri organized a Zoom meeting for them with Anita Díaz and Selena Durán, whom he introduced as the social worker who knew the girl better than anyone. Samuel realized that this woman and the lawyer had both grown attached to the child and wouldn't leave a single stone unturned until they found her mother. Angileri hadn't mentioned that Anita was blind and they didn't notice at first, because the Zoom image was blurry, but it soon became evident. That did away with any of Leticia's lingering doubts.

For Samuel, meeting Anita unleashed a tidal wave of painful memories, as if his heart had been torn open. He'd long suffered a cardiac arrhythmia, an uncomfortable condition that it was useless to pay much attention to, but he'd developed the habit of taking his own pulse on his neck and listening to his heartbeat. The hole in his chest widened into a yawn in that half hour watching Anita onscreen, so small and fragile, exactly like he had been at that age.

"When will she arrive?" he asked Selena Durán.

"In two weeks. I'll bring her to your house myself. We're both going to quarantine first as a precaution."

"How are you going to get here?"

"By car," she said.

"You're driving all the way from Nogales? That's a long way."

"We'll stop to stay with some friends of mine. They'll quarantine too and we'll be very careful."

"What do we need to have ready for Anita when she gets here?" Leticia asked.

"Nothing in particular. She doesn't need much, just stability and affection."

"I'm a little worried about her blindness in this big house crowded with clunky old furniture," said Samuel.

"Don't worry, Mr. Adler. Anita can see blurry images, like looking through a fogged-up window or like there's Vaseline on her eyes. In good light and with a magnifying glass she can read large font. She has a good sense of space and direction, she memorizes things easily, and she can quickly orient herself in any space; she doesn't stumble around."

After the Zoom call, Leticia entered into a frenzy of activity. They had a couple of weeks, but she didn't want to waste a minute. She started by moving herself into an upstairs bedroom so she could be near Anita's room, which she redecorated using lemon-yellow wallpaper sprinkled with daisies and butterflies. She also ordered a Disney bedspread, which Samuel thought was horrendous.

"This girl needs some cheerfulness in her life. She might not be able to see the pattern but she'll be able to make out some of the colors," Leticia decreed.

Armed with a ladder, a paintbrush, and a bucket of glue, she hung the paper on the walls according to instructions she looked up on the internet, while the old man and the dog tried to stay out of her way. She stocked the pantry and fridge with enough food to survive a siege and bought toys and audiobooks but decided to wait for Anita's arrival before ordering new clothes since she didn't know the child's size.

"I don't think Anita reads braille yet," Samuel said.

"She must be very behind in school."

"As soon as we can, we'll enroll her in the School for the Blind in Fremont; it's about forty minutes from here."

"She might not know enough English for that," Leticia said.

"She's been in this country for several months, she must speak at least a little. I'll use the rest of the summer to give her a good head start. Remember I was a professor for many years, Leticia. If I was able to help so many talentless students learn music, I'll be able to teach that little girl English and a bit more as well, I expect."

ON THE DAY OF Anita's arrival, Selena called to let them know they were half an hour away. Leticia had gone all out preparing Salvadoran dishes so that Anita would feel at home: beans, fried plantains, corn tortillas, and a cake, as well as horchata, a drink made of grains, seeds, rice, milk, and spices. They were both so anxious about the girl's arrival that they each had a splash of whiskey in their coffee to calm their nerves.

"What are we going to do if we don't connect with Anita, Mr. Bogart?" Leticia asked.

"That would be terrible. Bonding is a mysterious thing, it doesn't obey any known laws, it happens spontaneously or it doesn't happen at all; it's impossible to force it."

But they didn't need to worry about that possibility, because as soon as the girl stepped out of Selena Durán's dusty car, with her knapsack on her back, she immediately won their hearts. She looked like a little fawn with her skinny legs and wide frightened eyes peeking out over the required mask, wearing a secondhand dress and tennis shoes. She walked slowly, holding Selena's hand, hugging a rag doll to her chest. Leticia bent down and wrapped her arms around the girl, tearful.

"I'm your cousin Leticia. This is Mr. Bogart and Paco, the dog. Panchito the parrot is waiting for you in the kitchen. We also have two stray cats who eat here and sometimes sleep over, but they're half wild and don't have names," she explained in a shaky voice.

"Welcome" was the only thing Samuel could think to say.

He was wise not to try to hug the child; it would be a while before Anita felt comfortable around him. Samuel later learned about her distrust of all men.

The first few minutes were awkward, but conversation began to flow when Leticia served the horchata and tres leches cake. She gave Anita one of the gifts she'd bought for her, a doll that could walk around like a zombie thanks to several batteries in her stomach. Anita entertained herself for a few minutes feeling out how the doll worked, never letting go of her own rag doll. Samuel asked her if she knew any songs and managed to get her to hum a nursery rhyme, which he accompanied on the piano with some pretentious baroque flourishes. Anita loved this and offered him some other simple melodies, which suffered the same treatment at Samuel's skilled hands. Then Leticia ran a bath for the girl, because she was tired after the long journey, while Samuel sat down with Selena to receive the necessary instructions.

"I can't thank you enough for bringing Anita to us," Samuel said.

"No, sir, I'm the one who should be thanking you and Leticia for taking her in. She's been badly mistreated by our immigration system."

"Separating families at the border is inhumane; it's a disgrace to this country . . ." Samuel spat.

Selena talked more about Anita, explaining that her blindness was more or less comparable to the condition of a patient with advanced macular degeneration. An unfortunate car accident a few years prior had damaged her corneas, but in her case the damage wasn't progressive.

"I think there's a treatment that could help her," she added.

"You must mean a corneal transplant. I'll look into it," said Samuel.

"Marisol, her mother, told the border officer in her interview that she was fleeing her country because she feared for her life but that she also hoped she might get better treatment for Anita's condition in the United States. But this turned out to be a strike against her, because the officer interpreted it as an intention to abuse the U.S. healthcare system."

"That's a cruel assumption. Actually, there's a school for the blind relatively close by. I could take care of the cost. She will not be abusing the system," Samuel said.

"In time, I think that Anita would be capable of attending a regular school. She knows how to read and write. She's a good student and has a great auditory memory, she only has to hear something once and she can repeat it weeks later."

"That's excellent news: It means I can teach her music, if she's here long enough."

"The judge has authorized Anita to stay in this country until her mother is located. Then their case will go to court," Selena explained. "Frank Angileri was able to prove that the girl has been the victim of a disgraceful administrative mishandling. She's not the only case, unfortunately, but Anita's condition seemed to soften up the judge. I guess the last thing they want is for it to come out in the news that they'd deported a blind girl who'd been forcibly separated from her mother."

"How long will she be with us, do you think?"

"I couldn't say. She's been granted temporary asylum. In early February, Frank and I flew to El Salvador in search of Marisol Díaz. We weren't able to find her."

LETICIA AND SAMUEL HAD been isolated for months before Anita's arrival and had settled into a fixed routine, like an old married couple; they lived independently for the most part, respected each other's space, and enjoyed the little time they spent together. The forced co-habitation brought on by the pandemic offered them an extraordinary opportunity to get to know each other, and as they did, they better appreciated each other. Anita's arrival changed the rhythm of the house and their habits, but she also brought them closer together. With her, they started to become a family.

Anita's first night at Samuel's house was difficult. She was so frightened that she curled up on the floor, clutching her filthy doll, Didi. The yellow wallpaper and new bedding delighted her when she first arrived, even though she could only just make out the colors, but at night she was too scared to sleep alone because she'd never had a room of her own. This seemed logical to Samuel; that wallpaper would give him nightmares as well. It took almost an hour to get her into bed and she didn't fall asleep until well past midnight. The next morning Leticia found her once again crouched in the corner, silently sobbing, and discovered that she had wet the bed.

"It's no big deal, Anita, it's happened to everyone," she said, trying to console the girl.

"Before, when I lived with Tita Edu, I never wet the bed. I don't know why it happens here," the girl answered, wiping away tears.

"Shhh, honey, it's no big deal; all we have to do is change the sheets."

Leticia told Samuel what had happened, but the man was not surprised.

"She's too old to be doing that," Leticia commented.

"What can we do?"

"Back home she slept with her mother or grandmother. She might feel safer if she sleeps with me. Can I use Camille's bed, since it's bigger?"

"You can use whatever bed you like. But we'll have to move it to your room."

It was a difficult task. Samuel didn't have the strength he'd once had, but he was far from being an invalid, and despite his sprained ankle, they managed to swap out Leticia's single bed for Camille's. From the first night Anita began sleeping with Leticia, she stopped wetting the bed. Samuel thought the solution a bit extreme, but he accepted it without comment, because he remembered the fear he'd felt as a boy at night when he had first arrived in England. He would bury his head under the pillow so that no one could hear his sobs.

Sometimes Samuel still woke up in a state of terror with the same recurring dream: It was dark, the middle of the night, he heard the sound of branches scraping the window and the screech of an owl. He was lying on a hard, narrow bed, it was very cold, he was freezing, but he felt something warm under his body and understood with horror that he had wet himself. How many times in childhood had he experienced that moment of shame, humiliation, the muffled sobs, recriminations, punishments, and the taunting from the other boys? The memory of that period in his life was still vivid, which was why he felt infinite compassion for Anita. He knew exactly how she felt, why she called out for her mother in the night, why she sat for hours at the front door listening to the sounds outside and hoping Marisol might magically appear.

The last time Samuel saw his mother, she was waving goodbye on a crowded train platform. He was very small, wearing an oversize coat and a wool scarf, his shoes two sizes too large. He was leaving on a train with hundreds of other children. For many years that image had been confusing, fragmented, incomprehensible, but at some point in his youth he'd been able to put the pieces together and understand what had happened. The other children on the train were all Jewish, and, like the rest of the families on the platform, his mother had decided to send her child to England alone, to be taken in by strangers with no guarantees for his future, in order to save him from the Nazis' brutality. His mother had surely believed that it would be a temporary solution, that they would soon be together again.

. . .

MANY YEARS BEFORE, IN 1995, Samuel Adler had visited the Holocaust Museum in Washington, D.C. He had already been back to Vienna to see the neighborhood where he was born. In place of the building that had housed his father's clinic and his childhood home, he found a bank. He had also gone to see what was left of Dachau, Ravensbrück, and Auschwitz, a journey to the center of human depravation. There was very little left, but he saw the ruins of a few barracks, the barbed-wire fences, the watchtowers, and the chimneys of the crematoriums, enough to gather a full picture of the crimes that took place there. He walked through those sinister installations immersed in overriding silence; no birds chirped, not even a single blade of grass grew. He felt that the air was charged with the presence of the men, women, and children who had been murdered there, millions of lost souls.

At the Holocaust Museum he studied the lists of genocide victims and found his mother, Rachel Sara Adler, along with the names of his aunt Leah and his maternal family, but his father's name was absent. The Nazis had kept an up-to-date register of their actions—even the greatest atrocities were duly documented—but some records had been systematically destroyed after defeat.

For Samuel, that painful pilgrimage was inevitable. His roots had been amputated the moment he'd set foot on the Kindertransport train. He had lost his parents and grandparents without any proper goodbye or logical explanation. He had grown up waiting. Nostalgia and anguish were the most overarching emotions of those years. He lived a fragmented childhood, divided between the harsh present that he wished to escape and the nebulous fantasy of a family and home, which nourished his ever-fading memories of a mythic past.

He spent three consecutive days going to the museum from the moment it opened until closing time. He steeped himself in the testimonies, memorized the photographs, walked with the ghosts, cried inconsolably, and cursed with a rage that had built up over decades. He knew that his situation was not exceptional, that he was just one among millions of victims. He understood that his mother's only option had been to send him away, to give him a chance to live. He imagined that her suffering had been much greater than his own and that Rachel Adler had died with the name of her only son on her lips. On the trip, he accepted the fact that he would never be able to fully exorcise his demons; he would have to learn to live with them.

IN THE MONTHS THAT followed, Samuel and Leticia became grandfather and aunt to Anita Díaz, embracing their new roles so fully that they could hardly remember what their lives had been like before her arrival. They rearranged the house so that Anita could get around with greater ease, moving furniture, putting away rugs she might trip over, and placing so many lamps around that—according to Samuel—the house could surely be seen from outer space and might represent a hazard to local aeronautics. Leticia took care of everyday responsibilities—feeding and bathing Anita, brushing her hair—and Samuel kept her entertained and was in charge of her homeschooling as well. Anita did not have much of an appetite, so it was a constant struggle to get her to eat, but Samuel insisted that she sit at the table with the adults. Anita had good manners and always asked to be excused before getting up. "Thank you, Tía Lety, thank you, Mr. Bogart," she would say in English so that Samuel could understand. At first she avoided the old man, but she soon felt more at ease around him and began to seek him out. He wanted the child to be ready to attend the School for the Blind as soon as summer break ended and it opened up enrollment for new students. He ordered age-appropriate textbooks, all in English, and taught her for three hours daily. She was a quick learner. Since she couldn't write by hand, he lent her an old typewriter, which she could use with some difficulty, and he ordered a computer with a special keyboard for the visually impaired.

What Anita was most interested in was the piano. "It's easier than writing on the typewriter. I know when I mess up because it sounds bad," she would say. She was disciplined and understood that she had to practice her scales every day in order to train her fingers.

"The piano can be learned using visual memory, which is a problem for you, but also auditory memory, which comes easily. Most important, music requires emotional memory and muscle memory. Your fingers should remember how to play on their own, guided by your feelings," Samuel would say to her.

"I can play by ear," she said.

"Yes, but to be a serious musician you have to learn to read music and do your exercises every day."

Samuel started by writing music notes out very large in black marker, which Anita could read with her magnifying glass. Then he ordered some sheet music in braille and began to study the system in order to teach his new student. Anita would have to read and memorize the music by touch.

The strange situation of living confined with Leticia, Anita, and the animals reinvigorated Samuel's will to live. Ever since his wife had passed away, he'd felt that the losses, absences, disappearances, deaths, distance, separations, and neglect had only piled up. Also indifference: He'd long felt that any attachments he once held had withered and dried. He confessed to Leticia that he didn't miss his daughter or even the grandson he'd celebrated and spoiled as a child. Nadine had always said that a person can't choose their family and so must love and accept the one they're given, but Samuel did not agree; for him, affection wasn't something to be given away freely, it had to be earned. The only thing his grandson deserved was for life to throw him a few hard knocks, to dampen his arrogance and teach him some compassion.

But even for such a solitary man as Samuel, fondness for Anita came naturally. If they had been living in normal times, Anita would be in school and he would see her much less, but since she was always present, she quickly gained ground in his heart. Even when she wasn't near him, he could hear her moving through the house, see her playing with Paco in the garden or splashing in the hose on hot days. She spent hours exploring the overgrown vegetation, absorbed in mysterious games. In the short time she'd been under his roof she'd managed to fill every corner. The first few days she walked around hugging the walls, silent, staying as close to Leticia and as far away from Samuel as possible, but she soon forgot her shyness. She was very alert, memorizing distances between furniture, the locations of windows and doors, until she was finally able to move around with confidence, going up and down the stairs without holding on to the rail and chasing Paco down the halls. The dog immediately traded the old man for Anita as his favorite, following the girl everywhere she went, even climbing into bed beside her, where he stayed until Leticia kicked him out. Samuel could accept losing his best friend since the animal had clearly found his calling as a service dog.

"Paco's going to be so sad when Anita goes," Leticia commented.

"Is she going to go, Leticia? If it were up to me, she could stay and grow up here; she could become my granddaughter."

"That's only possible if they don't find her mother."

"Well, clearly I can't wish for that," he concluded.

AFTER SLIPPING ON THE ladder, Samuel had realized he would never again attempt to visit the attic. He had no idea what was up there in that cavern crammed with the detritus of family life that had accumulated and multiplied over the years. Poking around, Leticia had uncovered some secrets and dropped the name Bruno Brunelli several times, testing the waters to find out how much Samuel knew, but he wasn't going to satisfy her curiosity. It was a private matter, of little importance, and there was no need to bring up the past. He knew about Brunelli; his wife's affair with the pastry chef had lasted a couple of years and, logically, he had found out. It was such a trivial matter that Nadine hadn't even bothered to hide it.

Samuel was also aware that this wasn't Nadine's only infidelity. He knew that the longest and deepest relationship she'd had outside the marriage—the only affair that grew into true love—was with Cruz Torres, the last person he would've ever suspected. Nadine confessed it to him, drenched in tears, when Torres was deported. She didn't specify how long their affair had lasted, but Samuel calculated that it must've begun around the time they remodeled the house and ended eight years later, spanning a large swath of Nadine's mature years. He was retroactively jealous for a time, until he accepted that Torres, in Mexico, did not represent a threat to his marriage and that nothing could shake the mutual affection and companionship he shared with Nadine. He imagined that Torres had been a passionate lover, and that he gave Nadine something she needed at the time, something he hadn't been willing or able to give her. After sharing a life together for many decades, love can become fraternal and sex begins to feel incestuous, he thought. He couldn't expect absolute monogamy over fifty-five years of marriage.

In the meantime, Samuel had no doubt that they would soon have a vaccine. In his long life he'd learned that everything passes eventually, but he found it hard to imagine the future while stuck in the immutable present of the pandemic. What would the new normal look like? The windows and doors would be suddenly thrown open and humanity would totter back out into the world, hesitant at first. He imagined euphoric crowds taking to the streets and impromptu carnivals as people embraced with joy. But he would not be one of them. He had taken advantage of the long lockdown to distance himself from people he didn't like and free himself of the obligations that no longer interested him. He tolerated very few people, but he hid it so well that he'd earned a reputation as a friendly guy. No one could accuse him of being arrogant or selfish, only eccentric, which Nadine had always told him was endearing because of his British accent.

Before Anita's arrival, Samuel had clung to his work and studies to keep his mind active, fearful at the very real possibility of being lost to the fog of senility. With Anita's arrival in his home, however, he now felt confident he had enough challenges in his daily life to fend off the specter of dementia.

IN THEORY, LETICIA WAS so busy with Anita and the housework that she didn't have the time or energy to pursue her guilty pleasure of nosing around in the attic, but in practice it was another story. She immediately recruited the girl to help and the two of them spent entire afternoons searching for possible treasures from the past. Anita learned to use the ladder with confidence and to move between the beams and obstacles in the attic as if she could see perfectly. Samuel had given them permission to bring down Camille's and his grandson's old toys, which had been collecting dust for decades, as well as the artificial Christmas trees, complete with lights, which they propped in several corners of the house, seeing no need to wait for December. Anita commandeered a porcelain tea set and insisted that Samuel sip the horrible concoctions she brewed with leaves from the garden, so disgusting he had to add several spoonfuls of honey in order to get them down. The girl spent her days pushing Didi and Paco around in the English pram that had belonged to Camille, while her new doll—the zombie—lay abandoned. She liked to hold on to Paco's collar, out of fondness for him more than necessity, and she refused to let anyone help her. "I can do it myself" was her mantra. The child amazed Samuel. From a young age, he had been plunged into a harsh reality and never thought to create a better, imaginary world. But Anita, who had suffered similar heartbreak, seemed to live her life in some fantastical dimension. The attic, the garden, the empty rooms, were magical realms she could escape to.

Listening to the little girl's whispered make-believing, Samuel learned all about Azabahar, a distant star that Anita visited often, taking Paco along for the ride. Azabahar was a perfect world where Anita could be reunited with her absent loved ones. For the first few weeks with them, Anita spoke in an incomprehensible mix of Spanish and English, but soon, thanks to her lessons with Samuel, and the TV, English became more prevalent and Samuel was able to better understand her.

"Have you noticed that Anita talks to herself? She must have an imaginary friend. It's common among solitary children," he commented to Leticia.

"She's talking to her little sister," she responded.

"What little sister?" Samuel asked, confused.

"Claudia. She died in the same accident that left Anita blind. Claudia was three and Anita had just turned six. They were very close. That rag doll belonged to her little sister, which is why Anita loves it so much."

"How do you know all this?"

"Because I asked her, Mr. Bogart."

"She understands that Claudia is dead, right?"

"Yes. She's not hallucinating. She knows that Claudia isn't here. Poor thing . . . First her father died, then her sister, she lost her sight, her mother was almost killed, she had to flee her home and leave her grandmother, then when she got here she was separated from her mom and left all alone. It's not surprising she'd want to bring her sister back from the dead to keep her company."

"I don't know how she'll ever recover from all that . . ." Samuel murmured.

"She's strong. I expect she'll heal in time," Leticia replied.

.   .   .

FOR SEVERAL WEEKS, SAMUEL had been thinking about some changes he wanted to make to his will and had finally scheduled a Zoom meeting with his lawyer to leave his instructions, which he relayed to Leticia. When he died, the house would remain in a trust to support Anita, and she, as the girl's cousin, would administer it.

"Don't talk like that—it's like calling down death! And what will your daughter have to say about it? She's going to blame me: She'll say the maid tricked her poor senile father into changing his will."

"She's going to inherit the rest of my estate. She won't know about the trust until it's too late. I've already had two separate doctors sign off on the fact that I remain in full use of my faculties. You'll figure out how to deal with Camille. Nadine always felt this house should be a safe harbor for anyone in need, and I want to use it to finance Anita's education."

"Who knows if the child is even going to stay here?"

"Wherever she is, she's going to need an education, and if you sell this house, there will be enough to cover it. Or you could rent it out and receive a nice monthly income."

"Rent it? It's falling to pieces!"

"Don't exaggerate. Although I do suppose there are some things that could be fixed, once the pandemic is over," he responded.

"This place has so many empty rooms . . . You said that it used to be a brothel?"

"Don't tell me you're thinking of opening a house of ill repute, Leticia, for the love of God!"

"No, that would be too much work. But the rooms could be rented to students from the university. Like a dorm. What do you think?"

"If that's what you wish to do, go ahead. I'll be dead and buried. No cremation for me, I want to rest right beside Nadine for all of eternity."

"You're putting a lot of trust in me."

"I have full confidence in your abilities, as well as your honor, and the affection you have for Anita. Have you had any news from Frank Angileri?"

"He's optimistic. He's convinced that with the change in administration after the presidential election in November, they're sure to put more effort into reuniting the families."

"Those are high hopes, Leticia. The election is still far off and no one can guarantee the outcome," Samuel reminded her.

"Don't be such a pessimist!"

"I find it hard to stay positive in this rubbish world. But I'm starting to feel a desire to try to change it, something I've never really felt before."

ANITA

We're going to build a secret hideout in the garden, in the bushes where no one can find it, and we're going to make an extra special tea for a tea party with the angels and other magical creatures. I know just the leaves they like best. We can invite Paco too, but I'm not sure he'll want tea; he'd probably want a dog biscuit or a bone to chew. I might be able to get some treats for him but it could be hard to get a bone. We're also going to set a booby trap in the garden to catch any bullies or bad guys. I've planned it all out. First we have to dig a big hole and get a net like the kind the fishermen used at Tunco beach. The hole has to be hidden with branches and a little bit of trash, so the bad guy doesn't see it and he falls inside, then we throw the net on him and we catch him alive. We'll have to decide what to do with him. It depends. If it's Carlos or Mr. Rick, we're going to leave them to starve. If it's Gusano de Caca, for example, we might just throw some sticks at him and leave him there for one night, then we'll let him go.

Where did you get the idea that there were snakes in the garden, Claudia? There are no snakes here, that was in El Salvador. What they do have in this garden is a treasure buried by pirates. When we find it, we'll send the gold coins to Tita Edu, so she doesn't have to work anymore. The pirates were from a long time ago. There are no pirates anymore, they were all deported.

MR. BOGART MADE ME talk on Zoom to an eye doctor and I had to explain like three times all the details of the accident and what I can see and what I can't see, but he's still going to have to examine me in person anyway. I can't get an appointment right away, since he is only treating very urgent cases, because of the virus, and mine isn't so urgent. That's what he thinks. It seems pretty urgent to me, though, because I'm tired of being blind. Mr. Bogart told me that they're going to give me a transplant and Tía Lety explained that that means they'll take the eyes out of a dead person and put them in my head, and if I'm lucky, I might even get blue ones. The whole thing sounds scary. I don't want them to take out my eyes and I also don't want them to put anything from a dead person in me. Mr. Bogart says not to listen to Tía Lety, that what I'm getting transplanted is a tiny thing and no one's going to take out my eyes. Anyway, just in case, Tita Edu is praying to Saint Lucía, the patron saint of the blind.

I like this house, isn't it cool? Tía Lety explained that they call it the enchanted mansion because there are spirits here, but I'm not scared of them and I hope you aren't either, Claudia. They're nice ladies in very fancy dresses and they wander around without anyone noticing. Mr. Bogart says that ghosts don't exist, but he just says that because he has to. Tía Lety told me that one of the spirits is Mr. Bogart's wife, a very pretty, happy lady named Nadine. I can't see her yet, I have to wait until they fix my eyes, but if I pay close attention, I can smell her perfume. I recognize it from the bottle from her dresser that Tía Lety gave me. There's still a little left but I can't spray it because it made Mr. Bogart very sad when he smelled it. He locked himself in his studio and he wouldn't let me in, even though I knocked like a thousand times.

Tita Edu seemed a little strange when we talked to her, don't you think, Claudia? She kept saying over and over that I'm better off here in the North, that I should try to adapt and stay here, because that's what Mama would want and that's why she brought me here. She said I'm going to go to school and I have to get good grades and learn English and have my First Communion, but I don't want to do any of that without her and Mama. She also said that she's going to keep calling me on the phone and she's always going to love me with all her soul, but that I should forget about her because memories make us sad. But how could I forget my Tita Edu? That made me cry and then she started crying too and we both cried for a long time. When we didn't have any tears left, we agreed that I would never forget her and that she would come to see us here in California as soon as she finds someone to take care of Abuelo.

I asked Mr. Bogart if Mama can live here with us when she comes. She can help Tía Lety clean, because this house is so big, it has like five bathrooms and I don't know how many bedrooms. He said yes, and he gave me a hug, but he seemed a little sad. That happens with old people sometimes, Claudia: They get sad all of a sudden and no one knows why. When Mama comes, we're all going to live together and never be separated ever again. Can you imagine it, Claudia? It's going to be super, super magical!

SELENA AND SAMUEL

BERKELEY & SAN SALVADOR, SEPTEMBER 2020

Each week, Samuel called Selena Durán on Zoom to update her about Anita, but the hour often went by so quickly that they had to schedule another call the following day. There was so much to say about the girl, how she was adapting in this small family she'd been dropped into, her studies, the cornea specialist at Stanford who would be able to see Anita once the pandemic abated, how she'd gained some weight, even though she still had very little appetite. Samuel was like a doting grandfather, recounting insignificant episodes of things Anita did with Leticia, Paco, or Panchito. Sometimes he asked her to play the piano for Selena. He said that his student had such a good ear and was so hardworking that she could easily be a concert pianist one day; there were a few famous blind piano players, including a Japanese boy whom Anita never tired of hearing on You-Tube. The girl had always been musically gifted and soon she could identify the sound of every instrument in an orchestra and was even learning to appreciate jazz.

Frank Angileri sometimes joined the Zoom calls to bring them up to speed on Anita's case. He needed to move quickly and didn't have any help. Minors usually went in front of judges who were unwilling to view them as children. They were treated as delinquents: They had broken the law. But Frank always seemed optimistic and undaunted by the legal challenge. His plan was to get permission for Anita to stay permanently in the United States. If they didn't find her mother soon, he'd apply for residency, the so-called green card, since Anita could be classified as an abandoned child. The process would take two or three years. In the event that her mother was found to have died, Leticia could petition to adopt her. Angileri recommended patience, above all, because bureaucracy was slow and complicated.

The old man anxiously awaited the weekly call with Selena, as nervous as he would have been for a first date. That face-to-face check-in would've been impossible in normal times, because she lived in Arizona, but the pandemic had taught them to converse over a screen as if they were in the same room, even having tea together, she in her office and he in his studio. Samuel supposed that the young woman wasn't too bored by him, given that they often diverged from the topic of Anita and she opened up about her life, her strange family of women, whom he wanted to meet, her problems with work and with love. Selena, so clear in her professional objectives, seemed tormented by uncertainty when it came to matters of the heart.

"You're the father I'd like to have had," she once said to him.

"To tell the truth, I've not been a great father to my daughter, or a good grandfather to my grandson. It weighs on my conscience."

SELENA TOLD SAMUEL ABOUT Milosz Dudek, about how he rose to the rank of sergeant in his tours of Iraq and Afghanistan but left the military disillusioned and convinced only of the futility of the American occupation of those countries. He was grateful for his military experience, which had served to fortify his character and to get him away from his father's explosions, which had terrified him as a child and suffocated him in adolescence. He had no desire to live near his family in Chicago and only visited on special occasions; he didn't miss anything about the Polish community he'd been raised in. He had the appearance of a gladiator, a dogged work ethic, and a somewhat old-fashioned sense of integrity that manifested as a love of God, country, and family, but Selena was most attracted to his romantic soul. They first met when he retired from the military and entered civilian life as a truck driver, while she was still but a girl who'd barely ventured beyond her home and school, spoiled by the Durán women.

When he met her, Milosz believed, and continued to believe for a long while, that he could mold Selena, help her mature and guide her through life; he'd have married her immediately, but she was firm in wanting to finish college first. Milosz hadn't studied beyond high school and the few professional women he'd met made him uncomfortable because he felt that they looked down on him. He didn't understand why Selena wanted to waste so much time getting a degree in social work that would be of little use in her role as wife and mother. But Selena finished college without ever asking for his opinion and she brushed him off when he tried to give unsolicited advice. "You're a caveman, Milosz. That's why I love you; you're a project," she'd say cheerfully. The project consisted of modernizing that traditional man, and over time she achieved it to some measure. Milosz's project, however, lost steam along the way; the innocent girl he'd fallen in love with was in fact quite resistant to domesticity.

"I don't even understand why he loves me," Selena confessed to Samuel. "He's meticulous, tidy, punctual, so afraid of germs that he washes his lettuce with soap, and hates waste, chaos, or excess in any form. His life is regimented by schedules, distances, and routines. I, on the other hand, live day to day. I leave my things strewn all over the house and doors open, never have any idea how much money is in my wallet, lose my keys constantly . . . I'm a complete disaster."

She didn't tell Samuel, however, about her affair with Frank. She felt confused and embarrassed at betraying Milosz. Frank knew that she was engaged to Milosz; he'd seen the ring on her finger. But he had told her clearly that as long as she wasn't married, she was a free woman and he would keep trying to win her over. If she put off marrying the man for so many years, he concluded, it must have been because she wasn't truly in love.

Like all the lawyers and staff of Frank's firm, he'd been working from home since March. Hearings were suspended because the courts were on recess until further notice. That meant he wasn't able to move forward with Anita Díaz's asylum petition as the months of lockdown dragged on for much longer than anyone expected. When they spoke, he talked of how he missed restaurants, bars, travel, the gym, and tennis matches. Most of all, he missed spending time with Selena. He set up dates with her on Zoom and sent her gifts, from books and flowers to a meal service that delivered a keto-friendly dish to her apartment in Nogales every day.

Air travel was restricted and considered dangerous, but by June, Frank told Selena he couldn't stand to go another day without seeing her. He rented a car and camping equipment and drove to pick her up for a weekend trip to Patagonia Lake State Park. Even though it was summer, there wasn't a single tourist in sight and everything was closed; it was Frank's ideal romantic getaway. He was determined to use his short time to convince Selena that she couldn't live without him. His experience with camping was almost nonexistent, but he improvised, and in the span of just a few days he was almost able to sway her. He calculated that if he'd had three more days with Selena, he might've persuaded her to drop everything and move to San Francisco to spend the pandemic with him. He had big plans for their future: He would put her through law school so she wouldn't have to rack up student loan debt, and when she graduated, he would leave his firm. He didn't want to give the next twenty years of his life to Lambert and his associates; he'd open his own practice instead. He could picture the gold lettering on the door: *Angileri and Durán, Attorneys at Law.*

Meanwhile, Milosz kept trucking along, blissfully unaware of Frank Angileri and the increasingly important role he played in his fiancée's life. As the death toll increased and the hospitals became overwhelmed, the government tried to downplay the seriousness of the situation. Masks became a political symbol. On the road, he took certain precautions, but did not follow all the recommendations spouted by the so-called experts. Since he had to work and he couldn't guarantee that he was free of the virus, he had to stop visiting the Durán home and Selena as well, but he called frequently to tell his fiancée that he adored her and was counting the minutes until he could see her again, always taking the opportunity to ask where she was and what she was doing. These kinds of questions, which coming from Frank flattered Selena as proof of his love for her, annoyed her as evidence of distrust coming from Milosz. But he had good reason to be distrusting, she thought, ashamed of cheating on him.

"I love Milosz a lot, he's as loyal as a dog," she confessed to Samuel. "He's spent so many years waiting for me. Milosz doesn't have any doubts. For him, life is simple: All you have to do is stick to the basic rules of decency."

"What does he think of the work you're doing with these kids?" Samuel asked.

"He thinks that the government can't just open its doors to millions of immigrants, that we have to preserve the country and its values. But he understands that separating children from their families is horrible. He says he can't even imagine what he'd do if someone tried to take a child from him. He says it's totally anti-American."

"He's wrong, it's much more American than people think, Selena. Enslaved parents saw their children ripped away from them and sold off. Native Americans had their children taken away to become 'civilized' in horrific state-run orphanages. Thousands of those kids died of contagious illnesses and malnutrition, then were buried in unmarked graves."

"You're right, Samuel. Here only white children are considered sacred."

SAMUEL KNEW THAT SOMETHING had happened between Selena and Frank Angileri on the trip they took in February, months before Anita moved in with them. Selena had let it slip little by little, but it was enough to add two plus two to guess at what she'd left out. Even though he'd never seen them together in person, only a few times on Zoom, it seemed natural that Frank would be in love with her. Selena exuded a powerful attraction, like a gravitational force.

"It must be amazing to have had just one great love, like you did, Samuel," she said on one occasion.

"How many loves have you had, Selena?" he asked.

"Milosz is the only boyfriend I've ever had. We were supposed to get married in April, but then Covid came along and the wedding had to be postponed. He's given me an ultimatum: We get married as soon as they come up with a vaccine, or we never see each other again. He won't let me keep him waiting any longer; he wants to have kids and start a family."

"And what do you want?"

"I don't know if I even want to get married. I'm not ready to have kids, I want to go to law school and focus on work. Marriage is a commitment for life, that's a long time, don't you think?"

"It is, but when it's true love, you don't worry about that."

228 • ISABEL ALLENDE

"Then maybe I'm not in love."

"Maybe not enough. How would you feel without Milosz in your life?" Samuel asked.

"I'd be sad—he's the nicest man in the world."

"But you wouldn't feel lonely without him, would you?"

"No."

"I understand. There's another man, that's why you're so confused."

"Yes . . ."

"What does this other man have to offer, Selena?"

"We have a lot in common, even though he represents a world that's completely different from the one I've always known, a new environment, exciting ideas, projects, plans, travel, freedom. And no pressure to settle down, for now."

"Can he offer you the kind of love that your fiancé does?"

"I don't think I'd ever be the center of his world, like I am for Milosz. But he wants me to move in with him and if that goes well, in time our love could grow and solidify, I imagine."

"Not always, Selena."

"What would you advise me to do, Samuel?"

"Wait. You don't have to decide between one or the other."

"Milosz won't accept another postponement. He's put up with so much flakiness on my part already. I don't have the right to keep toying with his emotions."

"That's not a good reason to get married. You need to do what's right for you. Don't give in to the pressure from either of them—you might regret it later."

SAMUEL, FOR HIS PART, told Selena about his past, Nadine LeBlanc, his music, and the inevitable process of aging. The social worker always seemed interested in what he had to say. His memory had held on to the best and worst moments—the rest had been lost along the way—but Selena wanted to know the details. She had found out that, by one of those strange coincidences, Nadine had been one of the founders of the Magnolia Project, the nonprofit Selena worked for. In fact, it owed its name to her: Magnolia was the flower of New Orleans, Nadine's birthplace. Selena asked a lot of questions about Nadine, fascinated by her personality, her art, her activism, and her generosity. Samuel explained that as a wife and mother, Nadine was often neglectful, because she was too busy with her weaving, her friends, and her secretive activities that she seldom shared with him. When Selena informed him of his wife's involvement in the Magnolia Project, he wasn't at all surprised. He said that he and their daughter didn't love her any less for her lack of attention; to the contrary, they admired her greatly for everything she'd accomplished. Camille had fought a lot with Nadine, but she was also grateful to have freedom. There were advantages to having a mother who was always distracted and not constantly hovering.

"She didn't pay much attention to me either," said Samuel. "At first, I resented her for it. I thought that she didn't love me enough. But over the years I got used to it and stopped asking her for something she was incapable of giving. She was absorbed in her own life, she didn't need me or anyone else," he said.

Some of Selena's questions forced Samuel to relive painful memories. Days before falling unconscious on her deathbed, Nadine had said, "I'm going to be the first to go, Mr. Bogart. I hope you won't waste the time you have left." Looking back on the past, he realized, with regret, that he had in fact wasted his time, and that when he abandoned this world he would leave behind barely a faint trail of dust, one that would vanish in the first light of dawn. Before Anita came knocking at his door, he'd never done anything for anyone, a mere witness to the world for eighty-something years of his life, safeguarded from uncertainty by calculated caution. The pain of being orphaned as a young boy had caused him to withdraw and take refuge in his music. Nadine always said that indifference was a capital sin that had to be atoned for sooner or later. She was right. In his old age, the sin of indifference had become a fierce demon that stalked his nightmares and haunted him in moments of loneliness. He dreamed of being able to start again, imagining another life, one more like Nadine's, experiencing deep pleasure and deep pain, taking risks, facing challenges and defeats, a bold life.

"Nadine and I were together for decades, but each of us inhabited our own space. Still, I miss her dearly," he told Selena.

"She was a very special woman. How could you not miss her . . ."

"She shouldn't have been the first to go. In the months after her death, she appeared to me. I'm not a particularly imaginative man and I don't believe in ghosts, but I swear I saw her walking in and out of the rooms, going up the stairs, sitting at the table. I don't see her that clearly anymore, but sometimes I imagine I can feel her beside me. Did you know that Anita experiences the same thing with her sister?"

"Yes, I know. She had to have a psychological evaluation in Tucson, because she talked to herself all the time, didn't want to eat, wouldn't play with the other kids, and she wet the bed."

"That hardly happens anymore," said Samuel.

"I'm glad. She's suffered a lot."

Selena told Samuel that she'd spoken with Anita's grandmother Eduvigis, who explained that Anita started talking to her sister after the accident. In El Salvador she had been seeing a school counselor for a few months and was just starting to turn a corner with her grief when she was forced to flee the country. According to her psych evaluation in Tucson, the girl had suffered a regression in her emotional development. She needed counseling, just like all the other kids who had been separated from their families, but there was no government budget for that.

"I'll make sure she gets psychological support as soon as possible," Samuel promised. "I think Claudia's presence must be a comfort to Anita, just as Nadine's is to me. Let's call it a combination of love and a stubborn will to remember. Anita isn't crazy and I don't have Alzheimer's, I assure you."

"Of course not!" Selena exclaimed. "I'm not at all surprised to hear that the spirits of your loved ones visit you. I grew up with a psychic grandmother. I imagine life as a widower can be very lonely. Do you feel that way sometimes?"

"I used to, all the time. Not anymore. Thanks to you I'm happier now than I have been in many years. You have given me a purpose for this last stage of my life. I now have a fundamental responsibility and I can begin to repent for my sin of indifference."

"Are you talking about Anita?"

"Yes. What an amazing gift you've brought me, Selena!"

THE THIRD TUESDAY IN September, Selena called out of the blue. Samuel imagined it must have been something important, since it was not one of their regularly scheduled meetings. The agitated tone in her voice confirmed his suspicions.

"Are you alone, Samuel?" she asked.

"Yes, in my studio."

"Close the door, please. This is confidential."

"Just a moment . . . Anita can hear through walls and what she doesn't hear, she can infer. There's no secret she can't crack."

"She won't be able to hear what I'm saying over the phone, just be careful how you respond. Do you remember I mentioned Lola, our taxi driver in El Salvador?"

"Yes. What about her?"

"She just called me. There's a huge scandal. It's a series of crimes. They've discovered several bodies in the backyard of a home in

Chalchuapa. Some of the deaths date back several years, but the majority are more recent."

According to Lola, neighbors heard a woman screaming and called the police. They arrived an hour later, and by then it was too late. They found a young woman beaten to death with an iron pipe. They arrested the owner of the home, but at the insistence of the neighbors, who suspected terrible things had been happening there for some time, they dug up the yard and discovered human remains in several mass graves.

"It seems that all the victims are women and girls. But they expect to find even more bodies as they dig deeper," Selena said.

"Another despicable case of violence against women . . ." Samuel murmured.

"The property in question belongs to Carlos Gómez, an ex-cop who was fired several years ago for molesting a minor. It's the same man who shot Marisol Díaz."

"What!" Samuel exclaimed.

"He's been arrested. He's the main suspect, but they've also detained other men. They think it was a ring of human traffickers who kidnapped women and girls, then disposed of their bodies after they were tortured and murdered. Lola fears that Marisol might be among the victims."

"That would explain why you and Angileri didn't find anything when you went to look for her."

"It's too much of a coincidence, don't you think?" Selena said. "That man was out to kill Marisol and it's not unlikely that he managed it in the end."

"But how?"

"I don't think she was deported back to her country. My guess is that she was sent to Mexico to wait her turn to present her asylum case. Those refugee camps are controlled by criminals. It's quite possible that Marisol was kidnapped and taken back to El Salvador."

"By who? And why?"

"There's a lot of human trafficking at the border, especially of women and children. Carlos Gómez is part of that network, he has connections. He told me himself that he knows a lot of people."

"But it costs money to kidnap someone in another country. Where did Gómez get the money?"

"He's a security guard. And I doubt he had to pay money to anyone. Things among criminals are often paid in favors. Gómez needed to keep Marisol quiet and also wanted revenge for her rejection. It would've been easy for him to have her kidnapped in Mexico, taken first to Guatemala by land and then from there smuggled onto El Salvadoran soil, which would explain why there's no record of her entering the country," she said.

"You can't prove any of that, Selena."

"Well, I remembered that when I met Carlos Gómez on my trip to El Salvador, he mentioned that Marisol had shaved off her pretty hair. But how could he know that? She only cut her and Anita's hair when they reached Mexico, before riding the train. Gómez couldn't have seen her with short hair unless Marisol had been back home. And if she'd returned of her own free will, she'd have gone to visit her mother-in-law or her brother, but neither of them has seen her. Oh, Samuel, I'm terrified that Marisol is in one of those graves. What will become of Anita?"

"I will take care of her for as long as I can," Samuel replied. "But let's not get ahead of ourselves. We have to wait until the bodies are identified."

"There's something else that I didn't mention before, because it's really crazy."

And then Selena proceeded to tell him about her grandmother's vision. Samuel had never heard of Dora Durán before meeting Selena, but he now had great respect for her and her abilities. He knew that Selena had taken Dora to meet Anita in Nogales and that

234 • ISABEL ALLENDE

the woman had felt the girl's psychic power. He'd never believed in paranormal phenomena until he had the strange experience of seeing his wife's spirit. But there was a logical explanation for that, as the psychiatrist explained: hallucinations brought on by old age and deep depression. The diagnosis seemed accurate, given that Nadine's visits from beyond the grave stopped with the combination of therapy and medication, but he was never fully convinced by the doctor's assessment. He believed that just because something can't be explained doesn't mean it doesn't exist. He abstained from entering into debate with the psychiatrist, but he would give Dora Durán the benefit of the doubt.

"Marisol Díaz appeared to my grandmother in a dream. In it, she was underground. And she wasn't alone."

"Excuse me, Selena, but it sounds like the classic prophecy after the fact," he said.

"That was in June, Samuel. Well before they began to dig up women in Carlos Gómez's yard."

FRANK PATIENTLY EXPLAINED TO them via Zoom later that day that a psychic's dream would not hold up as evidence in immigration court. He could just picture the judge's reaction if he tried to enter it into the record at Anita's asylum hearing. The crimes in Chalchuapa didn't change the girl's situation, unless they could actually prove that her mother was among the victims. Frank immediately contacted his friend Phil Doherty, who provided him with all the available information on the murders. The street where the crimes had occurred was blocked off—not even the press was allowed—but Doherty had contacts thanks to his diplomatic post, backed by the power of the U.S. embassy.

The atrocity shook the country, despite the fact that gender violence was so commonplace that it was no longer newsworthy. The press published regular updates of the body count. They had to isolate Carlos Gómez and his associates in prison to keep the other inmates from massacring them. The president promised that justice would be served, and announced the creation of a special unit dedicated to crimes against women and children. Anita's grandmother Eduvigis Cordero went to the police station several times to report the disappearance of her daughter-in-law and the harassment she'd received from the alleged serial killer. Since the sinister discovery, Eduvigis was just one more of the people who had posted herself outside the barriers from dawn to dusk waiting to see what was pulled from the House of Horrors, as the press had dubbed it. Like her, they were all searching for someone who had disappeared. The forensic team, covered like astronauts, excavated the yard with an archeological precision, because the bodies were piled up one on top of the other and in many cases the bones had been jumbled together. In the initial excavations they counted twenty bodies. More continued to be uncovered.

Selena convinced Frank that they couldn't sit and wait for the victims to be identified. The process was going very slowly and there was speculation that some powerful men involved in the human trafficking ring were trying to meddle in the case. Around that time the San Salvador airport reopened, after being closed to foreign travelers for months during the pandemic, and Frank immediately bought flights for himself and Selena.

SELENA KNEW IT WAS finally time to confront Milosz with the truth: She told him that she would be traveling, for a second time, with Frank Angileri, the man she'd been having a romantic affair with for several months. She shared the news first by email and then talked to him over the phone, thankful for the pandemic as an excuse to avoid telling him in person. She had been fearful of her longtime lover's reaction, but it turned out that he already suspected something and was more or less prepared to hear it. By that point his patience had worn thin and he'd come to the conclusion that if she loved him as much as he loved her, no obstacle would keep them from being together. He could forgive many things, he said, but he could never get over her lies and betrayal, the fact that she'd been cheating on him for months. The conversation was tense but brief. Before hanging up, Milosz announced that he never wanted to hear from Selena again; it was time to turn the page and forget about her, for good. He was deeply pained, but this time the breakup was final, he said. There would be no reconciling.

Selena felt lighter once that tumultuous relationship, which had left her feeling exhausted and guilty, finally came to an end. After saying goodbye to Milosz for the last time, she broke down and cried with relief. She'd endured his pressures for eight years and finally, once she was free of him, she understood that his obsessive love had been like a weight on her shoulders, keeping her from moving forward. She wouldn't let herself fall into a similar trap with Frank. She loved him, but she didn't know him that well yet and she wasn't going to let him rush her into anything or get her tangled up in his plans. She needed space to think about what she wanted, as Samuel had advised her. Now, for the first time, her future belonged to her alone. She was eager to begin enjoying a relationship with Frank, but would insist they keep it light, with no strings attached.

ALL PASSENGERS ENTERING EL Salvador were taken immediately into quarantine, except for Frank and Selena, thanks to Phil Doherty. He was waiting at the gate to whisk them off to the airport's VIP lounge, accompanied by an immigration officer, masked and wearing latex gloves, who stamped their passports and welcomed them to the country. Then Phil took them to his home, where they would be at less risk of contagion than at a hotel. His wife prepared the guest room for them.

That night, Selena and Frank tried to make love as discreetly as possible, muffling their whispers and giggles, but there was little they could do about the squeaking of the bedsprings. They hadn't had a night together since their camping trip to Lake Patagonia in June and so took advantage of the situation, again and again, until dawn. A sleeping bag on the ground would do, but a cushy mattress was better.

The next morning, Phil drove the pair to the Medical Legal Institute, where the remains from the mass grave were sent to be identified after being exhumed. Among the many people waiting outside, they spotted Genaro Andrade, who recognized them and waved. Selena walked over to him.

"Have you had any news about your sister?" she asked.

"Nothing, and I've been here for two days straight. Many of us have traveled hours to be here."

"Are they providing updates?"

"Yes, when they have them. They've already identified three victims. They released the names, and the families were able to collect the remains to be buried. Are you guys going to be able to get inside?"

"We hope so. If we have any news of Marisol I'll call you immediately."

The director of forensic anthropology met with them in his office and explained the procedure, adding that he'd called pathologists from other cities to assist, since his team alone couldn't handle the huge caseload. Carlos Gómez had confessed to his involvement in the murders and provided the names of nine accomplices, but authorities suspected that the depraved crime ring actually counted many more members. In his testimony, he said that as far as he could recall, there were between thirty and forty bodies in his yard, although he wasn't sure of the exact number—he'd lost count. He didn't show signs of being particularly repentant, seeming instead to relish the notoriety.

The director led them to the autopsy room, where all the tables held bodies and more corpses waited their turn in the refrigerators. The first thing they noticed was the smell of death and disinfectant that their masks did little to filter out. Cleanliness and order reigned. The forensic anthropologists worked efficiently and respectfully, in almost total silence, just as horrified at the atrocity as Selena and Frank.

"This is our job," the director explained. "We're used to death in all its manifestations, but sometimes it's too much to bear. The worst is when we have to identify children . . ."

They approached one of the tables, where four people stood flanking a tiny body. One of the doctors explained that it was a two-year-old girl. His voice cracked and he cleared his throat behind his double layer of masks, choking back his outrage.

"We think the little body has been buried about a year. We'll do a DNA test to see if we can identify her; there are three or four families looking for girls who have disappeared, but they're all older. You don't even want to know how she died," he said.

"We're not here out of morbid curiosity, Doctor. We're looking for a young woman," Selena responded.

"I'm so sorry. Is it a family member?"

"It's the mother of a girl who is seeking asylum in the United States," she said, then proceeded to summarize Anita's predicament.

"Almost all of the remains we've found up to now belong to young women. Is there anything else that might help us identify her?"

Selena showed them copies of the pictures Eduvigis Cordero had provided, as well as the photos from her immigration file in Nogales.

"Her name is Marisol Andrade de Díaz. As you can see, Doctor, she arrived in the United States with her hair cut very short. She also has a space between her two front teeth. If she's among the victims, the body would be one of the more recent ones, no more than nine months old, because I spoke to her on the phone in December of last year."

"She also received a bullet wound to the chest. It hit just inches from her heart and went through a couple of her ribs. Would there be any signs of something like that left?" Frank asked.

"Possibly. We can check the bodies that have come in so far."

The doctor led them to the refrigerators, three lines of metal drawers stacked on top of one another, and he opened them one by one. Some trays merely contained bones and rotten rags, but the majority held bodies that were still whole, in various states of decomposition. None of them looked like Marisol or had hair as short as she would have had.

"They're still exhuming more remains that should be coming in over the next few days. If we find anyone meeting Marisol's description, I'll let you know," the director promised.

Selena began to feel weak in the knees and left to get some fresh air, guided by Frank and Phil. She made it outside before vomiting.

PHIL DOHERTY PERSUADED FRANK and Selena to forgo the picturesque pink taxi in favor of the much more secure embassy car, complete with driver and bodyguard, that he provided for them. He did, however, suggest they invite Lola to his house for a drink that night and, over multiple Manhattans, they told her of their experience at the Medical Legal Institute.

The next day, Frank and Selena went to Chalchuapa to see Eduvigis Cordero. They found her aged and very thin, but more than depressed, she seemed furious and eager to take action. A group of protestors was organizing a massive march at the national level. Via social media, they called for a day of strikes for all women. Protestors would refrain from going to work or doing any domestic chores and instead take to the streets to demand an end to femicide. Eduvigis had already gotten her friends and coworkers at the indigo plant involved in the movement.

"It's an open war on women. We are raped, tortured, and killed, and nothing is done about it. Enough!" the grandmother exclaimed.

Then they accompanied Eduvigis to the House of Horrors, which she had been visiting daily in hopes of gleaning some information. The black car with diplomatic plates was waved past security and stopped before a sturdy house on a large lot on the outskirts of the city. Eduvigis explained how the government was trying to downplay the atrocity, claiming that all the murders had occurred many years ago, but that this was a lie and in fact the majority were recent victims.

"These women need justice, just like the thousands and thousands of other women and girls who are murdered without anyone ever paying for it."

"We hope that this isn't the case for Marisol," Selena said.

"No one is going to convince me that Carlos Gómez didn't kill my daughter-in-law. They may not find her in his yard, but I'm certain she's no longer in this world," Eduvigis replied categorically.

"Until we can locate her, Anita's fate remains uncertain," Frank interrupted.

"I pray that my granddaughter will see her mother again, but I also pray that she will be able to stay with her aunt in the North if Marisol has been killed. What do I have to offer her here? My love, that's all. I can't protect her from the violence all around us or provide her with a decent education. I can't afford her eye surgery. And I'm not as young as I used to be; this tragedy has aged me. What would become of my granddaughter if she had to come back here?"

"We'll do everything we can to help her, Eduvigis, I promise you," Selena said, embracing the woman.

"And I promise you, ma'am, that if Anita stays in the United

States, I'll fly down and bring you up there to visit her. She misses you a lot," Frank added.

At that moment a large white vehicle exited the property and one of the guards explained that it was a mobile morgue, where they kept the bodies frozen until more room was available at the Institute.

"Did you see the body?" Selena asked the guard.

"No. There are two victims in there. All I know is that they're women," he replied.

They said goodbye to Eduvigis with the promise that as soon as they had any news, she would be the first to know. They returned to the Medical Legal Institute to wait along with the other mourners of disappeared loved ones.

A FEW DAYS LATER, Selena and Frank landed at the San Francisco airport. From there, they went directly to Samuel Adler's house, half hidden by its overgrown garden already showing signs of the autumn that would soon be upon them. It was early afternoon and the sunlight filtered weakly through the clouds, making the charming, old-fashioned home seem even more dramatic with its towers and pilasters. The garden gate was open and they walked in, Paco's barks announcing their arrival. The doorbell hadn't functioned properly since 1978.

When she heard them, Anita peeked out from inside, holding on to Paco's collar. Selena ran up the five steps to the front door and threw her arms wide.

"Is my mama with you?" the girl asked.

"No, Anita," Selena murmured, trying to hide her tears.

As if she sensed there was something she didn't want to know, the girl did not ask any further questions. She simply led them into the house, waited while they briefly greeted the rest of the family, then gave them a tour of her new computer with a special keyboard for the visually impaired, the half-dozen lit-up Christmas trees, which Leticia had sprayed with pine-scented air freshener, and other things she hadn't been able to show them on Zoom. She was still very thin but had more color in her cheeks. She showed them how she could use her magnifying glass to read the sheet music that Samuel wrote out for her in large print. But she wasn't overly enthusiastic about learning braille, because she didn't want to go to the School for the Blind.

"They're going to fix my eyes and I'm going to go to regular school, like before," she announced.

Finally Leticia was able to distract Anita in the kitchen. Selena and Frank seized the moment to speak with Samuel in his studio with the door closed.

"We have something to tell you, Samuel," Selena said.

"I imagine it must be important since you came all the way here. Pleased to finally meet you in person, Frank."

"We couldn't give you this news any other way. I don't know how to say it . . ." Selena blubbered.

"No need to beat around the bush. I'm too old for that."

"It's . . . It's about Marisol . . . We just returned from El Salvador, where we went to find out more about the crimes in Chalchuapa. We thought we could get more information if we were there on the ground. They found Marisol."

"Oh my God!" Samuel exclaimed, raising his hands to his chest, as he suddenly felt a kick to the heart. "Are they sure it's her?"

"Yes. She wasn't in the mass graves, she was buried in a more recent pit on the other side of the property, which is why she was the last to be exhumed. There's no doubt that it's her. Her brother identified the remains."

"An X-ray showed the bullet wound to her chest," Frank added. "She had only been deceased for a matter of months, so the body was still recognizable even though the hot, wet climate accelerates decomposition."

"We were with Eduvigis and Genaro when they buried Marisol. Samuel . . . Samuel . . . Are you all right?" Selena asked, alarmed.

"Yes . . . yes. This heart of mine just acts up sometimes. Nothing serious . . ." he replied, placing a pill in his mouth.

"You look very pale. I'm going to call Leticia."

"No, please don't. I'll be fine in a few minutes. Tell me everything you know."

"We don't want to rehash the details. They're atrocious. I hope that Anita never learns how her mother died. But she needs to understand that she'll never see her again," Frank said, rubbing his forehead as he choked back tears.

"Who's going to tell her? I couldn't bear to do it," Samuel murmured, shaking. "But the girl can't live her life constantly hoping, waiting, like I had to do at her age. It will be a heavy blow to her, but it's unavoidable."

"Why don't we wait a little while?" Selena suggested. "Anita is still so fragile, she needs time. She needs to get used to things here in her new home so she can start to get over the trauma of everything that's happened to her. With a lot of love and psychological support—"

"You're mistaken, Selena. This kind of trauma isn't something you ever get over. You simply learn to live with it," the old man interrupted.

"I can't bear to give her the news right now, Samuel. She's just starting to live a normal life. You and Leticia have become her family, she has love and is well taken care of, she'll be starting school soon, she'll make friends . . . How can I break the news of her mother to her now?"

"If you all agree, we can wait to see how Anita's asylum case turns out," Frank said. "Proof that Anita is an orphan changes everything."

"In the meantime, Leticia and I can prepare her for the blow, gradually. In truth I have no idea how to go about something like that, but we can try," said Samuel, who was beginning to regain his color. "You two take care of the legal side of things. The rest falls to Leticia and me. Anita will be safe with us."

EPILOGUE

BERKELEY, JANUARY 2022

Samuel and Anita were playing a sonatina on the piano when Selena and Frank arrived at the enchanted mansion that Saturday afternoon, as they often did. The pandemic had not ended but since most people were vaccinated, life had recovered some normalcy and it was possible to socialize.

Selena was now living in San Francisco and attending Hastings Law School. She'd adopted Samuel, Leticia, and Anita as family. Samuel, for his part, found in her the affectionate daughter he'd never had in Camille. She couldn't live with them in Berkeley, as they'd offered many times, because it was too far from the university, but if she'd been able to, she would have been welcome.

Selena and Frank's relationship had gotten serious, but Selena insisted on maintaining her independence. She refused to move into Frank's spacious apartment, instead renting a room in the neighborhood near her school. She knew he could be just as domineering and jealous as Milosz, although in his more understated way. "I have to train you before we can move in together and it's going to take a long time. You have a lot to learn," she told him. He laughed, but deep down he understood that it wasn't a joke. With the same frankness, Selena had turned down his offer to start a law firm together. "I'd just end up doing all the work and you'd take all the credit" was her response.

Saturdays were reserved for high tea at Samuel's house and this week they had a lot to celebrate: Anita's asylum, which Frank had just won for her, and her operation. Leticia was in the kitchen making a pot of tea that would meet the standards of a boss who had been raised in England. Samuel had very rigid notions about what that five o'clock ceremony should entail and not even fifty-something years in the United States had cured him of it. On a three-tiered tray, displayed in a prescribed order, sat a selection of sandwiches, pastries, scones, clotted cream, and jam. Tea in bags—or condom tea, as Samuel called it—would not do; they used only loose leaves in the silver teapots rescued from the attic, and they drank from the Limoges porcelain teacups that Nadine had inherited from her family. Leticia hated polishing the silver, but Anita helped since the job didn't require perfect vision. They liked to do it while watching a Spanish telenovela, because Leticia insisted that the girl needed to maintain her mother tongue so that she could always communicate with her Tita Edu.

That Saturday Selena and Frank would be seeing Anita for the first time since her corneal transplant. Her bandages had been removed after only three days, and according to the doctor, the operation was a success; they did not anticipate a rejection of the transplant. They had always seen her in shorts or pants but this time she was wearing a party dress that Leticia had made for her.

"I have to wear glasses and I can't rub my eyes. But I can go to regular school now," Anita informed them.

"She's going to enter fourth grade, because of her age, but academically she's ready for fifth," Samuel added.

"I see everything fuzzy for now, but soon I'm going to be able to see better," the girl said as she went into the kitchen to help Leticia, the dog at her heels.

Neither Samuel nor Leticia had had the heart to tell Anita the truth about her mother; every time they tried, words seemed to fail them. In light of their struggle, they hired a psychologist, who saw Anita twice a week. She was a specialist in children dealing with trauma, and she spoke Spanish because she had emigrated very young from Mexico. She understood that in a case like this in-person meetings were essential. Nevertheless, in the beginning Anita refused to talk to her, as if she intuited that the woman was the bearer of bad news. After three or four sessions, she finally began to open up. It was the psychologist's idea to bring the girl's grandmother up from El Salvador to be with her when they broke the news.

Frank helped Eduvigis obtain a tourist visa in under twenty-four hours, thanks to Phil. The old woman traveled by plane for the first time in her life. She arrived with three enormous suitcases full of gifts: coffee, tamarind candies, cheeses, even a box of fried chicken she'd bought at the airport before getting on the plane. She also brought a bottle of chaparro—a liqueur made from corn and sugar, typical to El Salvador—a gift from Lola that Eduvigis smuggled through customs. Tita Edu moved into one of the bedrooms that had formerly belonged to the ladies of dubious virtue, which Leticia made up with great care, and she spoiled her granddaughter rotten for an entire week before she finally shared the terrible news about her mother.

Anita seemed to handle the tragedy well, until Tita Edu returned to El Salvador. She held in her pain with a superhuman force so that her grandmother could leave without worrying. Once the old woman was gone, she gave herself free rein to grieve.

She went through a very hard period in which she alternated between attacks of sobbing and others of rage; she threw plates and cups to the floor, hid for hours with the dog, and began to once again wet the bed. But with the help of therapy, Paco's constant company, and Samuel and Leticia's patient attentions, she moved through the natural stages of grief. She followed Leticia around everywhere and slept holding her hand at night, with Didi on the pillow beside her. The woman learned to put up with Paco sleeping in their bed because she got sick of kicking him off only to see him worm his way back up beside Anita once he'd calculated that enough time had passed. Over the following months the girl's tantrums became fewer and further between, until they finally subsided.

One evening, during that painful time, Samuel announced to Anita and Leticia that he had something important to tell them. He summoned them to his sacred place, the music room, where they sat together in a close circle, with Paco at their feet, in the soft light of the Tiffany glass lampshades, surrounded by the beautiful musical instruments that Samuel had collected. He was not inclined to speak about himself, he was a very private man, almost secretive; he had only shared his most intimate thoughts and memories with his beloved Nadine. However, he had witnessed Anita's suffering for many weeks and he ended up feeling it as his own. Her tears washed away his legendary reserve. On that evening he began talking hesitantly but soon the dike that contained his oldest sorrows broke and all that he had held inside for so long spilled out. He told the woman and the girl about his traumatic childhood, about losing his family and being exiled to a strange and hostile place, about being an orphan, always lonely, always in fear, until Luke and Lidia Evans came into his life, bringing him comfort and love. He ended up sobbing and so did Anita and Leticia. Finally, he opened his violin case, pulled out his medal, and placed it in Anita's hand.

"What is it?" asked the girl, feeling it with her sensitive fingers.

"It's a magic medal. It belonged to a war hero, Colonel Theobald Volker. He lent it to me, but he died a long time ago and I never had a chance to give it back to him. I have had it since I was five years old."

"Why is it magic?"

"If you rub it, it gives you courage. It has always worked for me. Now it's yours, Anita. You can rub it as often as you need to, its power never wears out," said Samuel, pinning the medal on the girl's shirt.

The psychologist had warned Leticia and Samuel that despite the fact that Anita was beginning to accept what had happened and was open to the affection they both offered, it would be very hard for her to get over her fear of abandonment, because she'd been through too many losses at a very vulnerable age. Nevertheless, Samuel was more optimistic, because the girl spent hours at the piano, lost in the notes, and he knew better than anyone the power of music. It had mitigated the anguish and uncertainty of his childhood and given meaning to his existence. He hoped it might do the same for Anita.

One day the little girl, in a hushed and momentous voice, invited Samuel to Azabahar. The old man had heard the name in Anita's murmurings as she played alone, but she'd never openly mentioned it to anyone before, not even to Leticia. Samuel understood that she was placing great trust in him as she held out her hand so that they could cross the mythical threshold together. That day, Samuel got to visit Azabahar, the star where spirits dwell, and once he proved he could be trusted, he was invited back often. Just before she went under anesthesia for her eye operation, the girl gave Samuel permission to share her secret with Leticia, Frank, and Selena. She promised she would invite them soon as well.

"Leticia told me over the phone that Anita has stopped talking to Claudia," Selena commented to Samuel as they waited for the tea to be served.

"Claudia hasn't disappeared. She's with her mother now in Azabahar. Anita asked Nadine to come too. We all meet there," Samuel replied casually.

"What are you talking about, Samuel?" Frank asked teasingly, but also slightly concerned.

"I'm not senile yet, don't worry," Samuel replied, smiling. "I thought that Azabahar was simply Anita's refuge, a place she escaped to when she felt alone and frightened. But now I know that it's more than that. It's the mysterious realm of imagination, a place you can only see with the heart."

Author's Note

How does a story begin? There are as many answers to that question as there are novels, but in the case of *The Wind Knows My Name*, it starts many years ago, at a small theater in New York, where I saw a performance of *Kindertransport*, a play by Diane Samuels based on the true events of children saved from Nazi-controlled territory by organized rescue efforts. The protagonist is a Jewish girl who is sent to England by her parents to save her from the Nazi concentration camps. The heartbreaking decision of those desperate parents to send away their daughter and the trauma that it caused them and the child have haunted me for years. It's a life-and-death choice that no parent should ever have to make. What happened to those displaced kids? Some were received by kind families, others were met with indifference, some were exploited or abused—but they all grew up with holes in their hearts.

As a mother and a grandmother, I feel the pain of those families seared in my bones. After reading and watching movies and documentaries about the *Kindertransport* and listening to some interviews of the survivors, I started researching other instances in which children have been separated from their parents, like the Black children sold into slavery, or the Indigenous children taken away from their families to be "civilized" in brutal boarding schools in the United States, Canada, Australia, and other places, or the babies taken away from single mothers to be given into adoption in Ireland. I discovered that this tragedy has been happening for a very long time and it happens in places that are allegedly safe havens.

In 2017, the press reported about the systematic separation of children from their families at the United States' southern border. We learned of screaming children dragged away by border patrol officers, even breastfeeding babies ripped from their mother's arms. We saw harrowing photos of children in cages and the shameful conditions of minors in detention centers. It was a government policy aimed at discouraging asylum seekers, refugees, and immigrants.

Knowing that their children would be taken away, people often ask, who would risk crossing the border? The answer: only those who are running for their lives. And there are hundreds of thousands of desperate people in that situation.

Understandably, as this policy began to receive more press coverage over the next couple of years, there was a national and international outcry. Eventually the policy was revoked, but the practice continued. It may have discouraged many parents, but the influx of unaccompanied minors at the border has only increased.

TWENTY-SEVEN YEARS AGO, I created a foundation to honor my daughter, Paula, whose premature death broke my heart. The foundation's mission is to invest in organizations and programs that help vulnerable women and children. In the last several years, one of the ways we have done this is by working with refugees worldwide, especially at the U.S. border. Thanks to the foundation, I sometimes have the honor of meeting the extraordinary people, mostly women, who work tirelessly to alleviate the refugees' plight, like lawyers who represent children pro bono, social workers, psychologists, and thousands of volunteers moved by compassion and decency. I interviewed some of them as background for this book. They spent many, many hours sharing their experiences with me—often by phone or Zoom, due to the pandemic.

I have heard so many stories of loss and suffering, but also so many of courage, solidarity, and resilience! I met lawyers like Frank and social workers like Selena. And because the universe conspires to facilitate my work, I also met during my research a Salvadoran woman like Leticia and an old man who inspired Samuel. I consider it my job to listen, to observe, to ask questions. Then, as a novelist, in the quiet moments after these meetings I sit patiently and let fictional characters grow out of these experiences. Soon they are telling me about their lives.

Two amazing women, Lori Barra and Sarah Hillesheim, run the foundation with firm hands and soft hearts. Sometimes I despair at how little we can do with our limited resources, but they remind me that we cannot measure our impact in numbers—we can only measure it a life at a time.

And that's not unlike what I have tried to do in this novel: tell one story at a time. I hope the story of Anita speaks to you.

Acknowledgements

Johanna Castillo, my American agent, for her friendship
and help

Balcells Agency for their care and loyalty

Jennifer Hershey, my wise editor at Ballantine

Frances Riddle, my English translator, who
contributed to the final version

Jorge Manzanilla, as always

Elizabeth Subercaseaux and John Hasset for
reading the manuscript with great attention

Juan Allende for editing several drafts

Annie Toxqui López for her insights on El Salvador

Roger Cukras for keeping me fed, warm,
and loved during the writing ordeal

Lori Barra and Sarah Hillesheim for their work with
refugees and migrants in my foundation

Nicolás Frías for keeping me sane
(and everybody else around me when I am not writing)

Cathy Cukras for information about Anita's blindness

Cristóbal Basso for his knowledge about music
for the visually impaired

Sonia Nazario for reporting about refugees and
migrants at the U.S. southern border

Maria Woltjen and Olivia Peña from the
Young Center for Immigrant Children's Rights

Lauren Dasse, Gabriela Corrales, and Lilian Aponte
from the Florence Immigrant & Refugee Rights Project

Wendy Young from Kids in Need of Defense (KIND)

Susanne Cipolla and Keli Reynolds from
Olmos & Reynolds Law Group, LLP

Michael Smith and Sister Maureen from
East Bay Sanctuary Covenant

Sasha Chanoff from Refuge Point

Women's Refugee Commission

Jacob Soboroff for his book *Separated*

About the Author

Born in Peru and raised in Chile, ISABEL ALLENDE is the author of a number of bestselling and critically acclaimed books, including *Violeta, A Long Petal of the Sea, The House of the Spirits, Of Love and Shadows, Eva Luna, The Stories of Eva Luna,* and *Paula.* Her books have been translated into more than forty-two languages and have sold more than seventy-four million copies worldwide. She lives in California with her husband and two dogs.

IsabelAllende.com

Facebook.com/IsabelAllende

Instagram: @allendeisabel